WOL STARED INTO THE CREATURE'S EYES.

No, not a creature. For one thing, no mere animal could have crafted so impressive a weapon.

For another, the eyes that looked back at Wol were those of a warrior born who was prepared to do whatever it took to defeat Wol, just as Wol would not rest until her foe was dead.

I said I wanted a challenge, Wol thought, baring her teeth. "Today," she said, "is a good day to die!"

The alien said something in its language.

Wol then attacked.

The bloodlust rose within her as she leapt at her foe, *mek'leth* swinging ahead of her. They had taken away her honor, her family—all that was left to her was this.

Her foe did not limit its attack to its weapon. Claws, teeth, legs, all were used in service of its goal: to kill her. She, in turn, was bigger and had better protection. A glancing blow to her arm was absorbed by her gauntlets, where a like blow from her drew blood from her opponent.

Wol had no idea how long the fight had gone on when her opponent finally disarmed her. As her *mek'leth* went flying across the road, Wol grabbed for her foe's snout, then pulled the jaws apart, screaming her fury to the heavens as she did so. The alien tried to slice her torso open with its sword, and did succeed in drawing blood this time, but Wol was determined to score a victory. She yanked the alien's head backward, and heard the glorious snap of bone.

For Gene L. Coon, who gave us our first glimpse,
John Colicos, who gave us our first view,
and John M. Ford, who gave us our first insight

Honor is a code set not in stone nor on parchment, but in the blood and bone of warriors, in the souls that stir in their breasts, and the actions of their daily lives. It comes from the deepest part of us, coloring our every decision. It is an instinctive knowledge of right and wrong, that while not always in agreement with the laws of the land, is always in agreement with our hearts. Without a sense of true honor, we are nothing, for we have lost our sense of self, lost that which defines us as warriors, lost that which keeps our Empire strong.

—Engraved on the entryway to the hall
of the House of Jakvi

HISTORIAN'S NOTE

This novel follows the two previous *I.K.S. Gorkon* adventures in the *Star Trek: The Next Generation* novel *Diplomatic Implausibility* and Book 2 of the *Star Trek* duology *The Brave and the Bold*. It commences approximately six months after *Star Trek: Deep Space Nine*'s final episode "What You Leave Behind," and three years prior to the movie *Star Trek Nemesis*. That would put it toward the end of the Year of Kahless 1001 on the Klingon calendar, at approximately Stardate 53400 on the Starfleet calendar, and in mid-to-late 2376 on the human calendar.

A GOOD DAY TO DIE

CHAPTER ONE

The faces of the greatest warriors of the past ten centuries stared down at Klag, son of M'Raq.

Throughout the Hall of Warriors on Ty'Gokor, a huge, windowless, high-ceilinged room carved out of the very rock of the planet's greatest mountain, statues of the strongest *Habnagh* rendered some of the finest heroes of the Klingon Empire. They loomed over the warriors assembled for the induction ceremonies for the Order of the *Bat'leth*.

Captain Klag stood by a barrel of bloodwine. He found the libation to be barely drinkable, but then Klag had always had a more discerning palate than most when it came to alcohol. In order to accommodate the hundreds of warriors present for the induction ceremony—who would be spending the entire night in celebration—the High Council had ordered the bloodwine in bulk. An Empire still recovering from the economic ravages of a prolonged war was not going to acquire an especially lofty vintage for the occasion.

Still, they could at least have provided something less watery, Klag thought as he he refilled his mug by scooping it into the barrel.

Next to him, Klag's second officer and doctor did likewise. Lieutenant Toq and Dr. B'Oraq had come down with Klag from the *I.K.S. Gorkon* to cheer their captain as he was given one of the Empire's highest honors.

Around him, warriors shouted, sang, wrestled, laughed, ate, and drank. The sounds of celebration echoed off the high ceilings of the Hall, reverberating off the walls and the statues themselves, so much so that Klag could not determine the origin of this shout of triumph or that cry of pain that reached his ears.

Klag looked up at a statue far across the room from where they stood.

Toq followed his gaze. "Who is that, Captain?"

Shaking his head, Klag thought, *Youth.* "That is Ch'gran."

To Klag's relief, Toq recognized the name. "The lost colony."

"Yes." Klag gulped down some bloodwine. "Captain Ch'gran led the first fleet that attempted to colonize another world after the Hur'q pillaged Qo'noS. For many turns, the finest engineers constructed spacecraft, using whatever meager resources the Hur'q had left us. Many called them fools. Many called them wasteful. But Captain Ch'gran knew that we would never regain our honor, never be able to avenge ourselves on the Hur'q,

2

if we did not conquer space. Soon, seven mighty vessels had been built, and Ch'gran led them out into the vastness of the black sky—only to be lost forever."

"Not quite forever," B'Oraq said with a smile as Klag drank some more bloodwine. "Didn't they at last find the colony remains on Raknal V?"

"Yes," Klag said, "but that is a different story." He raised his mug. "To Ch'gran!"

Not only Toq and B'Oraq but several others who had gathered nearby repeated the toast. "To Ch'gran!"

Then they all gulped their bloodwine. Several warriors head-butted Toq, who returned the gesture eagerly. One did likewise with Klag.

"You tell the story of Ch'gran well," the warrior, who sported a commander's insignia, said after pouring some bloodwine in the general direction of his face—some of it even making it into his mouth, but most of it running through his brown beard.

"You honor me, Commander—?"

"Grakal, son of Kerr. You are Klag, son of M'Raq, are you not?"

"Yes."

"The hero of Marcan V!" Grakal turned to his companion, standing unsteadily behind him. "I told you it was him!"

"It cannot be," the other Klingon said. "Klag lost his arm at Marcan V."

"It is true, my right arm was taken from me at Marcan." He scooped up some more bloodwine. Grakal and the others looked at him with faces ranging from expectant to confused to so inebriated as not to care—but they obviously expected another story.

Who am I to deny them? "I served aboard the *Pagh* under Captain Kargan."

One of the drunker warriors raised his mug. "To Captain Kargan!"

"To Captain Kargan!" many of the others repeated, and drank their bloodwine.

Klag pointedly did neither, but continued his story. "The *Pagh* was one of twelve that faced six Breen and Jem'Hadar vessels on that great day at Marcan. The battle was glorious—many warriors died that day in battle, but they took the despicable Breen and the honorless Jem'Hadar with them."

Several members of Klag's audience—which had already doubled in size—cheered at that. Warriors were always up for a good story, drunken warriors even more so, and this was a story Klag had yet to tire of telling.

"When the battle had ended, only two ships remained: the *Pagh* and one of the Jem'Hadar ships. But we were both severely damaged. The fifth planet had breathable air, so Kargan ordered us to land. The Jem'Hadar did the same."

"So the fight was to continue on the ground?" B'Oraq asked with a smile.

Klag shot her a look. She, of course, knew this story, but she spoke as one who enjoyed hearing it again. "Yes. Our stabilizers had been damaged, so when we entered the atmosphere, we were thrown across the ship like riders on a bucking mount. By the time I regained my senses, I was on the deck, my right side pinned by the tattered remains of the command chair. I couldn't feel my right arm, but I could see it sticking out from the other side of the debris. With a mighty shove, I rolled the twisted piece of metal off me with my left hand—and then I stood to get a damage report." Klag took a long gulp of bloodwine. "My right arm remained on the deck."

"That is no way to lose an arm," Grakal said.

"No, it was not. I was furious—an anger that increased a thousandfold when I saw that I was the only one who lived through the crash. Our fine crew did not deserve to die such a death after having survived the Jem'Hadar!"

The warriors grunted and shouted in acknowledgment of this injustice.

Klag left out the great glee that he experienced upon seeing the corpse of Captain Kargan. A member of the influential House of K'Tal, and as great a fool as ever lived, Kargan had kept Klag under his heel for a decade. Too inept to inspire warriors to go into battle, but too well connected to be removed from duty by any honorable means, Kargan kept Klag as his first officer in order to cover his own inadequacies, blocking all opportunities for Klag to be promoted, and using Klag's greater skills to further his own lacking honor.

However, Klag saw no reason to pollute the story with Kargan. This was *his* moment of glory. "It was therefore left to me to finish what we had begun. After all, if I survived, some of the enemy might have as well—and that meant the battle was not yet over."

"The battle is never over as long as one of the enemy yet lives." The words were originally spoken by Kahless, now quoted by a woman who stood next to Grakal.

"Yes." Klag smiled at the woman. He drank down the rest of his bloodwine, then refilled his mug. "In fact, ten Jem'Hadar and one Vorta still lived amidst the wreckage of their ship. Armed with a *mek'leth*, I went to greet them."

"Only one warrior, with only one arm, against ten Jem'Hadar?" one warrior said, skeptically.

"Do you doubt me?" Klag asked. In fact, it had been only seven Jem'Hadar, but ten was a rounder figure....

Before the warrior could answer, one of his comrades slammed him in the stomach. "Let him speak, fool!"

Pointedly looking at each member of his audience save the skeptic—now doubled over in pain—Klag said, "The Jem'Hadar may have been bred for combat, but the heart of a warrior cannot be grown in a Vorta laboratory. Within minutes, I stood amongst the corpses of my enemies, my *mek'leth* stained with their blood and the Jem'Hadar's white drug. I was triumphant! Our victory paved the way for our forces to penetrate the Allicar Sector."

Grakal nodded. "Allicar was a great victory."

Toq, who had listened eagerly to Klag's story even though he probably knew it by heart, said, "To Klag! Single-handed defeater of the Jem'Hadar!"

By this time, over a dozen were gathered around to hear Klag's tale. They all cried, "To Klag!," gulped their bloodwine, and head-butted each other, laughing.

The woman who quoted Kahless spoke then. "How is it that you come to have two good arms once more, Captain? Have you one of those mechanical contrivances the Federation uses? Are you Borg now?"

Tossing his mug to the floor in disgust, Klag said, "I would never put a machine on my body and call it my limb!" He held up his new arm. "This once served as the good right arm of my father, M'Raq, son of K'Ton. He was one of the finest warriors in the Empire. My physician, Dr. B'Oraq," he said, indicating B'Oraq with his hand, "performed the procedure. Father and son have been reunited as one to forge a new path of honor!"

Several cheered at that. Klag took the moment of the cheer to grab a fresh mug from the pile next to the barrel.

"You should wear your scars proudly," one warrior said over the cheers, "not hide them behind false limbs."

Grakal asked, "Were you not listening? Do you truly think that he hides his glory? And why should he not give himself a new arm? One who survives battle should live to fight another day, not be handicapped by ancient customs."

"Do you find honor and duty an ancient custom as well?" the other warrior asked. He pointed at the statue of Kull, a contemporary of Kahless; the statue represented a warrior who was bereft of his left hand. "When Kull lost his hand in battle against Kinaan the Foul, did he have a sorcerer graft another's hand onto him?"

"No," Grakal said, "and Kull didn't use a disruptor to kill Kinaan, either. Mainly because they didn't exist."

B'Oraq looked sharply at the skeptical warrior.

"Should we abandon transporters because Kahless did not have one? Should ships that go at warp speed be scrapped because Kahless could not travel faster than light?"

"Bah!" The warrior walked up to the barrel and scooped up some bloodwine, then stomped off in search, no doubt, of a story more to his liking.

Meanwhile, the woman turned to Klag. She wore a captain's insignia. "It is an honor to meet you, Klag. I am B'Edra—I command the *Taj*."

Klag held up his mug. "You won the day at Orias."

"The *Taj* was one of many vessels that won that day." B'Edra did, however, return the toast. Both she and Klag drank heartily, as did B'Oraq, still standing next to Klag.

"Are you to be honored come the morning, Captain?" Klag asked.

"No. I am here at the insistence of my first officer. He was inducted several years ago, and he always returns for the new inductions if his duty permits. We were on undesignated maneuvers in a nearby system, and so I acceded to his request to participate." She smiled. "In truth, your presence is part of why I agreed, Captain."

This surprised Klag. "Why is that?"

"Your victory at Narendra III. Another warrior might have simply fought against the vessels that were enthralled by Malkus. But you gave them a chance to retain their honor and not die with their eyes blinded. I respect that."

Klag nodded his appreciation. A ninety-thousand-year-old tyrant named Malkus had had his consciousness implanted in an artifact that had been buried on Narendra III. Its accidental unearthing enabled Malkus to telepathically control all who dwelt on the planet as well as the seven ships in orbit. With the aid of a Federation starship, the *Gorkon* was able to stop Malkus. Klag had made sure that they fought only defensively: enough to keep the upper hand, but without dishonoring the warriors who were, after all, only victims, by forcing them to die when not even in their right minds.

B'Edra then turned to the physician. "You are also to be commended, Doctor. Klag's courage is already well documented, but yours is no less so."

B'Oraq tugged on the auburn braid that hung down over her right shoulder, secured by a pin with the emblem of her House. "You flatter me, Captain. I merely do what I can in service of the Empire."

"Not at all. Fools like that *petaQ*," she indicated the warrior who had stomped off, now engaged in—and losing—a wrestling match, "are legion. You challenge the fundamentals of what makes us Klingon—what makes us warriors." She looked around and raised her mug. Grakal and Toq were laughing over some shared joke, but they noticed her gesture and did likewise, as did a few others. "To B'Oraq! May she guide the way to a glorious future, where our warriors can continue to fight in this life in order to improve their honor and increase their glory in the next!"

Smiling, B'Oraq raised her mug in appreciation while the others cried, "To B'Oraq!"

"Oh yes, let us praise the butcher!" yelled a familiar voice from behind Klag.

What in the name of Kahless is he doing here? Klag thought, not even bothering to turn around. "Why are you here, Dorrek?"

Captain Dorrek of the *I.K.S. K'mpec*, the *Gorkon's* sister ship, stepped up to the barrel. "Let us praise the one who allowed her captain to soil the memory of a great warrior by stitching his remains onto the shoulder of an unworthy fool." He scooped his mug into the bloodwine barrel, then threw the mug against the wall. It clattered to the floor, bloodwine flying in all directions. "You dare much to bring this creature into a hall of warriors. I should think they shall have to fumigate the statues to remove the stench of her chamber of horrors from this noble place!"

B'Oraq tensed, her hand going to the *d'k tahg* on her belt.

Klag looked down upon Dorrek, who stood a full head shorter than Klag. "She has as much right to be here as you do. After all, she is a member of my crew."

"Yes. How fitting that a vulture who consumes the carrion of the dead serves with one such as you. You'd both be more suited to a Kreel ship."

Now Toq stepped forward, unsheathing his *d'k tahg*. "I will not hear such words spoken of my captain!"

"Stand down, Toq," Klag said. "Any challenge will be mine to make—and I will not take up arms against my brother here."

Both Toq and B'Oraq shot him a look.

Ignoring the look, Klag turned back to his younger sibling. "Again I ask you, Dorrek, why are you here? Surely, you have not come to wish your older brother well on his induction into the Order."

Dorrek looked up at Klag with his small, beady eyes, a direct contrast to Klag's wide ones. Dorrek had inherited his mother's crest, where Klag had gotten M'Raq's. The only obvious family resemblance between the two was in the sharply upturned eyebrows. "Believe me, brother, I would not have set foot on this planet knowing it had been sullied by your bootprints were I not ordered to. All the Chancellor-class captains have been summoned here to meet with Chancellor Martok and General Talak following the ceremony."

Klag had not known this—but his induction made his presence on Ty'Gokor a given, so such orders would not need to be cut for him. Instead, he simply sneered at Dorrek. "You accuse *me* of soiling this world, yet you stood by and allowed Father to wither away and die like some old woman! You supported his honorless path."

"He was our father. It was our duty to obey him. But that was never good enough for you, was it, Klag?"

"Ironic, is it not," Klag said with a smile, "that you hide behind filial piety when it suits your purpose, yet you make no such concession to me now, even though I am the older brother?"

Dorrek let out a growl. "Our father *earned* the right to be obeyed!"

"How? By allowing himself to be captured? By letting the Romulans prevent him from dying with honor? By refusing to reclaim that honor when he escaped from the prison camp? When, exactly, did he earn that right, Dorrek?"

Stepping forward, Dorrek started to speak, then stopped. "I will not do this now, Klag. Not here. This is a time of celebration, and I will honor those—*most* of those—who are to be inducted tomorrow. But know this—there is blood between us, and it will not end until one of us is in *Gre'thor*."

With that, Dorrek turned his back on Klag and disappeared into the ever-growing crowd of warriors.

Klag looked around for the first time since Dorrek's arrival. Grakal, B'Edra, and the others had disappeared into the crowd as well. Only B'Oraq and Toq remained by Klag's side.

Cursing, Klag scooped up some more bloodwine and drank it all in one gulp.

"Captain—" B'Oraq started.

"Be *silent!* We will not speak of this. We will drink and we will tell stories and we will sing songs of glory and battle and honor!"

Both officers exchanged a quick glance, then refilled their mugs.

Klag knew that both of them had questions, and he also knew that he had their support.

But right now, he wanted more than anything else to get excessively drunk.

Hours later, dawn rose on Ty'Gokor. At least, Klag assumed it did. The Hall of Warriors was enclosed, with no view of the outside world. All one could see in this place was history: that of the past, represented by the statues that gazed down upon all who entered, and that of the future, in the form of those who would be inducted into the Order.

Klag didn't feel nearly drunk enough.

B'Oraq, too, seemed maddeningly sober. Klag hadn't seen Toq in close to an hour, though he had looked very close to falling over then. The youth had last been seen standing with Grakal under the statue of *Dahar* Master Kor. Grakal had been telling Toq the story of the Battle of Klach D'Kel Brakt for the fifth time.

Klag had not seen hide nor hair of B'Edra—which disappointed him—nor Dorrek—which was a relief—all night. He wondered if the *Taj*'s captain had thought his treatment of his father to be distasteful.

He also wondered why he cared so much. Far too much of his life of late had been dictated by the whims of others. Kargan's influence kept him away from command for years. Kargan's death and Klag's own heroism at Marcan V had given him a command, but then only on others' terms. He had had no say in his crew.

But they had come together, won many campaigns, from the rebellion on taD to the defeat of Malkus at Narendra III, and it was all Klag's doing. *I have done this—I have at last brought honor to our House, after Father threw it away and after Kargan kept me from fulfilling it properly. Now, at last, I am to be inducted into the Order of the* Bat'leth! *And no one will take that from me!*

"Take what from you, Captain?" B'Oraq asked.

"Hm?" Klag hadn't realized he'd spoken aloud. "Nothing, nothing." He took a sip of his bloodwine, but the mug was empty. Looking down, he saw that the barrel too was empty. "*QI'yaH*," he cursed.

"Have you seen Toq?" she asked.

"Not since—" He cut himself off as he looked around. His eyes fell on the statue of Kor. Sculpted shortly after Kor's heroic death on the *I.K.S. Ning'tao*, it showed Kor as a younger man, leaning forward, each arm outstretched with a disruptor in each hand.

It looked almost the same as it did the last time Klag saw it, with one major alteration: Toq, who was now draped over the *Dahar* Master's arms, sleeping peacefully.

B'Oraq followed Klag's gaze, and then both captain and doctor burst into raucous laughter, Klag throwing his head back and bellowing his amusement to the ceiling.

It was the first real belly laugh Klag had indulged in since Dorrek had shown his hideous face, and it felt good.

"I'm reminded," B'Oraq said, "of a human saying I picked up at Starfleet Medical Academy. 'Youth is wasted on the young.'"

"Humans have almost as many sayings as we do."

"Yes, but ours are much more colorful. And most of theirs are from the great playwright Shakespeare, in any case."

Klag shook his head. "I always found Shakespeare to be overrated."

B'Oraq tugged on her braid. "You can't really appreciate him until you read him in the original English."

Their conversation was interrupted by cheers that

heralded the arrival of General Talak, Chancellor Martok's chief of staff. This meant that Martok himself could not be far behind.

However, another entered behind Talak: a Klingon, but not dressed in a Defense Force uniform. Rather, he wore a brown tunic, matching pants, and a black leather floor-length coat that bore the insignia of both the United Federation of Planets and the Klingon Empire on the chest.

"Captain, isn't that Ambassador Worf?" B'Oraq said.

Klag did not answer directly, but instead cried out, "Worf!"

The ambassador looked up and around the room at the sound of his name. Upon spying Klag and B'Oraq, he changed direction and went to greet them.

"What brings the Federation ambassador to our hallowed hall?" Klag asked when Worf was in conversational earshot.

Worf was far too taciturn to ever truly smile—a lifetime living among fragile humans had, Klag knew, taught the ambassador to restrain his Klingon passion—but he did smirk with pride as he answered. "The same as you, Captain. Chancellor Martok has added my name to the honor roll."

Klag nodded his approval. Worf had been involved in both Klag's mission to taD and his recent victory on Narendra III, and he had been a hero to the Empire in more ways than one. "The chancellor is wise. Though some may see this as a political move on his part."

"The irony is not lost on me," Worf said dryly.

"What irony?" B'Oraq asked.

"Twice," Klag said, enjoying the chance to tell another story, "the ambassador was cast out of the Empire. The first was when he accepted discommendation in order to keep the Empire from civil war. He did so to protect the secrets of the traitorous House of Duras. The second was when he opposed the Klingon invasion of Cardassia—an invasion masterminded by the changeling who impersonated Martok."

"In both cases," Worf said, "the reasons for my exile *were* political. This time, however, it is truly only honor being served."

."Come," Klag said, "let us find a barrel with bloodwine left and drink to your worthy induction."

Worf nodded. "I'd like that—but only if we drink to yours, as well, Klag."

Klag laughed. "It will be done!"

Within the hour, Klag had drunk six more mugs of bloodwine. The air felt stale, reeking with the musk of the assorted drunken Klingons, tinged with the overwhelming smell of the bloodwine, which now seemed to permeate every molecule that made up the hall.

Yet he felt more sober than ever. Klag, Worf, and B'Oraq exchanged more stories, with some other warriors coming and going—including Grakal, who had some disparaging remarks to make about Toq's constitution. Worf told of his capture by the Breen during the war, and his escape, aided by the Cardassian hero Damar. Klag told of the *Pagh*'s campaigns against the

Cardassians, including a well-fought battle at Quinor. Grakal finally told a story of his own, about taking Chin'toka—he had served as a lieutenant on the *Azrak* during that glorious battle.

"I remember Chin'toka well," Worf said somberly. "It was the site of one of our greatest victories, and one of our greatest defeats. We lost the *Defiant* there when—"

A bone-jarring pounding started then. It turned out to be the drums that loudly heralded the entrance of the chancellor. Martok was covered neck to toe in the heavy medal-covered cassock that signified his most high office. Behind him, a bearer held an ornate *bat'leth*. Klag saw that, rather than carry the weapon that had been the symbol of the Order for decades, Martok had instead brought with him the Sword of Kahless. Retrieved by Martok and Worf shortly after the end of the war, possession of the legendary sword, forged by the divine one himself, had cemented Martok's power as head of the High Council.

"Mar-tok! Mar-tok! Mar-tok!"

The cheer started with one warrior, then grew to fifty by the third repetition of the name. Klag had mixed opinions of the Empire's newest leader, but he knew that the one-eyed warrior was a distinct improvement on his predecessor, the ever-political Gowron. Martok was a commoner from the Ketha Lowlands who worked his way up the ranks to become a great war hero. In truth, he embodied the best of the Empire, so it was only fitting that he occupy its highest position. His road there had been hard-fought, but in the end, he had more than earned it.

"Mar-tok! Mar-tok! Mar-tok!"

As the chancellor stepped up to the stage, all the warriors who still stood turned toward him, cheering and drinking. Klag found himself joining them, as did B'Oraq and Worf.

General Talak stood next to the chancellor and cried, "Long live Martok! Long live the Empire!"

A general cheer rose up at that, some shouting Martok's name, some shouting *"Qapla'!"* and others just shouting. As they did so, two more Klingons wheeled a large board onto the stage. Attached to the board were about a dozen medals: the symbols of the honor that would be bestowed this day.

"Klingon warriors, I salute you!" Martok shouted over the din, his words serving to quiet that din somewhat. "At least, those of you still standing," he added with a laugh, as three unconscious warriors were carried out of the hall. Klag looked over at the statue of Kor to see that Toq had not been moved, nor had the boy budged on his own.

"This is a great day. A day when we honor those who have brought us glory, whose deeds will live on in song and story! And so, in this hallowed hall under the watchful gaze of our greatest heroes, you will receive the highest honor that can be given to a Klingon!"

More cheers went up at that, and Klag prepared himself to go forward.

But, though tradition stated that the chancellor's adjutant—in this case, Talak—would then read the honor roll, the general did not budge. Instead, Martok gazed out upon the crowd with his one eye and waited for the warriors to quiet down.

"Most of you," he finally said, "know the Order only as a great honor that we bestow. This night has been full of stories of our courage, our bravery, our honor, so I hope that you will allow me to tell one final tale. That of how the Order was founded."

Klag exchanged a glance with Worf. This was not a normal part of the ceremony. The ambassador simply nodded back at Klag. Obviously, Worf, a member of Martok's House, knew what was coming.

"The Order was formed over a millennium ago by Kahless's mate, Lukara, after his ascension. Kahless's divine wisdom was evident when coming from the lips of Kahless himself. Lukara was understandably concerned with whether or not her mate's words would live on after him. For conquest is only the beginning of the battle, not the end. As Kahless himself said, 'Power must not only be seized, but also held.' "

Interesting, Klag thought. He knew some of this history, but had never given it much thought. Most of the stories about Kahless focused on his life, not what happened after his ascent to *Sto-Vo-Kor.*

Martok now began to pace, speaking with the cadences and rhythms of a born storyteller, being sure to make eye contact with as many of the warriors in the room as he could. "And so Lukara formed the Order of the *Bat'leth* from among Kahless's most trusted followers." Walking over to the sword-bearer, Martok took the Sword of Kahless from him and held it aloft.

"Named after the very sword that Kahless forged in the lava of the Kri'stak Volcano, the Order was tasked not only with spreading the great word of Kahless, but also enforcing his doctrine. If a House Head was acting dishonorably, members of the Order would be sent to put him on the right path. If a warrior went back on his word to an honorable foe, the Order would ensure that he kept that word."

"The Knights Templar," Worf whispered.

"A not inappropriate analogy," B'Oraq muttered in reply.

Klag gave them both odd looks, then remembered that they both studied at Starfleet Academy. *No doubt it is some similar Federation organization.*

Certainly, Klag knew, the Order had long since fallen away from that particular duty. Although receiving the medal that signified membership in the Order was a great honor, it had never, to the best of Klag's knowledge, come with any special responsibility. It was but an acknowledgment of great deeds.

The inebriated, exhausted, yet exuberant crowd started to voice its pleasure with cheers and cries of "Mar-tok!"

Martok lowered the sword and continued. "Although no one has called upon the Order to serve their original function for many turns, that does not relieve any of you who are to be inducted today from your duty. You must be ever vigilant."

The crowd cheered its approval.

"You must live up to the ideals of Kahless!" Martok

raised his voice to continue to be heard over the swelling noise of the crowd. "And, should the need arise, you must call upon the Order to aid you in restoring honor to *any* part of the Empire! We are but a few months removed from one of the greatest victories in history. The war against the Dominion was on a scale not seen in this galaxy for millennia, and *we* were the victors!"

More cheers. Klag was not among them, but he did smile his approval. There were always those who would abandon the course of honor. Martok had had to deal with such creatures shortly after the end of the war. Klag was pleased to see that Martok had learned the lessons those battles had taught him and was preparing for potential future lapses.

"And so," Martok said, holding the sword back up, "let us go to glory!"

This time, Klag did join in the cheers. The sound echoed throughout the chamber, rising to a pitch so deafening Klag feared his eardrums would burst.

Talak stepped forward, holding a padd. "Come forward, Hevna, daughter of Larra."

Klag saw a woman approach the stage, a *mek'leth* in one hand, even as Martok reached onto the board to remove one of the medals. Proudly, Hevna stood as Martok pinned the medal onto her uniform. "Glory to you and your House," he said.

Nodding, she turned and returned triumphantly to her place, where she was greeted enthusiastically.

"Come forward, Grakal, son of Kerr."

Grakal stumbled toward the stage, barely able to keep to his feet. *A pity Toq is not awake to see the tables turned*, Klag thought wryly.

"Glory to you," Martok said as he steadied the drunken warrior with one hand while pinning the medal with another, "and your House."

After nodding, Grakal turned around, and proceeded to pass out, falling down the stage stairs.

This provoked gales of laughter from many of those assembled, Martok most of all. "How fortunate for Grakal," the chancellor said, "that tradition states that one must remain conscious *until* receiving the medal."

Klag threw his head back and laughed at the chancellor's remark, as well as its victim, even as he, Worf, and B'Oraq moved to help remove the insensate commander from blocking the stairs.

Once they had done so, Talak said, "Come forward, Worf, son of Mogh."

Turning, Klag saw the ambassador turn and walk to the stage. The cheers that met his announcement were at the same volume as the cheers for the other warriors, but Klag noted that they came from fewer mouths. Many thought Worf to be a hero to the Empire. He slew the traitor Duras; he killed Chancellor Gowron in honorable combat and installed Martok as his successor; he was the one who first saw the clone of Kahless on his manufactured return to Boreth, and his actions led to the clone's rise to the position of emperor. Others thought less of him for those very deeds—or they viewed him as an outsider because of his Federation citizenship. Some simply were unaware of Worf's role in those events, for others—primarily Gowron—had taken public credit for them.

However, Klag was sure to join in the cheers. Worf had overcome much, from the massacre of his family on Khitomer to Gowron's treachery, and he deserved the praise he received now. Klag had fought alongside him twice, and found him to be a true warrior and worthy of the honor Martok bestowed upon him.

Martok smiled as he placed the medal on Worf's heavy leather jacket. "Glory to you," he said, "and *our* House. This is a long time coming, my friend."

Worf simply nodded and turned around. Next to Klag, B'Oraq—who had remained quiet for most of the ceremony—cheered as loudly as she could for the ambassador.

Talak spoke now in a dull monotone. "Come forward, Klag, son of M'Raq."

Pride swelled within Klag's chest as he moved to the stage. He and Worf exchanged a nod as they passed each other.

From its sheath in his back, Klag pulled out the *mek'leth* with which he slew many Jem'Hadar and one Vorta on Marcan V. As he walked up the steps, he locked his eyes with Martok's one eye, and the chancellor looked back on him with the respect of a fellow warrior.

"Glory to you and your House." Martok placed the pin among the medals on Klag's floor-length cassock. It shone brightly.

Klag turned around to meet the cheers of the crowd.

Again, B'Oraq gave her vocal approval, as did Worf. Klag saw, to his joy, B'Edra raising her mug in appreciation.

Then he turned to see Dorrek—who had turned his back on the stage.

In truth, he thought, *I expected no less.*

When he rejoined Worf and B'Oraq, the latter handed Klag a mug of bloodwine. "Let us drink," the doctor said. "To Worf! To Klag! To the Order of the *Bat'leth!* To honor!"

They slammed their mugs together and drank heartily.

CHAPTER TWO

Me-Larr stood facing his foe in the circle.

His foe had a simple task: to draw blood before the first sun set. Me-Larr's was equally simple and related: to prevent his foe from doing so. If either of them violated the borders of the circle, that person would be banned from any form of combat or hunt for two seasons.

Me-Larr's foe was naught but a cub, a brown-and-black-furred youth named Em-Ran. His pack felt that Em-Ran was ready to join the Great Hunt. The Ruling Pack had disagreed; Em-Ran's pack challenged the ruling, as was their right.

Intrigued by the cub's audacity, Me-Larr had personally accepted the challenge. It was not necessary—indeed, many thought it a foolish risk. But Me-Larr felt that there was no true danger to him. At best, it was a pleasant diversion. At worst, Em-Ran would succeed in drawing first blood, in which case there would be no doubt as to his worthiness to join the Hunt.

Em-Ran lunged in a clumsy manner. Me-Larr batted the attack aside as if the cub were no more than an insect buzzing about his snout.

But then Em-Ran kicked at Me-Larr with his legs even as he fell backward. Me-Larr avoided this attack as well, but it showed forethought on the cub's part. He knew that his move was predictable, and used that to his attempted benefit.

However, Me-Larr did not become head of the Ruling Pack of the Children of San-Tarah by falling for such foolish attacks.

To Em-Ran's credit, he made fewer foolish attacks. He had the speed of youth, as expected, but he also knew to use *all* the weapons at his disposal: both arms, both legs, his claws, and his teeth. Indeed, at one point, he had almost succeeded in winning the contest by biting Me-Larr's shoulder, but Me-Larr was able to grip the cub's jaws, holding them open. He then threw the cub aside in an attempt to get him to stumble out of the circle. However, Em-Ran recovered enough to avoid that fate, thus keeping the fight going, and indeed he leapt right back at the older San-Tarah.

Me-Larr smiled. He had expected this to be an amusing diversion at best, but Em-Ran was proving to be worthier than that. The cub was relentless, never giving Me-Larr a moment to think. Not that much thought was required—Me-Larr's, after all, was the reactive posture. The onus was on Em-Ran, but he wore it well.

As the first sun lowered toward the horizon, Me-Larr's breathing grew more labored. True, he was the greatest fighter among the Children of San-Tarah, but the days when he would be considered a cub were long behind him, and even great fighters have limits. Em-Ran, however, seemed to have none, as his latest attack—diving for Me-Larr's legs in the hope of tripping him—was as ferocious as his first.

After Me-Larr kicked the cub to the side, Em-Ran coiled for another attack. Before he could employ it, however, drums sounded from nearby. Me-Larr whirled his head around to see that the first sun had taken its place behind the mountains.

"The challenge has ended!" cried Ga-Tror, the Fight Leader of the Ruling Pack.

For the first time since the challenge began, Me-Larr focused his attention outside the circle. Demarcated by a line drawn with a stick in the dirt, the circle sat in a clearing just outside the Prime Village. Most of the Ruling Pack, several members of Em-Ran's pack, and the inevitable gawkers had all gathered around the outside of the circle to see the battle. Few San-Tarah would turn down an opportunity to see a fight, fewer still to see Me-Larr engage in battle, even in so meager a contest as this. Me-Larr was, after all, the best of them, and any who challenged him would either prove themselves great by defeating the best or at least lose with pride, for against Me-Larr, one would be expected to lose.

Me-Larr turned to Em-Ran. The cub's breath was now as labored as Me-Larr's own. *Even the stamina of youth runs out eventually*, Me-Larr thought, and hoped that Em-Ran would, if nothing else, learn that on this day.

"You have failed in the circle," Me-Larr said, and Em-Ran's eyes burned with the magnitude of that failure. To have challenged the Ruling Pack was audacious enough, after all. Me-Larr, however, bared his teeth as he continued. "However, you have succeeded in your challenge. Few could last as long in the circle with me, and you proved more than your worth." He turned to face the rest of the Ruling Pack. "Unless any object," he said in a tone that indicated he would be very displeased if any did, "then I reverse the Ruling Pack's decision. Em-Ran will join the Great Hunt!"

Rousing howls came from the assembled crowd, particularly the other members of Em-Ran's pack. The cub himself was wide-eyed, his jaw hanging from his snout, his tongue lolling out of the side of his mouth.

"I—I can join the Hunt?" he finally said.

"That *is* what I said, Em-Ran."

Then he threw his head skyward and howled so long and loud, it echoed off the mountains themselves. After a moment, Me-Larr joined the howl, for at least a bit, before his breath once again left him.

Where do cubs get all that energy, anyhow? he asked himself, knowing that the older ones had asked the same questions when Me-Larr was young and carving a swath through the ranks of the Children of San-Tarah. He had slain the mightiest beasts, gathered the greatest spoils, and fought the greatest contests. Eventually, he had taken his place in the Ruling Pack.

In truth, there had never been any doubt that the white-furred cub would eventually lead them all. It had been many generations since any had seen one with his skill, his cunning, his strength, or his compassion. Though Me-Larr himself would be the first to admit that ruling the Children of San-Tarah took no special skills. The land provided more than enough food and raw material for shelter to allow them to live happy lives. The abundance had never shown signs of waning. It left the Children of San-Tarah to hone their arts, to improve their weapons and their skills at fighting. They had no other cares.

Me-Larr also knew that the day would come when he would become too old, when his breath would give out sooner than expected, and when even being able to predict the attack would not be enough to allow his old limbs to defend against it with any speed. When that day came, he would die proudly, knowing that his life had been led to the fullest, and that another would take his place in the Ruling Pack.

A horn sounded, heralding the return of the pack that had gone on today's hunt. A runner approached the circle on all fours, then prostrated herself before Me-Larr just outside the circle, where he still stood with Em-Ran.

"Great Me-Larr, we have returned with a *san-chera* fit for a feast!"

"Then we shall have a feast, for we have another for the Great Hunt." He indicated Em-Ran.

The runner stood upright. "I shall inform the pack,

Great Me-Larr. The feast will be ready by second sunset."

True to the runner's word, the center of the Prime Village was the sight of a great feast indeed. All those who lived in the village gathered around to pick from the carcass of the *san-chera* that had been brought down. Me-Larr noted with satisfaction that the hunters had done so with a minimum of damage—the beast died quickly and with no great loss of edible material. It was a fine hunt.

Fires had been lit all around the village, illuminating the celebration. Shadows of San-Tarah flickered on the huts that made up the village as they ate, drank, danced, and howled.

As Me-Larr was complimenting the pack-master on the quality of the hunt, another of the Ruling Pack approached him. "Me-Larr, may I speak to you?"

Excusing himself from the pack-master, Me-Larr turned and said, "Yes, Te-Run?"

Te-Run stared at Me-Larr directly eye-to-eye. A challenge. "I understand why you allowed the cub to join the Great Hunt. However—"

Me-Larr exhaled loudly. "However, you're worried that others will see this as a reason to challenge the Ruling Pack, since we will reverse our decisions even though the letter of the law was not followed."

At that, Te-Run looked downward, withdrawing her direct challenge, though her subsequent words proved that she was not finished with the conversation. "The cub in truth did not meet the criteria for the challenge. By tradition, you should not have allowed his petition."

Me-Larr gazed down at Te-Run, whose brown coat was flecked with gray. *Only a few more hunts left in her, I fear.* Te-Run had been a member of the Ruling Pack since Me-Larr was an infant. She was the smallest of the pack, but she brought a great cunning to her battles—and also to the Ruling Pack, where she served as primary keeper of the traditions and laws.

Which also means she worries the most. "I'm more concerned about the welfare of the people, Te-Run. The Great Hunt requires that our best hunters participate. It would be foolish not to make use of Em-Ran's skills."

Testily, Te-Run said, "You think I'm *not* concerned about the welfare of the people? I was in the Ruling Pack when you were still biting your mother's teat. My fear is that this can do harm to the Ruling Pack's ability to make pronouncements. If we are laden with contests—"

"Then we have more opportunities to show our prowess, to practice our skills. We are *fighters*, Te-Run. If we have the chance to fight, we should *take* it."

Te-Run exhaled. "I suppose so. Still—"

"Don't worry, old friend. All we have done today is find another great fighter in our midst. Now is the time to celebrate!" They approached the carcass of the *sanchera*. "Let us feast!"

Baring her teeth, Te-Run said, "Yes, let's."

They both leaned in and ripped out a chunk of meat with their snouts. The meat was still fresh and tender, and Me-Larr savored the warm, soft flavor of it on his tongue.

Nearby, several dozen San-Tarah danced to drumbeats provided by two of the pack who had hunted the *san-chera*—the duty of providing the music, as well as the food for the feast, was theirs. Me-Larr noted that two females—neither from the cub's pack—were vying for Em-Ran's attention. *He will have to get used to that*, Me-Larr thought. The head of the Ruling Pack remembered the attentions females used to lavish on *him* when he was Em-Ran's age....

CHAPTER THREE

Martok had called the meeting for High Sun in the amphitheater, which was located only a few dozen meters from Ty'Gokor's Great Hall. Klag—having sent B'Oraq and the still-insensate Toq back to the *Gorkon*, and said his farewells to Worf and B'Edra—proceeded there alone.

In contrast to the dark, windowless hall where the Order inductions had taken place, with directed light casting harsh shadows, the amphitheater was out in the open, the bright light of Ty'Gokor's sun beating relentlessly down on the rock. The oppressive heat on his metal-and-leather uniform sharpened Klag's senses, the discomfort heightening his awareness of his surroundings. He appreciated the effect, particularly after a full night of drinking.

The Great Hall had been constructed inside Ty'-Gokor's largest mountain, built to withstand ground assaults as well as orbital bombardment, a frequent method of attack in the early days of the Klingon Empire's expansion. Even now, Ty'Gokor was one of the best-defended planets in the entire Empire.

Similarly, the amphitheater had been carved into one of the nearby valleys that already had the basic formation. From what Klag understood, it was the preferred venue for the productions of Kovikh, one of the Empire's greatest opera composers of the third century of Kahless. Klag himself had never had much use for opera, but he still appreciated the significance of sitting in the same spot where the first performances of such great works as *The Battle of Gal-Mok* and *River of Blood* were performed.

Eleven other captains joined him, seated in the first row. Klag silently approved. None took an inferior position in a row further behind, and all showed their contempt for anyone who would claim a lesser place by keeping their backs to those spots.

Klag also noted that Dorrek, when he came out, took a seat as far from Klag as possible while still remaining in the front row.

Besides Dorrek, Klag knew only one of the other captains—Wirrk, who was a Housemate of Klag's security chief, Lokor, and commanded the *Kravokh*. In fact, the captain came to sit next to Klag.

"What do you want?" Klag asked in greeting.

"It is an honor to meet you, Captain," Wirrk said, his wide black eyes constantly darting to the new medal on Klag's chest, which flashed with reflected sunlight.

"Your deeds have been worthy of the songs composed about them. I hope that you find my cousin to be a worthy member of your crew."

"More than worthy," Klag said. "Lokor serves me well."

"Do you have any knowledge of what the chancellor has planned for us?"

Smiling, Klag wondered if it was his induction into the Order that made him a target for potential gossip, or simply that Wirrk's cousin served under him. "I have none," he said honestly, not bothering to add that he did not even know of this meeting until his arrival at Ty'Gokor.

"I hope it is some new offensive against the Romulans."

"The Romulans are our allies."

Wirrk spit in disgust. "For now, for as long as it suits them. They have been our allies before, after all, and much Klingon blood was spilled by Romulan treachery during those times. We would be well to strike before they can do so again."

Talak and Martok arrived just as the sun reached its zenith, a bit of promptness that Klag admired. It was a small thing, to commence the meeting right at High Sun as announced, but it showed Martok to remain a man of his word. Recent Empire history showed that not all chancellors were such.

All twelve captains, who, like Wirrk and Klag, had been talking among themselves, quieted as chancellor and general took to the stage.

"Welcome to each of you, fellow warriors." Martok

again surveyed the entire crowd, a much simpler task than it had been that morning in the Great Hall. "With the end of the Dominion War, the Federation is blazing a trail of renewed exploration in the Gamma Quadrant—and that is fitting."

Klag knew that the Federation had just sent a ship through the Bajoran wormhole on a three-month journey to reopen the Gamma Quadrant to exploration—those parts of the quadrant not controlled by the Dominion, in any case. Klag had been of the considered opinion that, following the victory on Cardassia Prime, the wormhole should have been destroyed. The Gamma Quadrant was more trouble than it was worth. He suspected the primary reason it wasn't—besides the bizarre unwillingness of the Federation to destroy things during times of peace—was due to its hallowed place in the Bajoran religion. It was allegedly the home of their gods. Klag's considered opinion on *that* was that the Bajorans should follow the Klingons' example and eliminate their gods. They, too, were more trouble than they were worth.

Martok continued. "But it is not enough. We are Klingons, and we must make our Empire strong again. It would be easy to become complacent—the Dominion is defeated, Cardassia is in ashes, and the Federation and Romulans are our allies, for the moment."

That last phrase cause Wirrk to nudge Klag in the ribs. Klag grunted a reply.

"But we are also depleted. And that is why we must push ourselves to expand."

That led to a cheer from most of the twelve, including Klag—though not, he noted, Wirrk. *No doubt he prefers conquest of the Romulans to expansion.*

"While it is true that we were victorious against the Dominion, that does not mean that our battle is ended. We have lost many fine warriors, and exhausted some of our greatest resources. Our best allies, the Federation, are as weakened by the conflict as we—more so, truly, for though they fought well, they are *not* Klingons."

Several grunts of agreement with those sentiments came from the captains, especially Wirrk. Klag did not agree. He had fought alongside humans and other Federation species enough times to know better than to judge them so harshly. He thought Martok had, too, though perhaps he was speaking to his audience, as it were.

Looking over, Klag saw that Dorrek was another who agreed with Martok's disparagement. *As if I needed more proof that my brother is a fool.*

"Our other allies, the Romulans, are not to be trusted. As long as they abide by the terms of our alliance, we will not take up arms against them—but we will not turn our backs on them, either, nor will we expect that they will be anything but our enemies in the future."

Wirrk muttered, "It is not enough."

"To compound matters, the Federation feels the need to send aid to Cardassia, further delaying their own recovery. We will not make the same mistake. The Chancellor-class vessels were created in an attempt to improve our ability to fight the Dominion. Now they will be at the vanguard of our new call to glory. The Kavrot Sector is a teeming mass of unexplored space, ripe for conquest. It is here that each of you shall go, seeking out new worlds for us to add to the greater glory of the Klingon Empire."

Klag nodded in acknowledgment. He knew that the situation was even more complicated than Martok could say in public. Only a few months ago, Klag had participated in a mission to taD—where he had first met Ambassador Worf—a conquered world that was rebelling against the Empire. Martok had told Klag then that other such worlds were fomenting rebellions of their own, and how they handled taD would reflect on the Empire's ability to maintain their hold on those territories. It was wise of the chancellor to improve the Empire's position by finding new worlds to place under the Klingon flag.

Then General Talak stepped forward.

Unable to hold back a sneer, Klag looked away.

Wirrk noticed. "Something troubles you, Captain?"

"It is a—family matter."

Nodding, Wirrk said nothing more, wisely choosing not to interfere in a dispute between two Houses.

Though, in truth, no real dispute existed, exactly. Kargan's death at Marcan V freed Klag from being under the heel of that honorless *toDSaH*, but Talak, Kargan's Housemate, still served as Klag's commanding officer. Though Talak was not as unworthy of his position as Kargan—that almost wasn't possible—Klag had very little use for the general, and his position as Martok's chief of staff had always been a point against the chancellor in Klag's mind.

"General Talak," Martok said, "has assembled a fleet. Each of you will be given a subsector of Kavrot to explore. If you find a world that is worthy of being added to the Empire's glory, you will contact the general immediately and begin the conquest. He will send his fleet to the planet to complete the securing of the world for the Empire."

Talak, who shared a crest with Kargan, but did not have as fat a face as the late captain, added, "I have prepared a list of the types of worlds we are particularly interested in, and the minerals, elements, and materials we are in especial need of."

"This is an open-ended mission," Martok said, looking at each of the twelve captains in turn. "It will continue until every parsec of Kavrot is at least charted and catalogued. Initial probes have indicated at least a dozen worlds that should meet the criteria for conquest, and hundreds more possibilities. Kahless once said that the unknown is the greatest foe of all. Today, each of you will go out and face that foe. And I have every faith in your ability to defeat it. I send you all to glory! I send you all to honor!" Martok raised a fist. "For the Empire!"

Klag stood and raised the fist that once belonged to his father and, along with the eleven other captains, repeated, "For the Empire!"

Next to him, Wirrk had done the same, but when he

lowered his arm, he muttered, "I'd rather be fighting Romulans."

Throwing his head back and laughing, Klag said, "Do not worry, my friend. I suspect that you will find all the fighting your heart desires. Think of it—an entire sector filled with foes we cannot even imagine. It will be glorious."

Wirrk spit. "It will be tedious. Charting solar systems like some kind of Federation science vessel. It is not the task of a warrior."

Grinning, Klag said, "I will make you a wager, Wirrk. I have a case of bloodwine in my quarters—from the K'reetka vintner."

That got Wirrk's attention. "What year?"

"Ninety-eight."

Laughing, Wirrk said, "What is your wager?"

"I predict that, within six months, both of our vessels will have seen combat on this mission. If we both survive the mission, we will reconvene here when the sector is fully mapped. If I am wrong, the case of bloodwine is yours."

"And if you are right?"

Klag laughed. "You can watch me drink it."

Wirrk stared at Klag for a moment, then joined Klag's laugh, and they head-butted enthusiastically.

Dorrek watched in disgust as Klag and one of the other ship captains, whom Dorrek did not know, laughed over some no-doubt-foolish bit of humor.

He had so been looking forward to taking the *K'mpec*

into battle against the Dominion. After living in the shadow of his unworthy younger brother, Dorrek had been given a chance to shine on his own. Klag had shamed Dorrek and the rest of their House in every possible way. But now, thanks to some joke of fate, they were equals: both commanders of Chancellor-class vessels, both going on similar missions to bring new territory to the Empire. Dorrek was not sure whether it was fitting or revolting.

Talak had a padd for each captain which contained detailed information on their specific assignments. As his older brother approached the general to take his, Dorrek saw a glance pass between the two of them.

Dorrek recognized the expression on Talak's face as he looked upon Klag, as Dorrek saw it in reflective surfaces every time he thought about his brother. Talak, Dorrek knew, was of the same House as the late Captain Kargan of the *Pagh*. *Perhaps the general also feels, as I do, that my brother stole Kargan's honor.*

Deliberately hanging back, Dorrek waited so that he would be the last to receive the orders. Most of the captains—including Klag—then transported back to their ships or left on foot for some other business on Ty'-Gokor.

As he took the padd from Talak, Dorrek said, "I would speak with you."

Talak wouldn't even look at him. "I have nothing to say to the younger brother of the so-called Hero of Marcan."

"In that case, we have much in common, General—for I have no use for my older brother, either."

Now Talak made eye contact. The general had steely gray eyes that peered out from beneath the ridge of his crest. His long hair had gone mostly white, but his beard was still a powerful dark brown. His scowl deepened.

"Very well, Captain. You may speak—briefly."

"Captain Klag shames me with his very existence, General. He had the good fortune to serve under a great commander on the *Pagh*, only to rob Kargan of the glory he deserved for the victory at Marcan."

Talak's facial expression did not change, but he did say, "Kargan was my Housemate."

"Indeed?" Dorrek said, feigning surprise. "Klag used Kargan to further his own honor, and then abandoned him when Kargan at last went to *Sto-Vo-Kor*. But that is the least of his crimes."

Now Talak nodded. "You speak of his mutilation?"

"Oh yes," Dorrek said, clenching his fists. "For over ten years, he ignored the wishes of our father. You know of M'Raq?"

"Only that he is the father of both yourself and Klag."

Dorrek managed to contain his disappointment. M'Raq had once been a great warrior, and it disheartened him that his deeds had not been immortalized. *But then*, he thought, *that was Father's wish*. "My father was captured by Romulans and not permitted to die. He escaped without giving the Romulans any intelligence about us and returned to Qo'noS. Klag refused to see him—until the day M'Raq died, when he descended upon our father's corpse like a predator and grafted his good right arm to his shoulder."

Still, Talak's face betrayed no emotion. Dorrek found it disturbing—was he getting through to the old man? *Am I cultivating an ally or sowing the seeds for my defeat by a most powerful enemy?*

"It would seem," Talak finally said after an uncomfortable silence, "that we both have our reasons for finding your brother unworthy of his rank and position."

This goes better than I had dreamed, Dorrek thought. "Yes. Perhaps we should put those thoughts to action."

However, Talak shook his head. "No. At least not yet. Klag has just joined the Order, and is obviously favored by Martok. And, whatever he may or may not have done at Marcan V, his deeds at Narendra III are unimpeachable."

Dorrek spit on the stone floor of the amphitheater. "With the help of *humans*."

"With the help of *Picard*," Talak said. "That human is a hallowed figure in the Empire, Captain, and Klag has fought beside him as an equal. That is a factor that cannot be underestimated."

Bristling, Dorrek had to at least concede that point. Jean-Luc Picard was the only outsider ever to serve as Arbiter of Succession, having done so a decade ago when Gowron succeeded K'mpec—navigating a civil war between Gowron and the House of Duras along the way.

Then, for the first time, Talak smiled. "But it can be overcome—eventually. We will wait. Klag is a *toDSaH* who has survived due to the skills of others far more worthy. Today, however, he, like you, has been sent to the Kavrot Sector—alone. He will not have Martok or Picard or Kargan to save him." The general put a hand on Dorrek's shoulder. "We will speak again when the time is right, Dorrek, son of M'Raq. My Housemate and your father will be avenged. On that, I give you my word."

"And I give you my word," Dorrek said, returning the gesture, "that whatever aid you will need to expose Klag for the coward and fool that he is, I will provide."

Talak nodded. "Good. Now, return to the *K'mpec*. You have a long journey ahead of you, and much glory to bring to the Empire."

Returning the nod, Dorrek stepped back and activated his communicator. "Dorrek to *K'mpec*. One to transport."

"*Qapla'*, Captain," Talak said.

"To us both," Dorrek replied as the transporter took him back to his command.

Immediately upon Klag's entering his quarters on the *Gorkon*, the intercom sounded with a message from Lokor, his chief of security.

"*Captain, the* I.K.S. Mekbel *has arrived with the crew replacements.*"

"Good. Instruct the transporter rooms to bring them aboard. Have the troops report to their *QaS DevwI'* and the others report directly to their duty stations." He paused. "Except for Commander Kornan and Lieutenant Leskit—bring them to me in my office."

"As you command," Lokor said. *"Sir, I must ask—will we be learning our new mission soon?"*

From anyone else, the question might be presumptuous, but Lokor was simply doing his duty. As the head of ship's security, he was concerned with maintaining order on the *Gorkon*. He had expressed concern with the deleterious effect of prolonged inactivity on the ground troops under the command of the *QaS DevwI'*. The *Gorkon* had been in space for almost five months, and the call for the fifteen hundred troops assigned to the vessel had been minimal. Several had been rotated off at Ty'Gokor, and most of those the *Mekbel* was transporting now were replacing those.

"Our new mission will be announced once we have gotten under way."

"Thank you, Captain. Out."

Klag sighed. *He won't thank me once he hears of the mission.* The Kavrot Sector was a huge expanse of space in the Beta Quadrant, far from the borders of other local powers. No other local governmental body of any consequence had territory bordering on that sector.

Unfortunately for Lokor, the mission was likely to be one of prolonged inactivity, leavened with bursts of action that would require their warriors to be at their finest. Lokor's unenviable task would be to make sure that the *QaS DevwI'* were able to keep the troops' frustration during the former at bay and have them be ready for the latter.

Before departing his quarters, Klag contacted the medical bay. "Dr. B'Oraq, this is Klag. What is Lieutenant Toq's condition?"

"*Unconscious,*" B'Oraq said in a tone that conveyed the smile Klag knew was on her face. "*He is not due on the bridge for another twenty minutes. If he has not roused by then, I will administer a stimulant that will render him capable of duty.*" She paused. "*I can't guarantee it will render him capable of coherent speech, but he will be fit for the bridge.*"

"Well done, Doctor."

"*While I have you here, Captain, I believe you wanted to commence* bat'leth *drills today?*"

"Yes." Klag had grown reaccustomed to having two limbs for everyday activities. The next step was to relearn the skills of a warrior—which was, after all, why he had chosen to undergo the transplant procedure in the first place. He wished to improve his prowess as a warrior and bring honor to his House. He could not do that until he adjusted to fighting with a *bat'leth*. "When my bridge shift ends today, we will meet on the holodeck."

"*Very well. Out.*"

Klag then exited his quarters and headed for the bridge. Morr, Klag's personal guard, fell into step behind him.

The turbolift door opened noisily to the bustle of activity that characterized the nerve center of any spacefaring vessel. Entering on the starboard side, he saw the second-shift crew at the science and communications stations, the fire and damage-control stations just beyond them from where he stood.

He strode across the bridge, his boots pounding loudly on the metal of the deck. The noise level reduced as soon as everyone realized that the captain was present. At the rear of the bridge, the four secondary gunner positions sat empty until such time as the *Gorkon* would be called into battle. Beyond that, assorted *bekks* worked the various engineering consoles. Ensigns Kal and Morketh stood at the operations and primary gunner positions behind the captain's chair, while Ensign Koxx occupied the helm control station to the chair's left. The chair itself remained empty—only the supreme commander of the vessel had the right to take that seat, and that was Klag until such time as he was removed.

May that day only come when I die in battle, this fine crew by my side.

Lieutenant K'Nir, the second-shift duty officer, rose from her position in the first officer's chair.

"Report," Klag barked at her.

"Holding position in standard orbit around Ty'Gokor, Captain," K'Nir said quickly. "Transporter rooms report all crew replacements on board. All systems show ready."

"Good. All of you are to remain on the bridge when your shift ends in fifteen minutes until I dismiss you."

As he spoke, the port turbolift door opened to let in

three officers, of whom Klag recognized two. Leading the way was the tall, muscular form of Lokor. His waist-length black hair was tied in intricate braids, making him instantly recognizable. The white-haired one behind him, who added to his uniform by wearing a necklace made up of Cardassian neckbones, gathered in combat over the past few years, was Leskit. The lieutenant had served as the *Gorkon*'s pilot during its shakedown and first mission before being rotated back to the *Rotarran*. Since then, Klag had gone through three pilots, each more incompetent than the last, culminating in the fool Vralk, who had gotten Klag's first officer, Commander Tereth, killed at Narendra III. Tereth had been a fine warrior and an excellent officer, and deserved a better fate. Naturally, Klag put Vralk to an ignoble death, happily twisting the *d'k tahg* that released the imbecile's spirit to *Gre'thor* himself. Command had finally seen fit to provide him with a pilot who had some skill.

The third had a commander's medal, and therefore had to be Tereth's replacement as Klag's first officer: Kornan. Toq had been second officer only for a few months, and both Klag and Command agreed that he was not yet ready to take on the responsibilities of a promotion, so Kornan was assigned. Klag knew that, like Leskit, the commander had served on the *Rotarran*, including several tours under then-General Martok himself. Klag noted that Kornan had unusually short hair and wore a sleeveless tunic instead of his standard uniform, though it had all the appropriate insignia.

"You have the bridge until then, K'Nir." He gazed upon the three officers. "Return to your post, Lokor. You two, with me."

Lokor nodded and reentered the turbolift. Klag walked the rest of the way across the bridge to his office, the footfalls behind him indicating that Leskit, Kornan, and Morr did likewise behind him.

Klag took his seat behind his desk. Morr, of course, remained outside the office, but the *Gorkon*'s new first officer and pilot followed the captain in and stood before him.

"Welcome back, Leskit," Klag said.

"Couldn't muddle through without me, Captain?"

"Apparently not, based on the animal Command sent to replace you. And his two replacements were far worse." Klag smiled. "Though I hope that you will endeavor to report for combat duty fully dressed."

Kornan shot the pilot a look at that. Leskit simply grinned. "That will depend on factors outside my humble control, Captain."

Klag laughed at that, then turned to Kornan. "As for you, Commander, you come highly recommended—most notably by Chancellor Martok. Yet, sometimes I wonder."

"Sir?"

"Your service record reads like one who has been replaced by a changeling. First we have the Kornan who served as gunner on the *Rotarran*. Then the ship won a victory against the Jem'Hadar while rescuing the *B'Moth*, and it is as if a switch was thrown. The old Kornan bore little resemblance to the Kornan who was decorated six times over the course of the war."

"I had—lost my way, Captain," Kornan said after a moment. "The chancellor helped me regain the path to honor, and I have not strayed from that path since."

Leskit leaned forward and pretended to speak in a whisper. "He's also gotten much more boring."

Snorting, Klag said, "Be that as it may, you will need to remain on that path. This is a crew of our finest warriors, Commander, and you have a difficult task ahead of you. Tereth was well regarded, and she died a death unworthy of her. You will be held to a lofty standard. See that you live up to it."

"I will, sir."

"Good. I chose you due to that—do not make me regret that choice."

Klag hoped that the reality of Kornan lived up to the billing. For the first time, Klag had had a choice in first officers—Command had assigned him the useless Drex when he first took command of the *Gorkon,* and Tereth had specifically requested the post when Drex was transferred off. This time, Klag chose from a variety of candidates, of which Kornan seemed best suited. The *Rotarran* had gained a reputation as a ship that knew only defeat before Martok had managed to restore the vessel's—and the crew's—honor. Kornan and Leskit had both been part of that, and part of the transformation.

And given the nature of our mission, those skills would be of even more use.

"The primary shift is about to start," he said, handing Kornan the padd that Talak had given him. "This will be our mission."

Kornan read over the padd. "It could be glorious," he said, looking up from the display.

"Yes. This is our chance to add to the Empire and make us even stronger. You will give our orders to the crew when the primary shift reports, and then you will take us to the Kavrot Sector."

"It will be an honor to do so, sir."

"Then report to your station, Commander. I will be on the bridge shortly."

"Yes, sir." Kornan turned and left the office.

Leskit hung back for a moment. "As I said, Captain—much, much more boring."

"That order was for you both, Leskit."

"Of course, Captain," Leskit said with a slight bow. "After all, we can't trust these younger pilots to find their way to the Kavrot Sector."

"Actually," Klag said with a grin, "I simply wish to have someone convenient to blame when we get lost."

Leskit laughed, and exited the office.

That left Klag alone.

Now to get up out of the chair.

The trick, really, was not to think about it. When he didn't focus on it, he got out of the chair with little difficulty. But the presence of a new first officer made him all the more self-conscious, which was why he made sure that Kornan and Leskit were dismissed. This way, when he did list to the right—and he knew that he would—he would not be shamed.

Why is this so difficult?

After putting it off for several minutes, he finally got up from the chair, and stumbled to the right. *"Qu'vatlh!"* he cursed in anger.

I will conquer this, he swore. *I will not let this defeat me.*

He entered the bridge just as Kornan was finishing providing the *Gorkon's* new mission to the crew. "And so we go for the glory of the Empire!"

The bridge was full, with both the primary and second shifts present. All of them cheered at Kornan's words.

Almost all of them, Klag amended with an amused look at the operations console. Toq was at his station, as duty required, but his eyes were half-open, and he did not cheer. Indeed, the volume of the cheers seemed to cause him pain. Next to him, Lieutenant Rodek, the first-shift gunner, looked at the young second officer with combined amusement and pity.

Kornan turned to Klag and nodded. Klag nodded back. Kornan then said, "Second shift dismissed." As the officers and *bekks* filed out toward the turbolifts and the rear exit, Kornan once again regarded his commanding officer. "The crew stands ready, Captain."

Klag moved to his command chair and sat in it.

"Our enemy stands waiting for us, Commander—let us face it."

"Yes, sir." Kornan sat in the first officer's chair to Klag's right. "Lieutenant Leskit, set course for the

Kavrot Sector. Proceed at full impulse, then execute at warp eight when we have cleared Ty'Gokor."

"Setting course and executing, as the commander commands," Leskit said with a smile.

Klag looked down at the medal that symbolized his latest honor. *There is an entire sector out there that has not heard the songs of Kahless. But they will hear them, loud and clear.*

Leskit announced, "We have cleared Ty'Gokor."

"Execute," Kornan said.

The *Gorkon* went into warp, heading out into the unknown.

CHAPTER FOUR

Wol walked up to the door that led to the *QaS DevwI'*. The twenty who served as the troop commanders on the *Gorkon* had their workstations in the room on the other side of the door. Wol, who was among the transfers from the *Mekbel*, had been given orders to report to Vok, the first among the *QaS DevwI'*. She had expected to be assigned to one of the middle groups. To be assigned to the most prestigious of the twenty was an honor indeed.

The Chancellor-class ships had a complement of one thousand five hundred soldiers, broken into three hundred five-soldier squads. Each of the twenty *QaS DevwI'* commanded fifteen squads. Vok commanded the first through fifteenth. First Squad was, of course, the elite. Those five received the highest duties, including serving as the personal guards to the senior staff. The Leader of the first was the captain's personal bodyguard.

Wol had no chance of attaining such a lofty position, but she hoped perhaps to be assigned to Ninth or Tenth Squad and be able to work her way up.

"Enter," sounded a voice from the other side of the door, which parted noisily to let her in.

The room was cramped, with twenty small desks in groups of ten that were face-to-face with each other. Only one was occupied: the one on the far left as she entered. The Klingon who sat at it was a barrel-chested man with stringy brown hair that extended to his neck. His facial hair consisted only of a small mustache and a chin beard. He stared at the computer screen on the desk, then looked up when Wol entered. As he did, a huge smile spread across his face.

"Come in, come in! You must be *Bekk* Wol. I am Vok—welcome to the *Gorkon*."

"Thank you, sir," she said, coming to an attentive pose to the right of the *QaS DevwI*'s workstation.

"I've read your file, Wol. You've been a credit to your ships. I'm especially impressed with your work securing the station at Mempa IX during the war."

Given that she had disobeyed orders to accomplish that, she was grateful to hear Vok say so. Krantor, the superior whose orders she disobeyed, was kind enough to die in the fighting and was never able to report it, and the other troops supported her because Krantor was a fool.

Wol said none of this. "I was merely one of many, sir."

"Don't be so modest, *Bekk*. Mempa IX was a crucial

battle, and your ability to adapt to the circumstances speaks well of you."

At that, Wol shot Vok a look. *Does he know——?* But that was impossible. With Krantor dead...

"In any case, we're lucky to have you here, and I've decided to have you fill a vacancy. The Leader of Fifteenth Squad was rotated off-ship. You will take his place."

Wol tried to control her reaction. "*Leader,* sir?"

"Of course." He laughed, a hearty one that came from the deepest recesses of his large belly. "Did you think I called you here simply to assign you as a mere soldier? I have received fifty new troops, *Bekk.* If I called each of them in here to hand them their assignments, we'd be deep in the bowels of Kavrot by the time I was finished. No, simple troop assignments are posted on the duty roster. Leaders, however, I prefer to notify personally."

Vok rose from his chair and started pacing around Wol, who continued to stand attentively. His corpulent form caused the medals on his uniform to clank as he walked, his boots treading heavily on the deck. Yet, for all his swagger, he retained a smile that reminded Wol of her uncle.

An uncle I'll never see again, she thought bitterly, then put the thought aside. Her days as a member of the House of Varnak ended long ago.

"Don't think I'm doing you a favor here. You'll have to earn the title of Leader, and if I think you haven't, you'll be sent to the three hundredth without a moment's hesitation."

Wol repressed a shudder. The three hundredth was the lowest of the low. They were the troops who considered assignment to waste extraction a better day than most.

"However," and that smile was still there, "I doubt it'll come to that. Anyone who can think on her feet the way you did at Mempa knows how to lead warriors into battle. Or into whatever else they may face. And that will be the biggest issue. The fifteenth is the lowest of my groups—you'll be, in essence, the worst of the best. That means you'll have the most to prove. I expect you to prove a great deal to me."

"I hope to go beyond your expectations."

Again, the belly laugh. In fact, Vok put his hands over his stomachs as he did so. "Well said, Wol, well said!" He walked back to his desk, grabbed a padd and a small piece of metal, and handed both of them to her. "These are your troops," he said, indicating the padd, and then handed her the piece of metal, adding, "and this is your insignia. All four of your troops have been serving on this ship since its shakedown—but this is their first time under my command. Your job is to make sure they're worthy of their promotion."

"And that I'm worthy of mine?" she asked without thinking, then immediately regretted it.

However, Vok just smiled. "That, too."

Wol looked for a moment at the small pin that denoted her as a Leader. It would be placed over the small symbol on her uniform's right biceps indicating that she was a simple *bekk*. Now she declared to all that she was something more than that.

Vok sat back down, the chair creaking from having to accommodate his girth. "You're dismissed, Leader Wol."

Nodding, Wol turned to leave. Then she stopped at the door and turned back around. *If he'll accept one breach of protocol, perhaps he'll accept a second.* "Sir, at Mempa, I was simply following orders."

That prompted a third belly laugh. "If that *toDSaH* Krantor actually gave those orders, I'm a *ramjep* bird. Now then, I believe I dismissed you. I have work to do, and so do you."

Still smiling, he went back to his computer screen. Satisfied, she turned and left.

So, he knows Krantor. Or, rather, knew him. That explains a great deal.

Never in her wildest dreams had Wol expected this. Her status as a Houseless female had left her options fairly limited. Even within the Defense Force, she never expected to advance beyond that of a soldier. To be given the responsibilities of a Leader was more than she could have hoped for.

Though still less than I could have been. . . .

Wol tried not to think about the past, about her time as the daughter of a great warrior—or her intended mating with a fine warrior that she herself sabotaged when she instead bore the child of the man she truly loved. Her lover was killed; her son was given to a cousin; she was exiled. She had wanted to die with her lover, but even that was denied her—and her father could not bring himself to have her put to death. *As if his discomfort mattered more than my ability to regain my honor.* But the House of Varnak did what was proper, not what was right, and she found herself going from a life with limitless options to one with very few.

So she changed her name and joined the Defense Force.

Years of service were mostly uneventful. She moved from post to post, doing her duty, slaying the Empire's enemies, and getting noticed by no one, save the occasional fellow soldier in need of someone to help keep a bunk warm.

Until Mempa IX, when Krantor tried to get them all killed and she stopped him, enabling them to take the base from the Cardassians instead of losing it so soon after the fleet had reconquered the world. Not willing to die to suit the whims of a fool, nor to allow Mempa to fall back into Dominion hands, she took over the operation, fully expecting to be killed for her effrontery, but secure in the knowledge that the day would be won. To her shock and gratitude, the only one who died was Krantor, and the rest of the squad stood by her. The fool was given posthumous credit for a victory he did not earn, and Wol was able to continue serving the Empire.

The day, only a few months previously, when she learned that the House of Varnak had been eliminated, thanks to its participation in a failed coup against Chancellor Martok, had been bittersweet. Most of her family was dead, and she lived on, when by all rights it should have gone the other way around.

The one thing she had never been able to find out

for sure was whether or not her son survived—in part because she had never been able to learn his name. The cousin who had taken her child in had many sons, and Wol never knew which was hers. Of course, if he did live, he was a man without a House also, since Varnak was disgraced and eliminated.

And she, who was once disgraced, was now a Leader.

She worked her way toward the barracks, located on the ship's centermost deck. The troops were housed in bunks that were arranged by squad. The deck consisted of a maze of corridors, each wall taken up with five bunks inset into the bulkhead that were stacked from deck to ceiling. Each bunk was two meters in length, one meter in width, and half a meter in height. That two meters of space and whatever you could cram into it was the only thing you could call your own if you were a Klingon soldier. The Leader got the bottom bunk, which could be climbed into easily from the deck; the others were accessible via a ladder.

It didn't take long for Wol to locate the fifteenth set of bunks, located in the forward section of the deck. She was not surprised to find that her few belongings had been placed at one end of the space that would serve as her two meters for the duration of her tour on the *Gorkon*.

A man roughly the size of a small asteroid approached the bunks from the other direction. Wol blinked in amazement. This *bekk* made Vok look diminutive.

His face—round, and with a thick black beard that

covered his cheeks, mouth, and chin—gazed down at her. His wide shoulders blocked out the ceiling lights, casting a massive shadow on Wol. "I am Goran."

"I am Wol, your new Leader."

Goran pointed a massive finger at her belongings. "I need to sleep in that bunk."

Wol started. The Leader always had the bottom bunk. It was the way of things. "That bunk is mine, *Bekk.*"

"I need to sleep in the bottom bunk." Oddly, there was no threat in Goran's voice, merely a statement of fact. "If I don't, the bunk will break. It is because I am the biggest and the strongest."

Wol quickly called Goran's service record up on her padd, and took particular note of his weight. The bottom bunk had the added reinforcement of the deck itself to support Goran's considerable bulk. The material of the upper bunks by themselves might not be sufficient. And the only way to prove otherwise was to risk Goran crashing through to her own bottom bunk. *Not really worth the risk.*

"Very well, *Bekk.* You will switch my belongings with yours and take the bottom bunk."

From behind her, a voice said, "An *opera?*"

Wol turned to see two warriors approaching. The older one had waist-length white hair and a horn-shaped beard; the younger had squinty eyes and light brown hair. The latter had spoken.

"Yes, an opera," the older one said in reply. "You have something against opera?"

"I have nothing against *good* opera." The younger

one was scowling. "I doubt you have the stuff to create such a thing."

The older one laughed. "Perhaps I don't. But I believe that I can provide something no other opera can."

Facing the two warriors, Wol asked, "And what would that be, *Bekk?*"

"Who are you?" the younger one asked belligerently.

"Who do you think she is, *petaQ?*" the older one said quickly, elbowing the younger one violently in the ribs and pointing at the insignia on her right biceps. "You must be our Leader."

"I am Wol."

"I am G'joth, son of Ch'lan," the older one said, then indicated his comrade. "This young idiot is Davok, of the House of Kazag."

To Wol's annoyance, Davok's eyes went to the left biceps of her uniform, which was bereft of any decoration, indicating that she had no House. By introducing him only by House rather than lineage, G'joth indicated that Davok had not been born to Kazag, but was brought into the House for other reasons.

Wol had neither House nor mother to identify her. "Is there a problem, *Bekk?*"

"No, Leader. Not yet."

"Ignore him," G'joth said quickly. "The rest of us do." He looked over at Goran, who had just clambered into the bottommost bunk. "Goran? Is that you?"

Goran looked up at G'joth. "Hello, G'joth. Are you in this squad also?"

Laughing, G'joth said, "Indeed I am. Oh, this will be

glorious. There's no one on this ship I'd rather have at my back than the big man."

"Thank you, G'joth," Goran said. "You can rely on me. Uh, you too, Leader Wol."

Wol acknowledged the amendment, then turned back to G'joth. "So what is this new perspective your opera will award us?"

"A true warrior's perspective. How many operas were written by actual warriors serving in the Defense Force? Oh, sure, some officers have gone on to compose some fine works, and of course you have the usual drivel about the lowborn merchant who becomes the greatest general who ever lived, but those are never actually written by lowborn merchants."

Laughing, Wol said, "Or by great generals."

"Good point." G'joth returned the laugh. "I will tell the truth."

"You're a fool," Davok said, climbing up the ladder to his bunk, which was the topmost. "Operas aren't about truth."

"*Most* operas aren't. Mine will be." G'joth climbed up behind him to his own bunk right under Davok's, the padd on which he'd been composing his great work tucked into his belt.

Another warrior approached, this a woman with straight black neck-length hair, holding a small duffel.

G'joth noted her arrival as he settled into his bunk. "Krevor! So you're our fifth."

"It would seem so, G'joth," the woman said.

"Nice to have the ambassadorial bodyguard make

it to Vok's elite," G'joth said with another laugh.

This one's as jovial as Vok, Wol thought. *No wonder the QaS DevwI' chose him....*

"I am Leader Wol. Welcome to the fifteenth."

"I am *Bekk* Krevor. I hope to bring honor and glory to our squad."

"We shall see. You've served as a bodyguard to ambassadors?"

Krevor nodded. "On our mission to taD, I was assigned to guard Ambassador Worf for the mission. I defended him against al'Hmatti rebels."

"Filthy *toDSaH*," Davok muttered from his bunk above.

"What was that, *Bekk?*" Wol asked.

G'joth spoke up. "Davok and I met Ambassador Worf on Narendra III. Davok is just bitter because the ambassador shot him."

"I was not expecting it," Davok said defensively. "He has no honor."

Krevor said, "The ambassador is one of the most honorable warriors I have ever met. If he shot you, I'm sure he had good reason."

"Oh, he had excellent reason," G'joth said. "Davok was awake at the time, you see."

In response, Davok simply turned over, his back to the rest of them.

Shaking her head, Wol said, "All of you get some sleep. The *QaS DevwI'* will address us first thing in the morning, and then you'll get your duty assignments. I expect to hear nothing but good words about the efficiency, skills, and obedience of the fifteenth from here on in. Anything less will be addressed quickly."

"You have nothing to concern yourself with," Krevor said confidently.

G'joth's eyes rolled up toward Davok's bunk. "Almost nothing, in any case." Then he turned back to his padd and his composition.

Wol climbed up to the second bunk, above Goran, who was already slumbering. It wasn't the best she could have hoped for, but it was far from the worst. This was the greatest opportunity she'd had since her father cast her out. She would not squander it.

The *Gorkon* mess hall was a loud, boisterous place. Taking up a full quarter of the ship's seventeenth deck, it consisted of several dozen tables arranged around a central dais. On that dais sat a large food replicator as well as dishes full of nonreplicated food. How much of the latter was present depended on a variety of factors: the availability of food, the availability of replicator power, and the whim of the ship's quartermaster. Today, there was almost nothing on the plates, which didn't surprise Rodek as he waited in one of the six lines for the replicator. After all, this would be a long mission, one that would bring them far away from any Klingon base or repair facility. This early in the mission, they would be depending almost entirely on replicated food, holding the real thing in reserve in the mighty vessel's cargo holds in case replicator power needed to be diverted to a more needy ship's resource down the line.

Rodek had always found replicated food to be a mixed blessing. By not requiring as much cargo space to store food, they were able to conserve room for other functions, and allow more crew to serve on board. In the days prior to the Federation alliance—whence derived this impressive technology—a ship this size would only have three-quarters of the same crew, if not less, owing to the storage needs for food and liquid.

The other side was the appalling taste.

On the *Gorkon,* at least, that difficulty was alleviated somewhat, thanks to the good graces of the now-departed Lieutenant Vall. An engineer without par, Vall was no warrior—yet somehow managed to survive in the Defense Force, when his prospects for survival, and service to the Empire, would have been much better placed at the Science Institute or in some other civilian post. But he had insisted on being where the glory was, and had used his superior technical skills to compensate for his woefully inadequate martial ones.

Up to a point, anyhow. Eventually, the life of a warrior proved more than even he could handle, and he volunteered to be a puppet governor on a thrall world of the Empire called taD.

However, Rodek thought with a smile as his turn in line came up, *we were able to reap the rewards of his prowess.* For the first time since he joined the Defense Force, Rodek ate well from a replicator. Vall had finetuned the devices to the point where even the *rokeg* blood pie was all but indistinguishable from homemade.

Rodek ordered half a pie, as well as some *pipius* claw and half a heart of *targ*. The one thing the replicator could not provide was living matter, so no *gagh* or *racht* would come from it—and the quartermaster had apparently not seen fit to take any out of stasis on this night. *Pity*, Rodek thought. He had felt the urge to feel the wriggling of serpent worms down his gullet.

While he stood in line, the traditional song before the meal was sung. Since the *Gorkon*'s shakedown, every meal had opened with a song, and tonight it was provided by one of the troops, a beardless youth whose name Rodek did not know. His rendition of "*Mahk Jchi*," an ancient song that was sung in an old dialect of the Klingon tongue, was excellent. However, Rodek preferred the recording his father, Noggra, had given him when he left to serve in the Defense Force; it included an insistent drumbeat that drove the rhythm of the song.

After obtaining a mug of *chech'tluth*, he proceeded to what had quickly become known on the *Gorkon* as the secondary bridge: a five-person table in the aft port corner of the mess hall where Rodek and Toq had eaten virtually every meal together since the end of the ship's shakedown. Others had come and gone from the third, fourth, and fifth seats, but the second officer and gunner had remained there, hence the nickname.

Toq was already seated, his plate containing only a bit of *zilm'kach*, his mug holding a liquid with no odor that Rodek could determine.

"I half-expected you to be in your quarters, Toq," Rodek said as he took his seat, dropping his plate to the table.

"I thought I should eat *something*." The second officer spoke in a subdued tone.

Laughing, Rodek said, "That *cannot* have been your first all-night celebration."

Toq simply nodded weakly, and drank some of his liquid concoction. "I had thought myself made of sterner stuff."

"Well, at least you did not disgrace us *too* badly—and you still stood your post for the entire shift. For that, at least, you are to be commended."

"I would rather be commended for being conscious for the captain's induction. I will never redeem myself in his eyes." Toq sounded miserable.

Rodek was about to say that he remembered his first experience with such prolonged celebration—but, of course, he didn't. In fact, Rodek knew nothing of his life prior to four years ago. A shuttle accident near Bajor had robbed him of any recollection of his life prior to the accident. Noggra had done what he could to remind him of the life he had led, but no amount of prompting or mental therapy had been able to restore his memories to him. Though he had, by all accounts, led an honorable life as the son of an advocate, something drew him to the Defense Force. Rodek knew that Noggra had hoped his son would follow his father into the legal profession, but he had also done nothing to discourage him, especially once the war with the Dominion escalated.

"Why am I not surprised to find the two of you here?"

Looking up, Rodek saw the familiar face of Leskit, along with their new first officer. "Where else would we be?" Rodek asked with a grin.

"No doubt the benches have conformed to the shape of your rear ends." Leskit sat down, dropping a plate laden with half a heart of *targ* and a small piece of *bokrat* liver onto the table. Next to him, Kornan did likewise, his plate holding the same items.

Rodek laughed. "No doubt."

"You have done well in your time on this ship," Kornan said after a moment of silence, "both of you. It will be an honor to stand for you on this mission."

"I'm sure it will be," Rodek said. Kornan's words seemed to be sincere, but they lacked—something. Rodek wasn't sure what it was, but Kornan rubbed Rodek entirely the wrong way.

"This is a truly fine vessel," Kornan added. "After years on a bird-of-prey, it will be good to serve on a warship such as this."

"Assuming, of course," Leskit added, mouth full of *targ* heart, "that there is any war to be had."

His voice still weak, Toq said, "There will be war. If we must, we shall ask B'Elath to sing."

Leskit winced. "No one's shoved her out an airlock yet?"

"Who is B'Elath?" Kornan asked.

"One of Kurak's engineers," Leskit said. "She has the voice of a hoarse *grishnar* cat, only less tuneful. She used to massacre 'The Campaign at Kol'Vat.' "

"She still does," Toq said.

"But every time she does," Rodek added, "the next day we go into battle."

Kornan asked, "And are you victorious?"

Grinning, Rodek said, "We are still here, aren't we? I don't know what kinds of ships you have served on in the past, Commander, but on *this* ship, victory is the order of the day."

"I would expect no less," Kornan said, almost by rote.

Rodek chewed on his *pipius* claw. He should not need to explain this kind of thing to his first officer—his first officer should be reminding him of it. Rodek knew that his own passion and fire were sometimes lacking—it irritated him, and he had tried to overcome it. The *Gorkon*'s successes had aided in that regard, and he had hopes of someday regaining his warrior's fire, even if he never regained his memory.

Looking at Kornan, he started to see what others sometimes saw in Rodek himself. And it disgusted him.

Kurak stood with her left hand gripping her right wrist while their new first officer walked through the engine room. Kornan was the third first officer Kurak had had to tolerate since the *Gorkon*'s launch.

Just another year of this, she reminded herself. In a year's time, her nephew would be of age to begin his training as an officer in the Defense Force and then, at last, she could quit this mad place. *The House of Palkar must always serve the Empire*, she thought bitterly; those words had been drilled into her since birth, and the deaths of her parents, brothers, and grandparents during the war had left her as the only able-bodied adult in the House who could serve.

Soon, though, it would be over. She could return to the Science Institute, go back to designing ships instead of coming up with idiotic methods for fixing them on the fly. How any self-respecting engineer could work under these conditions was beyond her—jury-rigged repairs and half-done reroutes was no way to operate machinery, and every day she spent in the Defense Force being forced to work with no proper time or facilities for testing tried her patience.

That she hadn't gone mad was, in her opinion, a testament to her mental strength.

Her only concern now was the duration of this mission. No time frame had been specified, and they would be far from the center of the Empire. She would be trapped on this vessel until the Kavrot Sector mission was complete, even if that took her past the year she had left to her.

She watched as Kornan checked the readouts on the various consoles. Around her, the engineering staff—a collection of unworthy fools, the lot of them, who barely comprehended the tools they wielded—stood stiffly at attention, awaiting the commander's pleasure.

Kornan himself, at least, was worth looking at. The *Gorkon*'s original first officer, Drex, looked like a *ramjep* bird; as for his successor, Kurak had no aesthetic interest in females, though Tereth, unlike Drex, was at least competent to do her job. Kornan, however, had a strong presence, a fierce face, an impressive, if short, mane of black hair, a strong beard that resembled two spears pointing downward, and a powerful musk.

Ironic, she thought, *that he would come along with Leskit's return.*

At last, Kornan finished the inspection. He walked over to Kurak, his muscular arms—exposed by his sleeveless uniform shirt—clasped behind his back.

Kurak braced herself for the inevitable criticisms. She'd been hearing them ever since she first signed on during the war: *You're supposed to be one of the finest engineers in the fleet, why isn't this engine room up to standards, you designed the* Negh'Var, *yet this is the best you can do,* and so on. The captain had been particularly irritating on the subject. As if improvements to engines could ever be done in the field...

Instead, Kornan smiled. "You've done well, Commander. I'm sure Makros would be proud."

"What?" Kurak said. Makros had been her mentor at the Science Institute. His patronage was responsible for her being given not only a commission but the field rank of commander upon enlisting. He died during the war, when a Breen ship attacked the shipyard where he'd been working. She couldn't imagine anyone in the Defense Force who wasn't a general or an engineer knowing who he was.

"Makros. He was a great engineer. I'm sure he's in *Sto-Vo-Kor* now, coming up with better ships for the warriors of history to use in battle." Kornan smiled, showing impressively sharp teeth.

"Well, I will have to disagree with you, Commander—Makros would be appalled to see me working under such obscene conditions."

"Perhaps, but we are lucky to have you on the *Gorkon*. I will provide you with the full report of my inspection by the end of the shift. I do have some changes that will need to be implemented due to the nature of our mission, particularly regarding duty shifts."

"I look forward to reading the report, Commander." For the first time in her career, Kurak spoke those words and meant it.

As he left, and Kurak ordered her subordinates back to their stations, she admonished herself, *Didn't you learn your lesson with Leskit? Form no attachments.* She almost let herself go to that old razorbeast, and then he left.

Of course, he's back now. And it is going to be a long mission....

The rest of the shift went as expected. The *Gorkon* was traveling at warp eight toward Kavrot. The battle damage from Narendra III—which had been minimal in any case—had long since been repaired. So at shift's end, Kurak retired to her cabin. As a commander, she was entitled to her own room, which was a luxury even on a ship this size. One of many things she had to thank Makros for.

Kurak still hated it. Her closet back home had more

space than this and similar claustrophobic holes that she'd been calling home for the past few years.

Just one more year.

The door closed loudly behind her and she collapsed on the bunk, the hard metal a comfort. She supposed she should eat something, though she couldn't motivate herself to get up and go to the mess hall.

Besides, Leskit might be there. And I still haven't figured out if I want to take him to my bed or beat him to a pulp.

Not that the two are mutually exclusive. . . .

Then the door chime sounded. She wondered who it could possibly be. "Who is it?"

"Kornan."

She blinked. "Enter."

The door parted to reveal Kornan's muscular form. "I said we would discuss your inspection further at the end of the shift, Commander."

Kurak sat up. "So you did."

"I'm afraid that I'll have to perform a more detailed inspection, first."

She frowned. "Of what?"

A grin formed on Kornan's face. "Of the chief engineer."

At that, Kurak laughed. It felt good. She hadn't laughed since—

Since Leskit was last on board.

Kornan approached her. She could smell his excitement from the moment he walked in the door. It, in turn, excited her—

—but not as much as she'd hoped. Kornan was certainly attractive enough, but she wasn't sure she was ready to get involved again.

Not after the way things ended with Leskit.

But things got out of hand with the old pilot. He'd never intended more than a romp, and she wasn't really willing to give more than that in any case.

And yet...

Her hesitation obviously was coming through, as Kornan hesitated. "What is wrong?"

"I just came off duty, Commander, and I'm not really in the mood for an inspection." She smiled. "At the moment."

Kornan leaned close to her face. His scent now filled her entire body. "It will be a very long mission," he whispered in her ear.

She pushed him away. "Then you have plenty of time."

"I may grow impatient." He smiled.

She smiled back. "That's your concern, Commander, not mine." Then she guided him toward the door. As it opened, she said, "It's up to you to determine how badly you want to make that inspection."

He left, a lascivious grin on his face.

As soon as the door closed, Kurak let out a growl. *Why did you let him go? He made you laugh.*

Of course, so did Leskit. And, as Kornan said, it is a long mission we have ahead of us. Let us see where things lead.

Instead, she sat down with the intention of catching

up on the technical journals she'd downloaded at Ty'-Gokor. Given the distances they'd be traveling, it might be months before she saw a new one, and she wanted to be as up to date as possible.

And in just a year, I'll be able to write for them again....

CHAPTER FIVE

Nine weeks passed.

Klag was sitting in his office, sipping a *raktajino* and reading over assorted reports, when the door chime rang. Setting the padd aside, Klag grunted in acknowledgment. The door opened to Kornan.

The first officer held two padds of his own. "We will be in sensor range of the binary star system in an hour, and we have received the latest dispatches from Command, sir."

Wearily regarding Kornan, Klag asked, "And what joyous tidings have we received from the Homeworld?"

"Apparently, the *K'mpec* has found a planet worthy of conquest."

"*What!?*" *We have spent nine weeks charting useless rocks, yet Dorrek, of all people, has found something of use?*

Kornan held out one of the padds. Klag leaned forward and snatched it. "The planet is called Brenlek," the first officer said. "Captain Dorrek has called in General Talak's fleet, and they anticipate subjugating the populace within the week."

Klag read over the dispatch, which indicated that Brenlek was rich in both uridium and dilithium, and had a native populace that Klag's younger brother described as "easy to conquer" in his report.

"In addition," Kornan continued, "the *Kravokh* defeated an alien ship that appears to be part of a small confederation. They're investigating further to see if they are worthy of being conquered."

Snorting, Klag thought, *Well, it may not be Romulans, but at least you have your battle, Wirrk.* And now Klag was halfway toward winning his wager with the *Kravokh*'s captain.

Though at the rate we're going, I will never fulfill my half.

"I have scheduled a battle drill for tomorrow," Kornan added.

"Good. Hold it an hour earlier."

Kornan blinked. "Sir?"

"You posted the time for the battle drill, yes?"

"Of course, sir."

"Then coordinate with Toq to have the drill commence an hour sooner—make the crew think it's an actual attack. You'll find the results to be more telling that way."

"An excellent idea, sir."

Klag snarled. "Dismissed."

As Kornan left the captain's office, Klag thought, *Tereth never announced battle drills*. Then he again cast aside the thought as unworthy. Kornan needed to be judged on his own merits, or lack of them, not on the fact that he was different from his predecessor—hardly an offense he could avoid.

The captain checked the time—it was only a few more minutes before another *bat'leth* drill with B'Oraq.

Good, he thought as he looked again at the padd with the *K'mpec's* report on Brenlek. *I'm in a fighting mood.*

Rising from his chair, he once again listed to the right. *"Qu'vatlh!"* he cursed.

He exited the office and headed straight for the bridge's turbolift. Morr fell into step behind him seamlessly as ever. "I will be on the holodeck," he said to Kornan, who now sat at the first officer's station.

Wol was heading to the armory when she encountered two *bekks*—Maris and Trant from the seventh. They both acknowledged her with a quick nod, then went back to their conversation. She might have been a Leader, but she was still only from the fifteenth. Her rank gave her the respect granted by the nod, but no more than that.

Trant had a full, well-trimmed red beard with two braids that protruded down from his chin. For his part, Maris's beard was somewhat weak—just a couple of thin moustache hairs that grew out of the area above the corners of his mouth and some hair on his chin. They went on with their conversation, which appeared to be about the grooming habits of Avok, the Leader of the seventh.

Lieutenant Toq then climbed down from a ladder.

Wol stood at attention at his arrival, and the two *bekks* did likewise, though with less dispatch. "Lieutenant," she said.

"As you were," Toq said quickly. This was Wol's first time meeting the young lieutenant, though she had heard nothing but good things about him. According to G'joth, he had been a bridge officer who challenged the second officer when his carelessness almost got the ship destroyed. Since winning his duel and taking over the position of third-in-command, he had excelled at the position. Krevor had opined that he should have been given the first officer's position after Tereth's death. Meeting him now, Wol saw why that had not happened—Toq was barely old enough to have a beard, much less be one life away from captaining a warship.

As was proper, the three of them fell into step behind Toq. Maris and Trant continued their conversation. Maris said, "I like *your* new beard."

"What is *that* supposed to mean?"

Maris laughed. "It just means that I like what you have done."

"No one laughs at me and lives, Maris."

Trant's voice was unusually harsh for one who had just been paid a compliment. Wol was about to say something when Trant struck Maris with the back of his hand, sending the other soldier sprawling onto the deck.

Maris immediately unsheathed his *d'k tahg*. "So you want a fight, do you?"

"Your jealous rantings do you ill," Trant said with a sneer, doing the same with his own knife.

Wol could not believe what she was seeing. She supposed that Maris could be jealous, but she had heard nothing to indicate it in the *bekk*'s tone.

"Why would I be jealous of you?" Maris said.

"Stop this!" Wol barked.

"Stay out of this, Leader," Trant said. "This is between me and the dead man who dares to laugh at me."

Maris shook his head. "Stupid *petaQ*. I was complimenting you!"

Trant thrust his *d'k tahg* with a shout. Maris eagerly blocked it and screamed a shout of his own. The two of them were suddenly a mass of limbs, fighting with no art, no skill. Punches, kicks, and knife strikes hit seemingly at random.

"That is enough!" Toq cried. "Leader, help me pry these two infants apart, so I can send them to their cribs!"

Nodding, Wol reached for Trant's arms, grabbing one easily and pulling it behind his back. Trant growled and tried to stab Wol by thrusting his *d'k tahg* backward, but he had no leverage, and Wol was able to grab his other arm and keep him in place with a simple hold.

Meanwhile, Toq hooked his left leg around Maris's shin and brought him down. Maris let out a cry of pain, even as his *d'k tahg* clattered to the deck. Toq reached down, grabbed Maris by his sash, and yanked him violently to his feet.

"Look at yourselves! Brawling over a *beard*? You are warriors of the *seventh*, and yet you behave like children!" Toq slammed Maris into the bulkhead. Then he reached down and picked up the *bekk*'s *d'k tahg*. "This is a symbol of honor—of your very self. It should be saved for *honorable* combat. By using it for such a frivolous gesture—and by letting it be taken from you so easily—you dishonor yourself and this ship. I am ashamed to serve on the same vessel as the likes of either of you." He added this last to Trant, still struggling and failing to break Wol's hold.

"He insulted my honor!" Trant shouted.

Wol rolled her eyes.

Toq spit on the deck. "He did no such thing. Are you so desperate for a foe that you manufacture one from the air?"

Trant hesitated. "Perhaps. But when there is no foe to be had—"

"Then you wait until one presents itself." Toq walked up to Trant and spoke directly into his face. "There is no glory in this type of brawl. If you think there is, you belong in a tavern with drunken laborers, not on board the Defense Force's finest vessel." He looked at Wol. "Let him go."

Wol released her grip. Trant yanked his arms free in an unnecessary gesture of defiance. Then he sneered at Toq. "You have made an enemy this day, Lieutenant."

"I have done my duty as second officer of this ship, *Bekk*. And this will be reported to *QaS DevwI'* Vok and to Lieutenant Lokor."

Wol spoke up, then. "That is not necessary, sir." With a glower at Trant, she added, "And you have made no enemies this day. This is a matter for the troops. We will see to it."

Toq stared at her. A youth he may have been, but he was no fool. He knew that it was his duty to report this, but he also knew that it would only serve to cripple the seventh to no good end.

"You are to be held responsible for their behavior, Leader," Toq said. He handed Maris his weapon, then turned on his heel and continued to the mess hall.

As soon as the lieutenant was out of earshot, Wol looked at both troops.

"We are in your debt," Maris said. "We would probably be on waste-extraction duty with the two-seventy-fifth right now if you—"

"You are very much in my debt, both of you," Wol barked. "You have both indeed made an enemy today, but it is *not* Toq—it is me. I swear to you, if I learn of *any* dishonorable behavior on either of your parts, I will kill you both. And I *will* collect on that debt, of that you can both be *very* sure."

Maris had the good grace to look vaguely contrite. Trant was still snarling.

Then Wol turned on *her* heel and continued to the armory without another word.

For the first time in nine weeks, Leskit laid eyes on Kurak.

It was in the mess hall, which had gotten progressively quieter over the course of the last couple of months. Leskit remembered the dark days on the *Rotarran*, when they had lost engagement after engagement with the Dominion. The mess hall had always been quiet there, too, and the number of incidents among the crew rose to dangerous proportions. It took a successful rescue of the cruiser *B'Moth* and a victory against the Jem'Hadar to finally restore joy and honor to the ship. But the *Rotarran* was just a bird-of-prey with a comparatively tiny crew. This was a warship with a complement of almost three thousand. If this enforced inactivity went on much longer, it would make the *Rotarran* look like a party.

At first Leskit was surprised to see Kurak. She generally preferred to eat in her cabin. *Of course,* he thought with wry amusement, *perhaps the toned-down atmosphere suits her nature.* Leskit had considered contriving some excuse to go to engineering at various times over the past two months, but he couldn't convince himself of anything that wouldn't make him look foolish. Besides, while Leskit himself was sure of his own motives, he was less sure of Kurak's.

The last time they'd seen each other was in his cabin on this very vessel months ago, as he was preparing to ship back to the *Rotarran.* He had been hoping for one final coupling, but she was due in engineering.

"Perhaps some other time," she had said, in a tone that gave Leskit hope.

"Perhaps."

"Or perhaps," and here she had reverted to the harsher tone, the one that kept all the engineers on the *Gorkon* in constant fear for their lives, "I will curse your name and never speak to you again."

Leskit had laughed, then. "I believe that's what my mate said to me the last time we spoke."

"A wise woman, I'd say. Good-bye, Leskit."

Yes, he thought now, *the next move is most definitely hers. And, since she's had nine weeks to make it, I suspect that that is the end of it. Ah, well.*

However, as Leskit moved toward the "secondary bridge" to join Rodek, Toq, and Kornan, Kurak approached him. She held a plate of *gagh*—the quartermaster had finally taken some out of stasis, which, according to Kornan, had been done by way of improving morale. Leskit wondered why Kornan hadn't ordered it sooner. In fact, Leskit's own plate was piled high with the serpent worms, lathered in *grapok* sauce, and garnished with a bit of *taknar* gizzards.

"Commander," he said formally. "What do you want?"

"It is good to see you, Lieutenant. How is your mate?"

Leskit smiled. "You'd have to ask her. Our son is doing well, however. You'll be happy to know that his poetry is improving with age."

Kurak scowled. "It could hardly get any worse."

Leskit had given Kurak a love poem his two-year-old had composed. It had been a ploy to get her to laugh, and at that—and other things—it worked marvelously.

"Was there anything else, Commander?"

"I simply wanted to tell you to be careful when you're leaving orbit. You tend toward a course that fights the planet's rotation. It's an unnecessary strain on the engines."

Snorting, Leskit said, "It's also an irrelevant one. This ship is hardly a fragile—"

"I'm giving you an order, Lieutenant. Take better care of the engines."

"And if I don't?"

Finally, Kurak smiled. "Then I will be forced to take action."

With that, she turned and left the mess hall, plate of *gagh* in hand.

"What did the commander want with you?" Kornan asked as Leskit sat down.

Toq grinned. "Finally picking up where you left off?"

"What do you mean?" Kornan asked.

Leskit bit into his *gagh*. "Our chief engineer expressed a concern over my handling of the *Gorkon*'s exit from standard orbit."

Rodek laughed. "That's *it*?"

"What more would she want?" Kornan asked.

"Probably what they had before," Toq said to Kornan with a mouthful of *gagh*, then turned to Leskit. "Unless she found you inadequate."

"Unlikely," Leskit said. "She probably realizes that she won't be able to improve on perfection."

"For what it's worth, Leskit," Rodek said as he finished off his *pipius* claw, "you are the only one who has fired that particular disruptor. Her bed's been as empty—"

"As yours, Rodek?" Kornan said angrily. "Except I am sure in Kurak's case it is by choice."

"I wouldn't presume to guess what goes on in that woman's head, Commander," Rodek said—with, Leskit noted, only partial deference to Kornan's rank.

"That doesn't surprise me," Leskit said after a brief, ugly pause. "As I said, she probably couldn't improve on perfection."

Toq gulped down some bloodwine. "There are more attractive women on this ship. Some of them are *very* athletic."

"Yes, well, that's the only exercise they are likely to get," Rodek said with disdain, "unless we find a planet worthy of our time and attention."

Gnawing on his gizzards, Leskit said, "That's the problem with having the unknown as a foe. Sometimes it doesn't show up for the fight."

"Why do they send us on such a mission?" Rodek asked. "Are we Starfleet vessels that waste time charting solar systems and studying quasars? We're *warriors*. We should be engaging enemies in battle, not making maps for the generals back home."

"Others have engaged in battle," Toq said. "The *Kravokh* and the *K'mpec* have both—"

"I don't care about the other ships!" Rodek ripped off a piece of *ramjep* meat from the bone. "We won a great victory on Narendra III, our captain has been inducted into the Order of the *Bat'leth*, and *this* is our reward?"

"Patience," Leskit said, "patience. You can rest assured, we will see battle before long."

"What makes you so sure?" Rodek asked.

"Because the one constant of traveling in space is that nothing remains constant. Yes, we're bored now, but it won't last. It never does."

Toq asked, "Getting philosophical in your old age, Leskit?"

"Perhaps. But you would do well to make use of my experience, boy."

"I am not a boy," Toq snapped. "And I am also your superior, *Lieutenant*."

Leskit grinned. "My humblest apologies, Second Officer Toq, sir. I did not mean to undermine your authority." Silently, Leskit was impressed. *The boy's grown a spine in the last few months. Good.* The child who'd challenged the former second officer and killed him without any great effort had truly become a warrior. It had been hard to judge that, what with over two months of tedium, but the fire was there—and, more crucially, the assuredness.

We'll need that once our foe—whoever or whatever it is—decides to show itself.

Leskit noted that Kornan had been silent. Then, without warning, the first officer gulped down the remainder of his *chech'tluth*, slammed the mug down on the table, glared at Leskit, then got up to leave the mess hall without a backward glance.

"What was *that*?" Toq asked Leskit.

"How should I know?"

"You've served with him," Rodek said.

Angrily, Leskit said, "That doesn't make me his keeper." He finished his own bloodwine, then got up and chased after Kornan. His words to Rodek and Toq notwithstanding, Kornan's sudden sullenness was more in keeping with the old Kornan, the one who skulked about the *Rotarran* like one possessed by *jatyIn*, and Leskit hadn't the first clue what brought it on. *And given the other growing similarities between this ship and the Rotarran of late, it's best to cut this behavior off at the neck where possible.*

He caught up with Kornan in the corridor. "Now what—"

Kornan whirled on him, his *d'k tahg* unsheathed. "Understand something very important, *Lieutenant*— she's *mine*, unless I say otherwise. You would do well to stay away from her."

Leskit looked down at the blade in shock. Kornan had never pulled his blade on Leskit in all the years they'd known each other, except for good-natured sparring; based on the look on Kornan's face, what the first officer was thinking was neither good-natured nor as harmless as sparring.

"Who, Kurak?" he asked. "You and she are—"

"We will be. I have sworn it."

Unable to suppress a bark of laughter, Leskit asked, "Have you sworn this to *her*? She might, after all, have something to say on the subject."

"That is not relevant."

"Oh, you think that, do you? In that case, my good friend, I suggest you pray fervently that Kahless himself returns to help you, because he's the only one that will stay her wrath if you cross her."

Leskit then turned his back on his comrade and reentered the mess hall. Part of him expected the *d'k tahg* to lodge itself in his back, but Leskit was fairly certain that Kornan wouldn't stab a shipmate in the back over a woman.

Of course, he hadn't expected Kornan to take an interest in Kurak—nor for her to return the favor, though all the evidence indicated that she hadn't yet.

Let them do as they wish, Leskit thought, suddenly feeling very tired. *I'm too old for games. As Toq said, there are other women on this ship.*

B'Oraq watched as Klag sparred with Morr. The young *bekk* was one of the most proficient *bat'leth* fighters on the *Gorkon*—which was both why he had been assigned to be Klag's bodyguard and why Klag now used him as a sparring partner as he relearned the weapon.

At first, Klag had fought against holographic foes, but the captain himself found them unsatisfying after a certain point. They were useful in order for him to refamiliarize himself with the basic maneuvers—the parries, the thrusts, the defenses—but in order to truly regain his form, he needed to fight against a foe with instincts.

And nobody on this ship has better instincts than Morr, she thought.

Certainly Klag didn't. The captain was trying his best, and Morr was very obviously holding back, yet Morr still had the upper hand.

Klag swung his *bat'leth* around, leading with his right hand. Morr parried the blow easily by holding his *bat'leth* vertically braced against his entire left arm, then raised that arm upward to parry, throwing Klag backward. He then guided his weapon around into a downward stroke with his left arm, which was a much slower maneuver than doing the same with his right—which would have been a quick upthrust, as opposed to the full second it took to bring the weapon back down with his left arm. B'Oraq knew that Morr was doing this to make things easier on Klag, and wondered if Klag himself realized it.

Metal clashed against metal as Klag—barely—was able to parry the blow. Had Morr chosen to thrust with his right arm, Klag would not have been able to defend himself.

Nine weeks, and he can barely defend a simple thrust. This is not good.

What concerned B'Oraq the most was that the only thing she saw in Klag's eyes was fatigue. No fire, no bloodlust—and not nearly enough *interest* in what he was doing. *That's been a shipwide problem these past few weeks.*

Again, Klag swung around, leading with his right arm, and again Morr parried, but this time he simply shoved his weapon forward, then rotated the weapon ninety degrees, slamming the outermost of the four blades into Klag's left forearm. His uniform protected him from the blade, but the impact was sufficient to make him lose his grip on the *bat'leth*. Morr then slammed the hilt into Klag's jaw, and the captain fell to the deck.

B'Oraq ran over to Klag, running a scanner over him. "You'll be fine," she said after a moment. "Just the usual bruises."

"How encouraging," Klag muttered. Then louder,

but still with a noticeable dearth of enthusiasm, he said, "We will begin again."

"Captain—"

Before B'Oraq could continue, however, the intercom sounded. *"Kornan to Klag."*

"Klag."

"Sir, we have completed our scan of the binary system. We may have found a planet worthy of our attention."

The captain was on his feet like a shot. Now the fire was in his eyes. "I'll be on the bridge momentarily."

Without a backward glance, he left the holodeck.

To her surprise, Morr stayed behind. "Doctor—" He hesitated.

"What is it, *Bekk?*"

"Klag is my captain. My task is to protect him, but I cannot—" Again, he hesitated.

B'Oraq sighed. "Speak freely, *Bekk.*"

"He should not be leading with his right arm. Its reach is shorter now than it was before Marcan V, and it leaves him vulnerable."

"You could tell him this."

Morr shot her a look that indicated he thought she was insane. *"You* could, perhaps, but not I. He is my *captain.* I must go to his side now, but—" A third hesitation. "He has not gotten better, Doctor. In fact, I believe he is getting worse."

With that, the captain's bodyguard left the holodeck.

Interesting that he was willing to risk Klag's wrath by not accompanying him immediately to the bridge, but not willing to risk the same by criticizing him.

Of course, the two were not equivalent. The former might draw some ire from Klag, and might not; the latter, however, could easily mean Morr's death. Somehow, B'Oraq doubted that Klag was so foolish, but she could see why Morr would not take the chance. The doctor was in a unique position. She had been able to bully Klag into getting the new arm in the first place, and he had come to trust her judgment over the past few months. A lowly, easily replaceable *bekk* had no such assurances.

But sooner or later, Klag was going to have to face the hard reality that his skills with the *bat'leth* would never be what they once were.

Given that regaining his full warrior's skills was his primary motivation for replacing his right arm in the first place, B'Oraq had the feeling that Klag would not face that reality with much grace.

Sighing, she exited the holodeck, shutting it down, hoping that whatever they found on the bridge was truly a new world for them to conquer. *Klag needs something to cheer him up....*

CHAPTER SIX

As soon as the turbolift door rumbled open to allow Klag access to the bridge, he said, "Report."

Kornan, who had been seated at the first officer's position, rose. "Lieutenant Toq has discovered a sixth planet in the binary system."

Klag approached the command chair, but stopped short of it, turning his gaze on his second officer. "The long-range scan indicated a five-planet system."

"Yes, sir, it did," Toq said. "However, there was one reading that seemed—odd. I recalibrated the sensors, and discovered that there was a sixth planet. Actually, sir, it's the fourth planet from the sun. For some reason, the area around the world contains some kind of subspace anomaly that interferes with sensors. Preliminary indications are that the planet's air is breathable. But I cannot be completely sure without a closer look, sir."

Smiling, Klag moved to his command chair. "Give the order, Commander Kornan," he said as he sat.

Kornan also smiled. "Yes, *sir*. Pilot, set course 111 mark 19."

"Course long since laid in, Commander." Leskit, too, was smiling.

It's odd, Klag thought, *when Leskit first reported aboard for the shakedown I was concerned about his manner. Now I find that I missed it while he wasn't here. It is good to have him back.*

"Execute at warp six."

Klag almost questioned Kornan's ordered speed, then recalled their distance from the star system. To go any faster than that would be to overshoot their destination in less than a second.

As the *Gorkon* went into warp, the turbolift door opened to Morr, who took up his position at the captain's office door. Klag admonished himself for not even noticing that Morr was tardy, so eager was he to get to the bridge to learn the details about this world. *No doubt, B'Oraq kept him behind to question him about my bat'leth skills.*

Rodek then spoke. "Sir, I recommend we engage the cloaking device."

Kornan turned to face the tactical officer. "Why?"

"The planet was hidden. It may be so for a reason."

Then Kornan turned to Klag. The captain considered the gunner's words, and knew that they were sensible ones. He gave Kornan a nod.

"Engage cloak," the first officer said, and the bridge lights dimmed a moment later.

"Now entering star system," Leskit said.

"Go to impulse power and take up position five hundred thousand *qelIqams* from the planet."

"As the commander commands," Leskit drawled, operating his console.

Toq's voice then sounded from the operations console behind Klag. "Sir, there is a possible problem. In order to get accurate readings from the planet, I need to do an intensive scan. Such a scan might give away our position—even while we are cloaked."

Nodding, Klag added, "Which would defeat the entire purpose of being cloaked." He thought a moment, then turned to the pilot. "Lieutenant, enter random course changes. Move us around in as patternless a manner as possible. Coordinate your movements with Toq so he can still make his scans."

"Sir," Kornan said, "the scan will take longer, in that case."

Klag stood up; he also turned to face his first officer, handily covering his inevitable move to the right as he did so. "We've waited nine weeks, Commander. I believe a delay of another hour or two will not be fatal." He strode toward his office. "Keep me apprised of your progress."

He hoped for a race of worthy foes, one that had hidden their planet behind these subspace anomalies to protect some great secret, one that he could find and exploit for the Empire.

Perhaps even a foe I can defeat by hand. He had been pleased with his progress in the *bat'leth* drills. With each session he felt more confident. He desperately wanted to test his mettle against a real foe, not a hologram or a warrior who was sworn to protect him. Morr had taken it easy on him—it was inevitable. Klag was, after all, the captain, and even if he ordered Morr to go full-out, he doubted that so loyal a warrior as Morr had proven to be would be able to do so.

No, I need an enemy. A true enemy.

He entered his office. Gazing over the mass of padds on his desk, he decided to finally read the detailed report on his brother's discovery and planned conquering of Brenlek. For the first time since Kornan had brought him the report, he felt he could read it without retching.

Kornan sat at his position, watching the viewscreen as it showed a stable starfield, which then shifted as the *Gorkon* changed position.

From the science station to Kornan's left—just behind Leskit—Toq said, "Commander, I have a preliminary report."

Getting up from his chair, Kornan walked over to the console. Several displays showed various bits of sensor data. Kornan found that he could comprehend only about half of it. It related to subspace, that much was certain, but...

"What am I looking at, Lieutenant?"

"I am still not sure, sir, but I am fairly certain that this is not a natural phenomenon. It seems as if some force has thinned the boundaries between subspace and normal space."

"Kurak to bridge."

"Kornan."

"Commander, how much longer is this foolishness going to continue? We're lumbering around space like a drunken lout, our sensor capacity is at maximum, and we're cloaked. These systems were not designed to work simultaneously in this manner."

Turning to Toq, Kornan repeated the engineer's question. "How much longer?"

"I will need at least two more hours, Commander."

"That is not acceptable."

Peering down at the sensor readings, Kornan thought a moment. "We can get more accurate readings if we are closer." It wasn't a question.

"Of course, sir. But—"

At Toq's hestitation, Kornan angrily prompted, "Yes?"

"Sir, as I said, I am still not sure what these subspace anomalies are. They are difficult to detect, but if we get any closer, we risk interacting with them, and I cannot predict what their effect on the *Gorkon* will be."

"We are warriors, Lieutenant. Risk is our business." He strode to his station. "Engineering, we will endeavor to cut our investigating time." As he sat, he looked at Leskit. "Pilot, bring us to within two hundred thousand *qellqams* of the planet."

"Yes sir." Leskit made the course change. "Am I to assume that once that is accomplished, we are to resume lumbering around space like drunken louts?"

Kornan glowered at the older man. "Yes."

Leskit had been Kornan's friend and comrade for

many years, but just at the moment, Kornan was unclear as to why he had grown so close to the old *toDSaH*. *First to presume to interfere with my pursuit of Kurak, then to display such effrontery on the bridge . . .*

Once they were in position, Toq said, "Resuming scan."

Ten minutes later, a collision alarm sounded and the lights brightened, indicating that they were no longer cloaked.

"Cloaking device offline!" Rodek cried.

At the same time, Leskit said, "Helm unsteady—I'm losing attitude control."

"What is happening?" Kornan asked.

"We're drifting," Leskit said. "Attempting to regain helm control."

Klag then entered from his office. "Report!"

Toq finally reported something useful. "We have drifted into a subspace eddy. There are more of them this close to the planet."

"This close?" Klag turned to face Kornan. "How much closer are we?"

Kornan gritted his teeth. "Engineering was expressing concern with the time we would need to sustain maximum sensors, the cloak, and the random maneuverings, so we moved closer to the planet to expedite Lieutenant Toq's work."

"I've regained control," Leskit said. "Taking us out of the eddy."

Turning to Rodek, Kornan barked, "Damage report!"

"Cloak still offline. Structural integrity field went offline for point-three seconds, causing some minor hull damage, which is being repaired. All other systems normal, sir."

"Time to repair the cloak?"

"Unknown, sir. Nature of the damage still being assessed."

Rodek gave his report concisely and expertly. Kornan appreciated that. Then he turned to see that his captain was glowering at him. Kornan appreciated *that* as well. "Captain, the eddies are difficult to detect, and Lieutenant Toq has not been able to map them."

"Which makes one wonder why you risked getting this close to them, Commander, especially since our defenses are now reduced."

Kornan said nothing. The first officer needed to have the trust of his captain, and he needed not to be weak in front of the crew. If he consulted the captain for such a minor course correction, he would be seen as useless. On the other hand, when there were risks to the ship involved, the captain *should* be consulted. And Kornan's time on the *Gorkon* to date had given him little opportunity to determine which kind of captain Klag was.

"Sir," Toq said before Klag could go on, "I do not believe that the lack of a cloak will be much of an issue. Since we moved closer, I have been able to get full sensor readings of seventy percent of the planet. The air *is* breathable, and there is sentient life—I am detecting several artificial structures and a system of roads. But I am detecting no artificial electromagnetic emissions. Indeed, even natural EM levels are astonishingly low."

Klag's face broke into a huge grin. "Really?"

Kornan tried to remain straight-faced, but even he could not prevent himself from smiling a bit. A preindustrial society would make for fine conquest.

It also meant that the need for stealth had passed. Kornan hoped that would be a mitigating factor in Klag's mind.

"Sir, there is something else," Toq said. "It's only preliminary, but the geological indications are that this world is rich in kellinite."

Everyone on the bridge shot a look at Toq then. The mineral, which was used in shipbuilding, was fairly rare, and two of the Empire's best sources had been destroyed by the Breen during the war. Indeed, the kellinite shortage had made it difficult to replenish the ships lost in battle, and had slowed the postwar rebuilding of the fleet to a crawl.

"This is a great discovery, if it is true, Lieutenant," Klag said slowly.

"Yes, sir," Toq said with what Kornan thought was an unnecessarily proud smile, given that it was only a geological indication so far.

"In fact, this has the potential to be a far greater discovery than Brenlek."

"Quite possibly, sir, yes."

"What a pity for poor Dorrek."

Kornan frowned. He remembered Toq mentioning at

dinner one night that there was bad blood between Klag and his younger brother.

"Of course," Klag assured Toq, "I am primarily interested in the good of the Empire."

"Naturally, sir."

"The fact that it makes my arrogant *petaQ* of a brother look bad by comparison is merely a fortuitous side effect."

"Yes, sir."

Klag nodded. "Excellent. The next priority is to map those subspace eddies."

Blinking, Kornan said, "Sir, should we not—"

"What we should do, Commander," and Klag spoke in a low, menacing voice, "is not risk stumbling into something that can take our cloak offline and deactivate our structural integrity field, even if for only point-three seconds. We cannot claim this world—this world that may combine easy conquest with riches for the Empire—until we have scanned one hundred percent of it rather than seventy, we cannot do that until we achieve orbit around it, and we cannot do *that* until we know we can do so without being destroyed. Once you have determined that we can orbit this world without risk to my ship, we will go in."

"Yes, sir." Kornan hoped he didn't sound as meek as he felt.

To the ensign at the communications station, Klag said, "Have Lieutenant Lokor report to my office. We will be needing troops soon enough, I think. Inform me when you are ready to move the ship into orbit, Commander," he added to Kornan as he went back to his office.

As soon as the door closed behind the captain, Leskit said, "Odd—I thought that risk was our *business*."

Several people laughed at that, including Toq, but they were all silent once Kornan gave them each looks of anger.

He saved the last such look for Leskit. *There will be a reckoning, "old friend," of that you can be sure.*

Kurak shifted uncomfortably in her chair. She had no great desire to be here in the wardroom. She hated having to leave inferiors in charge of engineering during her shift. It was bad enough that she had no control of the place for half the day, but she had learned to live with that over the years. To compound it, however, with being called away for idiotic discourses in the wardroom or the mess hall or the captain's office simply irked her more.

Also present in the room were Toq, Leskit, Kornan, and Rodek. Rodek was the only one she found remotely tolerable—she had served with him once before, on the *Lallek*—and that was only because he mostly left her alone and was less obnoxiously Defense Force than the others. Toq, on the other hand, was the textbook example of the eager young *petaQ* that the military encouraged and she despised with every fiber of her being—he reminded her far too much of most of her family.

As for the other two, they were conspiring to drive her mad, both personally and professionally. In the case of the latter, Leskit's crazed maneuvering had put half her staff into paroxysms, and Kornan's attempt to improve things by moving them closer to those subspace eddies only made the problem worse.

Now they were going to get even *closer* to this planet. The meeting was to determine how best to do this.

"I believe we can navigate the eddies with this course," Toq said. He called up a display on the screen. It showed the planet they had found in green, a latticework of subspace eddies around the world in red, and a path for the *Gorkon* to take in yellow. The yellow path required maneuverings that made what Leskit was doing earlier look positively ordinary.

"That should not be difficult," Leskit said with a confidence that Kurak might have found attractive under other circumstances.

She snapped, "This isn't a bird-of-prey, Leskit. We're a quarter of a *qellqam* long."

Leskit just shrugged. "If we go slowly enough, it can be done more easily. The eddies don't move, do they?"

Toq hesitated. "They have shown no signs of doing so yet."

"Then we can take our time." Leskit grinned. "It's something we've gotten good at these past weeks."

"The eddies are too close together once you're within fifty thousand *qellqams*," Kurak said, refusing to be mollified. "If you stray into one of them, we may lose the structural integrity field for even longer. And with that kind of maneuvering, the hull will be strained past its limits."

"We'll need to divert more power to the field," Rodek said. "Once the cloaking device is repaired, we can take power from there. It's useless as a tactical tool now in any case."

"And wasteful," Toq added. "There doesn't appear to be anything on that planet that can detect us, cloaked or uncloaked."

Kurak stood, slamming her fist on the wardroom table. "What is wasteful is using this ship to thread this needle when it isn't necessary. It is obviously fit for conquest. We should call in the fleet, with their *smaller* ships, let them maneuver that labyrinth, and allow us to continue on our mission."

Kornan also rose and glared right at Kurak with deep black eyes. "Our orders, Commander, are to approach the planet. The purpose of this meeting is to determine how that is to be done. Am I understood?"

I understand just fine, Kurak thought. *As long as the Defense Force brainwashes you into doing every stupid thing some idiot with a captain's medal says, you will continue to do those stupid things.*

Aloud, she simply said, "Very well." She looked up at the display, then saw something. Under most circumstances, she might not even bring it up, but doing so would make her job much easier. Looking at Toq, she said, "Give me your padd, Lieutenant."

Toq handed it to her. She entered some commands, and a new course was overlaid in blue. It matched the yellow course up to a point; after that it had three fewer course changes, but a longer travel time. "If time is not of the essence, I suggest we take this route instead."

Leskit laughed. "Indeed. What is the rush, after all?"

Toq laughed as well. Rodek did not, though he did smile, nor did Kornan.

"Very well." Kornan had not sat back down. "I will take this to the captain. Stations."

With that, everyone got up to leave. Kornan, though, didn't move, and as Kurak approached the door, he spoke. "A moment, Commander."

After the other three had left, she said, "Yes?"

"I simply wish you to be aware, Commander, that your concerns *will* go noted from now on. I have been reading your reports, and those of Captain Klag and Commander Tereth. I know that you have had difficulty in getting your viewpoint heard on this ship. That will change, rest assured."

Kurak regarded Kornan. She had no idea if this was unvarnished truth or simply a way to impress her in the hopes of finishing that inspection he tried to start nine weeks ago.

Ultimately, she didn't care. Having a first officer who appreciated her intolerable situation could only make her life easier. "Thank you, Commander. You can rest assured that, should that be the case, I will be most grateful."

Then she left, thinking, *If you truly are sincere, all the better. If you aren't, then you won't get what you seek.*

Klag looked up from the preliminary sensor scans of the planet to direct a questioning gaze at Lokor, standing on the other side of the captain's desk. The head of security somehow managed to stand ramrod straight yet still look relaxed; his lengthy, intricately braided black hair framed his square-jawed face like a mane.

In response to the gaze, Lokor looked down at his own padd. "I recommend we deploy twenty squads to start, with another forty on standby. That should be enough to secure the primary cities." He tossed the padd onto Klag's desk. "If you want to dignify these settlements with the word 'city.' "

"They would appear to be primitive, yes. What concerns me is the presence of these subspace eddies. We can guarantee they will interfere with scanning equipment. I am concerned that there may be similar interference with weapons."

Lokor frowned. "Why?"

"Instinct. These eddies are there for a reason. They're not natural, that much is certain, and I agree with Rodek's initial assessment: They're there for defense. If so, we have to be prepared for the possibility that our disruptors won't work. They can already neutralize two of our most important technologies, and I will not risk losing this campaign because I did not anticipate that they could neutralize a third. Make sure all the troops are armed with at least two bladed weapons each, and instruct the *QaS DevwI'* to make sure that all are proficient in the weapons they carry. If anyone isn't, keep their entire squad on board."

"Yes, sir." Lokor retrieved his padd and made notes onto the display. "Which *QaS DevwI'* do you think should have the honor?"

The captain thought about it for a moment. This was

their first true ground campaign since their shakedown. Every other use of the troops had involved cleanup or securing a site after the action had been completed. Therefore the honor belonged to the second and third highest ranked on the ship. "Klaris, seconded by B'Yrak."

"I would recommend Vok lead the charge, Captain."

Klag blinked. Lokor had not hesitated, which meant that he had given the matter some thought before the meeting.

Or, perhaps more to the point, he hadn't needed to. The main reason to keep Vok's troops on board the *Gorkon* was to keep the ship secure. On a vessel this large, there were many security concerns, and it was often the most elite troops who were called upon to enforce that security. That was why the captain's bodyguard was always the Leader of First Squad.

The fact that Lokor was recommending having Vok's team lead the charge on the planet meant that his security concerns were minimal.

Seeing no reason to dance around it, Klag said as much. "You feel that the ship's security can be trusted to lesser warriors, then?"

"Yes. Engineering is the only potential trouble spot, but that's nothing new." Lokor grinned viciously, showing especially sharp teeth. "Besides, they are all united in their hatred for Kurak, but also restrained by the fact that none of them actually wants her position. It keeps things—well, not stable, but at least predictable."

Klag chuckled at that. "Very well, then. Inform Vok

that he is to lead our charge to the planet. Klaris will be second."

"Yes, sir. Thank you, sir, this is much better than the holodeck solution."

Frowning, Klag asked, "What holodeck solution?"

Lokor shot his captain a glance. "I assumed Commander Kornan had discussed it with you. Lieutenant Toq and I created a holodeck program that would simulate conquering a world. It was intended to alleviate the—"

When Lokor hesitated, Klag smiled. "Boredom?"

"Yes, sir."

Klag nodded. "Understandable. And it was a good idea. Did the commander approve it?"

"He did."

Another nod. "He was wise to. And not to worry, Lieutenant—this mission is far from over, and the program, I assume, isn't going anywhere. It may still prove useful."

"Yes, sir, I'm sure it will. If that is all?"

Klag thought a moment. "When you are done speaking to Vok, report back to the bridge. I want you there when we achieve orbit, in case the more detailed sensor data necessitates adjusting our forces."

"As you wish, sir."

With that, Lokor left.

Klag leaned back in his chair. He was impressed with Toq and Lokor's ingenuity even as he was disappointed with Kornan's continued mediocrity.

What was most maddening was that Kornan hadn't done anything *wrong* as such. He had shown no cowardice, put the ship in no significant danger, and done nothing to undermine Klag's authority. He simply wasn't as good as—

Tereth.

And, as satisfying as it might be, Klag could not remove a first officer without proper cause. *General Talak would love any excuse to strip my captain's medal from my arm, and that would give it to him,* he thought angrily.

"*Bridge to captain.*" It was Kornan's voice.

"Klag."

"*We have achieved orbit, sir. Toq has begun his scans.*"

At that, the captain smiled. "Excellent."

Time enough to deal with Kornan later. Right now, we have a world to conquer.

"I have never been so bored in my entire life," Davok announced as he sat down at the mess-hall table.

G'joth alternated between stuffing *zilm'kach* into his mouth and tapping on his padd as Davok took the seat next to him. The *zilm'kach* was too soft; everyone was falling all over themselves over the presence of *gagh* on the menu, but G'joth had never been able to stomach the stuff.

"You need a hobby," G'joth said as he tried to figure out which adjective to use to describe the *bekk's bat'leth*.

"Like opera composition?" Krevor asked with a smile.

"Novel writing, actually."

Goran frowned. "I thought you were writing an opera."

"I was, but the music didn't sound right."

Leader Wol arrived then, taking a seat between

Krevor and G'joth. "And here I thought that you simply were tone-deaf."

"He *is* tone-deaf," Krevor said. "You've heard him hum."

"I happen to have a magnificent singing voice," G'joth said archly. "You'll find out tomorrow night when I sing before the meal."

"It couldn't be any worse than B'Elath," Krevor said with a shudder.

Wol frowned. "B'Elath?"

"One of the engineers." Krevor shuddered a second time. "The worst singing voice in all of creation. If you're lucky, you'll never be subjected to her rendition of 'The Campaign at Kol'Vat.' I'm told the Romulans use a recording of it for torturing prisoners."

Goran spoke up. "*QaS DevwI'* Vok says that every time B'Elath sings that song before supper, we win a great victory the next day. Besides, I *like* the way she sings."

"We should get her to sing tomorrow night, then," Davok said, poking at his *gagh* without actually eating any of it. "Maybe then I won't be so bored."

"Tomorrow night's *my* turn," G'joth said.

"And that's the other benefit."

Wol swallowed her *gagh*. "A victory would be a good thing. I helped Lieutenant Toq break up a fight between two *bekks* from the seventh earlier today."

Davok sneered. "Why did you break it up?"

"They were fighting because one of them complimented the other."

G'joth couldn't believe it. "You're joking."

"I wish I was," Wol said. "One of them said the other had a strong beard, and the other attacked him. It was ridiculous."

"You should have let them fight," Davok said, finally picking up a couple of worms. "At least then we'd have something to talk about besides G'joth's novel." He swallowed the *gagh*.

Ignoring the gibe, G'joth asked, "Can you call a *bat'leth* 'sturdy'?"

Wol and Krevor exchanged glances. Wol shrugged. "You could. Why would you want to?"

"I need the right adjective."

Davok snarled. "You need a better hobby "

Wol turned to Krevor and, through a mouthful of *taknar* gizzards, asked, "Did you cut your hair?"

Krevor's hands moved self-consciously to her straight black hair. G'joth hadn't noticed before, but it had been growing past neck-length over the past few weeks, and now Krevor had hacked it back to what it was when she first joined the fifteenth. "I prefer to keep it this length," she said. "It was shorn in battle against the al'Hmatti when I was protecting Ambassador Worf."

Snorting, Davok said, "Not much of a trophy."

"You'd rather I do what Lieutenant Leskit does?" Krevor asked. "Wear Cardassian neckbones on my person like some kind of museum exhibit?"

"True warriors are not afraid to display their victories," Davok said.

Krevor shrugged as she swallowed her *gagh*. "You display yours your way, I'll display mine my way."

The intercom then sounded with Lieutenant Lokor's voice. *"First through Twentieth Squads, report for combat. Twenty-first through Sixtieth Squads on standby."*

"At last!" Davok practically leapt out of his chair.

G'joth got up more in a more leisurely manner, taking a moment to swallow one last bite of *zilm'kach*. The novel wasn't really coming along very well anyhow. *Perhaps I should try verse....*

CHAPTER SEVEN

Me-Larr watched with glee as the two Children of San-Tarah tried to beat each other senseless.

El-Yar claimed that Bo-Denn had stolen a small keepsake from her. Bo-Denn denied the accusation, and the item had not been found in his hut, or El-Yar's, or anyone else's. However, the item was small and easily disposed of in the river, and Bo-Denn's disdain for El-Yar was no secret, and went back many seasons. Declaring the solution was but a formality for the Ruling Pack, since they hardly needed Te-Run's expertise to know that such a dispute was resolved by unarmed combat. It didn't even require a circle.

The fight had commenced after the meal, when the day's hunt had been consumed. El-Yar's white fur almost glowed in the flickering light from the assorted fires that had been lit around the village, whereas Bo-Denn's black-furred form seemed to have a glowing outline around it.

Although Bo-Denn was both larger and more powerful than El-Yar, El-Yar was much faster, with sharper claws. More to the point, she knew how to use them. She had spent most of the fight on the defensive, but her attacks drew blood, where Bo-Denn had made many attempts to gain the upper hand, with little success.

Screaming, Bo-Denn suddenly dove at El-Yar. Me-Larr watched with amusement. *No art to it*, he thought, *but art matters little if one achieves results*. Bo-Denn's greater weight meant that he might very well crush El-Yar and be victorious.

Sure enough, Bo-Denn landed on top of El-Yar, knocking her to the ground. He lay across her, his bulk pinning both her head and her right arm to the ground.

"Now you die, liar!"

You should have pinned both arms, Me-Larr thought even as El-Yar reached with her left arm and grabbed the back of Bo-Denn's neck, then ripped out a chunk of fur and flesh with her claws.

Bo-Denn screamed in pain, but did not move. *Perhaps he hopes to suffocate her.*

Around them, members of the pack goaded on one or the other of the contestants. Me-Larr was not in the least bit surprised to see that most of those cheering El-Yar were the women, while Bo-Denn's primary support came from the men.

A three-note horn blow cut through the fighting, the cheering, and the screams.

Those sounds all stopped almost at once. El-Yar ceased her struggles, and Bo-Denn even rolled off her. Suddenly, the Children of San-Tarah had a concern far beyond that of an accusation of petty theft.

Three notes meant something that had not happened since Me-Larr was a cub. Then it had been three of the packs rebelling against the Ruling Pack and attempting to take over the guidance of the Children of San-Tarah. That effort had failed, owing mainly to the valiant Yi-Rak, who died quelling the uprising, as well as a much younger Te-Run. Since then, the only combat the San-Tarah had engaged in had been of their own choosing: on hunts, or in disputes like that of Bo-Denn and El-Yar.

The messenger who had sounded the alarm ran into the village, horn in hand, looking for Me-Larr. The head of the Ruling Pack ran toward her to make finding him easier on her; the others of the Ruling Pack did likewise, and they converged near one of the fires.

"We are invaded," the messenger said.

"By whom?" Te-Run asked.

"I do not know. I have never seen their like before. They appeared as if from the air. They have no fur, save for a mane atop their heads, their faces are flat, and they are armed quite well. They are moving toward us."

Me-Larr did not hesitate. Some threat had come. Perhaps it was more from beyond the clouds, like those whose sky-battle blotted out the stars generations ago. Perhaps they came from beneath the ground, or from the other side of the world. Ultimately, it did not matter. None might violate San-Tarah land without a fight, and no force existed that could defeat them in battle.

"To arms!" he cried. "A foe has come! Tonight we shall prove to them that the Children of San-Tarah are defeated by no one!"

All those present howled in reply, then ran to their huts to retrieve their weapons.

Wol materialized in the middle of a dirt road, the rest of her squad alongside her.

The only illumination was provided by the shoulder-mounted lamps that each member of the fifteenth carried. Among the many deleterious effects of the subspace eddies in the space around this world were that the stars were blocked from view, so the sky provided no illumination at night.

However, the shoulder lamps combined with some not-too-far-off firelight to give the Klingons—who had night vision far superior to that of most bipedal sentients in the galaxy—enough of a view to quickly get the lay of the land. The road on which they stood had tall, brown-leafed trees and shrubs on either side. *Good cover for an ambush*, she thought. A village—the source of that firelight—could be seen about a quarter of a *qellqam* in one direction, a mountain in the other. The former, from what Wol could see, was constructed from simple huts made out of local flora. *These people would seem to be easy prey.*

However, the fifteenth did not have the honor of taking the village—which was apparently the closest to a first city that this world had. Their job was to secure the primary road leading into that city. Although calling it a road was, perhaps, giving this dirt path too much credit....

Wol held her disruptor pistol in one hand, a *mek'leth* in the other. *QaS DevwI'* Vok had warned them that energy weapons might not work on the surface of this world, so they needed to be prepared to fight with older, bladed weapons. No one really found that much of a hardship. Goran had decided not to take his hundred-year-old disruptor with him for fear of harm coming to the old heirloom. The *bekk* claimed that it had been used in the service of *Dahar* Master Kor on Organia in the campaign against the Federation's Kirk, which Wol didn't entirely believe.

Vok had in fact ordered that everyone take two secondary weapons, and they had to be proficient in both of them. In practical terms, that meant that most had to bring something besides their *d'k tahg*. The exception, once again, was Goran, who had a *d'k tahg*, naturally, but never used it, as his hand was larger than the blade's grip, making it impractical for the giant's use. He instead carried a *tik'leth* on a holster strapped to his back, as well as a *bat'leth*.

For her part, Wol had always preferred the flexibility of a *mek'leth*. Unlike the two-handed *bat'leth*, it could be wielded with one hand and was faster on the parry and strike.

The first order of business was to test the disruptors. Wol unholstered hers and attempted to fire it at a bush.

Nothing happened.

"*Qu'vatlh*," she muttered. "It seems that the concern about disruptors was justified."

"You mean," Davok said with a sneer, "the officers were *right?*"

G'joth laughed. "It does happen occasionally."

"We'll just have to do this the old-fashioned way," Wol said. "Stations."

Davok and G'joth took up posts on the far side of the road, with Wol and Krevor holding position where they had materialized, and Goran placing his mountainous self in the dead center of the road. *Can't get much more secure than that*, she thought.

Wol expected very little from this campaign. Once they took the first city, the *Gorkon* would break orbit and get a message to General Talak. The general's fleet would come and finish the job the *Gorkon* started, and then they'd move on to the next place. *If there is a next place*. In truth, Wol had hoped for a worthier foe than a group of primitives to have to conquer. True, their world provided many natural defenses. Apparently the area surrounding the planet not only prevented the *Gorkon* from using subspace communication beyond a certain range, but also disruptors and torpedoes—the former would not fire and the latter's explosive capabilities were neutralized. But that didn't bother Wol, as it just meant the ground troops were even more important.

She removed the hand scanner from her belt. Unfortunately, it worked no better than the disruptors. "The scanners aren't functioning, either." Then she smiled.

"It would seem that we truly shall have to depend on our instincts."

"Good," Krevor said with a grin.

"This will make an interesting addition to my poem."

Wol shone her shoulder lamp on her subordinate. "Poem? An hour ago, it was a novel."

"Novels are tedious."

"Especially *your* novel," Davok put in, causing a snicker from Krevor.

G'joth shrugged, ignoring Davok. "I was thinking about it on the way down here, and I realized that the themes I wished to convey would work better in a poem. Besides, a writer needs a challenge, and constructing an epic tale in verse is a far more worthy endeavor than attempting to do so in—"

"Quiet!" Krevor hissed.

Even as Krevor spoke, Wol smelled it, too. Unfamiliar scents were approaching. The only thing Wol knew for sure was that whoever it was was covered in fur. *Some form of animal life*, she thought, remembering hunts from her younger days on the grounds owned by the House of Varnak.

Wol readied her *mek'leth*. Next to her, Krevor unsheathed her *d'k tahg*. Wol noted that the other woman's blade was undecorated and worn, just as Wol's own was. *The joys of being a Houseless provincial—you take whatever d'k tahg you can get.* "Proper" Klingons had their own personalized weapons. Wol had had to relinquish hers when her father cast her out....

Three furred bipeds leapt out of the bushes straight

at Krevor and Wol. They wore no clothing as such, though several straps, pouches, and belts made of animal hide decorated their persons. They had pointed ears atop their heads, long snouts instead of noses, with lipless mouths at the ends of those snouts that covered teeth as sharp as a Klingon's and long tongues. Their fingers—three fingers and a thumb per hand—ended in sharp claws, as did their padded feet.

As soon as they were visible, they howled. Even as Wol raised her *mek'leth* in defense, she heard howls from all around her. *This is a coordinated attack,* she thought even as one of the creatures swung a weapon at her. The metal blade clanged loudly against her *mek'leth*. She parried, shoving her opponents' blade downward, even as another of the creatures attacked with a similar blade.

Wol had never seen a sword of this like. Its blade curved upward from the hilt to a much sharper degree than that of her *mek'leth*, initially angling out from the hilt and then around into a deep crescent shape. That crescent then split in two, with one blade going straight upward, the other continuing to form the rest of the crescent. Each of the two blades ended in a V formation, granting the sword four points with which to attack.

Even as she elbowed the second creature in the stomach with one arm, she brought her *mek'leth* down on the first. However, the creature parried with the ease of a master sword wielder.

Now Wol wished she had brought a *bat'leth*. These creatures' two-bladed swords were as long as a *bat'leth* blade. Wol had fought *mek'leth-to-bat'leth* against single foes and won, but never against two. *I need to even the odds.*

A *qutluch*, the traditional weapon of an assassin, flew through the air past Wol's ear and lodged directly in the second creature's throat. Davok had a *qutluch* that he claimed he took off someone who tried to use it on him years ago.

Making a mental note to thank Davok later, Wol turned her attention to the first attacker. They stood facing each other for a moment, Wol's shoulder lamp shining directly into her enemy's face.

Wol stared into the creature's eyes.

No, not a creature. For one thing, no mere animal could have crafted so impressive a weapon.

For another, the eyes that looked back at Wol were those of a warrior born who was prepared to do whatever it took to defeat Wol, just as Wol would not rest until her foe was dead.

I said I wanted a challenge, Wol thought, baring her teeth. "Today," she said, "is a good day to die!"

The alien said something in its language.

Wol then attacked.

The bloodlust rose within her as she leapt at her foe, *mek'leth* swinging ahead of her. They had taken away her honor, her family—all that was left to her was this.

Her foe did not limit its attack to its weapon. Claws, teeth, legs, all were used in service of its goal: to kill her. She, in turn, was bigger and had better protection. A glancing blow to her arm was absorbed by her gauntlets, where a like blow from her drew blood from her opponent.

Wol had no idea how long the fight had gone on when her opponent finally disarmed her. As her *mek'leth* went flying across the road, Wol grabbed for her foe's snout, then pulled the jaws apart, screaming her fury to the heavens as she did so. The alien tried to slice her torso open with its sword, and did succeed in drawing blood this time, but Wol was determined to score a victory. She yanked the alien's head backward, and heard the glorious snap of bone.

The alien went down, dead.

Wol turned and growled, looking for a new enemy to take on, but saw that the rest of her squad also stood victorious. Davok bled from a wound in his cheek, G'joth's left arm hung useless at his side, and Krevor now walked with a pronounced limp. Only Goran seemed unscathed.

"They fight well," Goran said.

Wol's shoulder lamp illuminated ten alien corpses bleeding on the road and off to the side. Five of them lay at Goran's feet. Davok walked over and extricated his *qutluch* from the neck of the one he'd killed.

"Vok to all squads. We have met with resistance in the first city. We need to fall back and regroup."

The bloodlust dimming as her rational mind once again took charge, Wol opened a channel. "The main road is secure, repeat, the main road is secure."

"Well done, Leader. Sixth, remain to cover our regrouping—take as many of them as you can. Fifteenth, keep the road secure. Twentieth, set up a base camp one qell'qam

outside the first city. All other squads, head for that base camp. Take as many of these alien petaQ as you can! Qapla'!"

"We are running from battle?" Davok snarled. "This is madness! These creatures are—"

G'joth interrupted. "If Goran hadn't taken out five of them so quickly, those 'creatures' would have killed us all, Davok."

More howling sounded, mixed with the cries of Klingons as they fought. "The fighting is moving this way," Wol said. "Take positions." Then, remembering that Goran's position was the middle of the road, she added, "Goran, go with Davok and G'joth—we have to keep the road clear."

Soon, Klingon warriors, led by *QaS DevwI'* Klaris, started to run down the road, occasionally with aliens hanging off them or attacking them. Many were bloodied, some were badly wounded. Even as they passed, some of the aliens leapt from the surrounding shrubbery to attack, but Goran took care of those.

Wol heard movement behind her. She unsheathed her *d'k tahg* and threw it at the noise, which was from within one of the shrubs on the side of the road. "Hold station," she instructed Krevor, then went to retrieve her weapon.

The blade had lodged in the torso of one of the aliens. Covered with black fur, much of which was now matted down with blood, the alien slashed at Wol as she came closer, and muttered something in its tongue.

Ducking the swipe, Wol swung her *mek'leth* at the alien's throat—

—only to have it blocked by the alien's arm. The blade cut into fur and flesh and bone, blood spurting all over the shrub, the alien, and Wol herself. Though it wounded the alien further, it also, in essence, disarmed Wol, as her enemy then pulled its arm back, the *mek'leth* still lodged therein. Even as it did so, the alien reached down and swung upward with its sword, which had apparently fallen to the side.

Wol tried to fall back, dodging the attack, but her enemy was too fast, and the removal of her *mek'leth* too sudden. The straight blade sliced into her belly, followed quickly by the curved blade cutting her side.

Fire lit her entire torso, but the pain only gave her focus. Again, the battle lust rose, and she welcomed it. The blood roaring in her ears, she screamed to the heavens and lunged for the alien.

Peculiarly, the alien did not follow up its attack, nor resist Wol going for her throat. Wol had been throttling it for several seconds before she realized that her foe had already died—a bit late, but the *d'k tahg* finally claimed the alien's life.

Clutching her wounds with her left hand, she retrieved first her *d'k tahg*, then her *mek'leth* with her right and resheathed them.

She looked down at the furred alien. *I do not know if there is a place in* Sto-Vo-Kor *for your kind—but if there isn't, there should be.* After the Dominion War, this was almost a privilege. Jem'Hadar fought because they were bred to. Cardassians and Romulans fought out of a sense of duty to their country. But these people—they didn't fight just because they needed to, but because they wanted to. There was a joy to their combat that was almost Klingon.

The Leader returned to her post at the road, arriving just as Krevor sliced the throat of an alien that was attacking two wounded troops. From the city, she could hear howls. *Are they cries of victory?* she wondered.

Vok was, unsurprisingly, the last Klingon to come through, just as Klaris had been the first. A warrior's first duty was to fight for the Empire, but the *QaS DevwI'* were additionally responsible for the welfare of the troops. Just as Klaris would take command of the twentieth as they secured the new base camp, Vok would make sure that everyone who could move got out safely, and that those who could not would not be taken prisoner. If he had left the city, it meant that there were no living Klingon souls left behind.

Or, if there are, they won't be for long. Wol noted that no members of the sixth came down the road.

"Move!" Vok cried as he gestured for Wol's squad to go ahead of him. As one, Wol, Goran, Krevor, Davok, and G'joth ran down the road, following the other troops.

Davok muttered, "I still think this is cowardly."

"Did you say something, *Bekk* Davok?" Vok asked.

"He said nothing," Wol said, glowering at her subordinate. She also instantly regretted speaking. It was taking all her energy to make her legs work. Her left arm clutched her torso hard—she was half-convinced that if she let go, she'd fall in twain.

Vok did not pursue the matter. "You did well, Leader. Securing the road permits us to regroup and contact the *Gorkon*. Obviously, we will need more troops," he added dryly. "These are no mere primitives."

"No, sir," Wol said, clenching her teeth. The road was now taking them uphill. "They are true warriors, in the spirit of Kahless."

"Bah," Davok said. "They are overgrown *targs* with fancy swords. We have just grown soft from months of inactivity. I say we go back and show them the true mettle of Klingon warriors."

Wol closed her eyes for a moment, assuming that Davok's time in her squad—and in this life—had just been severely curtailed, but Vok just snorted. "You may *say* what you wish, *Bekk*. However, since you are merely crew, I am free to ignore your words for the mewlings they are."

Before Davok could say something else stupid, they arrived at the base camp: a large clearing in front of a cave opening, bordered by several rocks and boulders. Wol thought, *The twentieth's scouts did their jobs well.* The clearing had only one, uphill approach, and was very easy to defend. Two lamps had been set up to provide enough illumination to see by, so Wol shut off her shoulder lamp to preserve its energy cells; the rest of the squad followed suit.

Wol presumed that the base camp would get only temporary use. True warriors did not defend for very long.

One large tree overhung the clearing, and Wol saw

Moken, a soldier from the twentieth, seated on one of the branches, serving as a lookout.

Klaris approached Vok. "Base camp is secured."

"Good." Vok opened a channel on his communicator. "Vok to *Gorkon*."

"*Klag.*"

Vok proceeded to give a report on the troops' inability to secure the first city. When he finished the report, he added, "They fight like Klingons, Captain."

"*Then they can die like Klingons. We will beam down forty additional squads to your position. I want that city taken, Vok, and their leaders brought before me.*"

"Enemy approaching!" That was Moken from his lookout position.

Wol whirled around and instantly regretted it, as pain ripped through her wounded torso. She saw one of the aliens, a small one with white fur that seemed to glow in the light of the lamps, running toward the base camp. The alien appeared to be alone and unarmed. Like the other warriors they had fought, it wore no clothing of any kind, save for a belt with a pouch attached.

"Probably a messenger," Wol muttered.

"No doubt, Leader," Vok said with a smile. "Captain, one of the aliens is approaching."

"*Keep this channel open,*" Klag said.

"Yes, sir." To Leader Morr of the first, he said, "Activate translator."

Morr acknowledged the order and moved to do so. Idly, Wol wondered if the Leader preferred this ground campaign to his usual duties of guarding the captain's person.

The alien arrived just outside the periphery of the clearing, but did not enter it. He reached into the pouch, and placed a round stone disk with some kind of character carved into it on the ground in front of him.

"What is that?" Vok asked.

At that, the alien looked up in surprise. "You speak our language?"

"No, but we have technology that permits us to understand each other."

The alien squinted. "What is 'technology'?"

Vok laughed at that. "A tool that allows us to speak with you and you with us." A pause. "You fought well."

"As did you. Since you can understand me, I can speak the message the Ruling Pack had hoped to convey. The Children of San-Tarah wish to inform you that your next attack on us will be even more costly for you."

"We could say the same to you," Vok said, baring his teeth. "We did not expect such fierce warriors. Rest assured, you will not surprise us a second time."

"No doubt. However, we also wish to propose an alternative. The Ruling Pack wishes to speak with your Ruling Pack."

A look of distaste spread over Vok's usually pleasant features. "You wish to talk *peace?*"

Again, the alien—the San-Tarah—squinted. "What is 'peace'?"

Many of the Klingons laughed at that. G'joth was

among them, and he said to Wol, "I like these people more and more."

Frowning at the San-Tarah messenger, Vok asked, "You do not wish to end the fighting?"

"Of course not. The Ruling Pack simply wishes to discuss how the fight may proceed."

Vok continued to frown at the messenger. Wol wondered what was going through the mind of the *QaS DevwI'*.

Then, finally, Vok said, "Translator off." After Morr obeyed the order, Vok continued. "Captain?"

"Tell the San-Tarah that I will meet with their Ruling Pack as soon as they can arrive at the base camp. That is the only place I will agree to meet them. In the meantime, Dr. B'Oraq will beam down to tend to your wounded and I will have the remaining forty squads on standby transport to points surrounding their first city, including two more squads to your position. They are to stand ready, but not attack unless directly provoked by the San-Tarah or given a specific order from you, Vok. And you will not give that order until I say so, is that understood, QaS DevwI'?"

"Perfectly, Captain."

Wol smiled. The captain was no fool. If the San-Tarah wished to negotiate, then Captain Klag would make sure that the Klingons would be speaking from a position of strength. It was one thing to drive off twenty squads who were not expecting great resistance, quite another to drive off almost sixty who were prepared.

"Inform me when the Ruling Pack has arrived. Out."

Once the connection was closed, Vok instructed

Morr to reactivate the translator. "Our captain will speak to your Ruling Pack as soon as they arrive here."

The San-Tarah's ears flattened. "Your—your captain will not meet us in the Prime Village?"

Vok glared at the messenger. "The next time our captain sets foot in your Prime Village will be after we have taken it by force. If the Ruling Pack wishes to speak, they may do so here. If not, then the battle will continue as before." Then Vok let loose with one of his belly laughs. "It makes no difference to us, Child of the San-Tarah. You brought us this choice, and now we have made it. If you withdraw that choice, then we will attack and destroy you. If you don't, then our leaders will meet here."

A long hesitation, and then the messenger finally said, "Very well. The Ruling Pack will arrive at first sunrise." Then he ran off back down the road.

Davok turned to G'joth. "What other way of fighting is there?"

Wol was wondering that herself. Before she could agree with Davok's concern, though, the red light of a transporter effect shimmered in front of her, and eleven more warriors beamed down. *Or*, she thought, *ten warriors and one doctor.*

Vok immediately said, "Leader Wol is the worst hurt, Doctor."

"Ridiculous," Wol said even as B'Oraq approached her. "There are others in far worse condition."

B'Oraq stared at her hand scanner, slammed it on the side, then growled and put it away. "Sit down, Leader, it looks like we'll have to do this the old-fashioned way."

When Wol did not follow that instruction, Vok said, "Don't make me order you, Wol."

Sighing, Wol sat on one of the rocks and reluctantly took her arm—now soaked through with her own blood—away from her wounded torso.

"That's an impressive wound, Leader."

"It was made with an impressive weapon."

Davok growled. "I fully intend to take one back with me as a trophy when this is over."

"Live until this is over before making rash promises, Davok," G'joth said with a laugh.

Wol would have shared in the laugh, but the doctor started treating her wound, which sent searing agony through her entire chest.

B'Oraq looked at Wol and then chuckled.

"I amuse you, Doctor?" Wol asked angrily.

The doctor tugged on the braid that sat on her right shoulder. "My apologies, Leader, I was simply thinking about how much more pleasant it is to treat Klingons than humans. Humans scream at the slightest bit of pain. It's distracting."

"Enter," Klag said at the sound of the door chime to his office. He was standing in front of his desk, studying the dismaying report from Toq. As the door ground open to reveal Kornan, Klag looked up from the second officer's tale of woe regarding the ineffectiveness of long-range communications, sensors, weapons, and the cloaking device as long as they remained in orbit. Propulsion, short-range communications, transporters, and shields seemed to be working, as long as the ship didn't actually collide with any of the subspace eddies.

"Captain," Kornan said, "I would never question your judgment in front of the crew."

"Good," Klag said emphatically. Klag wasn't especially sure Kornan had any business questioning it in private, either—that was a privilege a first officer had to earn, and Kornan had done little to do so these past nine weeks—but was willing to hear the commander out. Especially given the likely subject of the objection.

"I do not see the benefit of *speaking* to these San-Tarah. They are primitives. Perhaps more aggressive than we anticipated, but—"

"It is more than that." Klag put the padd with Toq's report down on his desk. "They are not merely more aggressive. We attacked them by surprise by materializing out of thin air at night—and still, they were able to drive us off. That bespeaks a worthy foe."

"True, but it simply means we should use more forceful means to subjugate them until General Talak can bring his forces."

Klag held his tongue on the subject of the general—who, thanks to the interference, hadn't even been informed of this potential conquest. "True. However, there is also what the messenger said about the subject of these talks. These are not Federation diplomats discussing ways to not fight or Romulan emissaries attempting to maneuver for the upper hand. The translator wasn't able to render the word 'peace' into a word they could comprehend. What they wished to discuss was a way to continue the fight. For that, I am willing to hear them out." Then he picked the report back up. "Besides, our own capacity for war-making has been severely curtailed. Your job while I am gone, Commander, is to find ways to improve that. The *Gorkon* has been reduced to a glorified troop transport. I want that to change."

"Yes, sir. I have already asked Lieutenant Rodek for alternative methods of attacking the planet from orbit."

Klag smiled. "Good. In the meantime, I will see if the San-Tarah's methods for continuing the fight are worthy of being heard."

Returning the smile, Kornan asked, "And if they are not?"

"We have already tripled our forces on the planet, and we have the capacity to quintuple that if needs be."

"Yes, *sir*," Kornan said enthusiastically.

"*Vok to Klag.*"

Looking up, the captain said, "Klag."

"*Sir, a group of ten San-Tarah are approaching the camp.*" Klag heard the *QaS DevwI'* chuckle as he added, "*And the sun is just coming up, too.*"

"Our foes are prompt. I am preparing to beam down. Signal the transporter operator when they have arrived."

"*Yes, sir.*"

Moving toward the door, followed by his first officer, Klag said, "You have command of the ship, Kornan. Instruct Lokor to have *all* remaining troops on standby."

Klag exited his office, gave a nod to the bridge crew, and entered the turbolift. His new bodyguard—one of the soldiers from a lower-echelon squad—followed silently.

As soon as he arrived in the transporter room, the operator said, "We have received a signal from *QaS DevwI'* Vok, sir. The delegation has arrived."

Stepping onto the platform, his bodyguard next to him, Klag nodded. "Beam us down."

Moments later, Klag found himself standing on solid ground. Immediately, he was awash in sensations he had not felt in far too long. Truly, this world had never been touched by technology, and so was as pure a planet as Klag had ever visited in his life. There were designated hunting grounds on several Klingon worlds that were preserved, but even they paled in comparison to this. Just standing here, Klag felt *alive*: the scent of wild animals, the sound of birds flying overhead, the feel of the wind blowing through his long black hair.

This prompted Klag to try to recall the last time he had gone on a proper hunting trip, and realized that it was before the war. *Too long*, he thought ruefully. *When this world is conquered, perhaps I will come back. If the fauna is anything like the sentient life, it will be a fine place to hunt.*

Dozens of Klag's warriors—some injured—surrounded him on all sides save directly in front. Vok stepped forward, his normally jovial face looking understandably more grim than usual. He pointed to the ten aliens who stood just in front of Klag. They were bipedal, each covered head-to-toe in fur of varying colors. None wore anything that could truly be called clothing, though the one standing in the center had the most decoration. Klag presumed him to be the leader.

That instinct proved correct when that one stepped forward and said, "I am Me-Larr. I lead the Ruling Pack of the Children of San-Tarah. Do you lead your Ruling Pack?"

"I am Captain Klag—and I rule the warship *Gorkon*."

"Ship?"

"Yes." Klag started to walk back and forth, indicating the troops around him with one hand. "What you see before you are but a fraction of the warriors who are under my command. Right now, they and the thousands more on the *Gorkon* await only my word before they slaughter you in battle."

"A worthy task," Me-Larr said. "My next question, then, Captain Klag, is this: What is the eventual goal of your fight?"

Klag stared at Me-Larr for a moment. The white-furred alien's words of praise for the worthiness of their task of combat appeared genuine, but nuances did not always survive the translation process. On the other hand, Vok's report indicated a people who valued battle as much as Klingons did.

The captain also noted that Me-Larr did not look Klag directly in the eyes when he spoke to him, and he wondered what, if anything, that signified.

Finally, he said, "The *Gorkon* is but one of thousands of ships representing a great Empire that stretches across many stars and hundreds of worlds like yours. Our—our Ruling Pack," he said with a smile, "has instructed us to find new worlds to bring into our Empire. *That* is our goal. And I intend to fulfill it. In the unlikely event that I find my own vessel inadequate to the task, then I shall send for more ships. One way or another, Me-Larr, this world will belong to the Klingon Empire."

As Klag spoke, he saw something in Me-Larr's eyes—which still had not made direct contact with Klag's. *An understanding, perhaps?*

"Tell me, Captain Klag, what would belonging to the Klingon Empire entail?"

Interesting. "Your people will become *jeghpu'wI'*—a part of the Empire, though inferior to Klingons. You will serve us in whatever way your planetary governor sees fit. Your planet will serve us as well. There are minerals in your world's crust that we have need of."

"Will we still be permitted to hunt? May we still fight?"

Very interesting. "Possibly."

"I wish to discuss something with the Ruling Pack. May we have a moment to do so, Captain Klag?"

Under any other circumstances, Klag would have refused. *Then again, under any other circumstances, we would not have gotten this far. But their mettle has earned them at least the right to be heard.*

Me-Larr spoke with the other nine San-Tarah for several minutes out of earshot. As they did so, B'Oraq approached. "Captain, I've healed as many of the injured as I can. Most can return to battle immediately, but I need to bring some of them back to the *Gorkon.*"

"Do so."

B'Oraq nodded, and activated her communicator. "B'Oraq to transporter room. Six to transport directly to the medical bay."

Klag smiled with pride. Vok's report included dozens of wounded, but only five needed the extensive treatment B'Oraq required the medical bay for. *Excellent.*

"I'm afraid we must beam you to the transporter room, Doctor. The subspace interference makes site-to-site transporting problematic."

"Very well."

A few minutes later, after B'Oraq and the five wounded disappeared in a red glow, Me-Larr reapproached the base camp. Klag noticed that the planet's second sun was starting to peek over the far mountains, lengthening some shadows in the forest around them, severely curtailing others.

"Tell me, Captain Klag, would it be preferable for you to conquer us yourself rather than have to call in your other ships?"

In that moment, Klag understood the look he saw in Me-Larr's eyes earlier—or, perhaps more accurately, what Me-Larr gleaned from Klag. Somehow, the San-Tarah leader knew what was in Klag's heart.

However, Klag was hardly about to reveal that he knew this. "Why do you ask?"

Now, Me-Larr stepped forward and looked Klag directly in the eyes. They burned with the fire of a true warrior, and Klag was impressed despite himself. "If you continue on this course, you may well take this world. But you will not take us. From the Ruling Pack on down to the newest litter of cubs, we will fight you. We will not allow ourselves to be defeated. You may bring as many of your ships as you wish, and it won't change that. However, I do not wish that to happen. I am my people's caretaker, and though we would prefer to die fighting, we would prefer not to die at all even more. So I propose a way for us to settle this in a manner that is just as fitting but less wasteful."

Klag had a hard time wrapping his mind around the idea of warfare being wasteful, but let it go for the moment. "And that is?"

"A series of five martial contests, pitting the Children of San-Tarah against the fighters of the *Gorkon*. If you and your subjects win the majority of the contests, the Children of San-Tarah will cede themselves to you. You will have brought San-Tarah into your empire."

Throwing his head back, Klag laughed heartily. *Oh, I like these people!* "And if by some chance you defeat us?"

"Then you go and your empire stays away from San-Tarah forever."

Me-Larr was fortunate that he made his offer when he did. Klag had not reported San-Tarah to General Talak yet. He did not wish to claim a victory that was not yet won, and until they achieved orbit, they could not verify the existence of the kellinite and other exploitable resources on this world. Since they achieved orbit, they had not been able to communicate beyond the planet itself. Right now, he was the only one who could act on the Empire's behalf with regards to San-Tarah.

Truthfully, even the *Gorkon*'s full complement could not subjugate an entire world. All they needed to do was hold the first city long enough for Talak's fleet to arrive and provide a proper conquering force. That would be hindered by the subspace eddies' effects on weaponry and scanning equipment, but not fatally so.

However, Klag was loath to waste the time and the lives of these noble aliens in such a manner. Not when an alternative—one that allowed all sides to keep their honor intact—presented itself.

So Klag made a decision.

"Assuming the contests meet with my approval, I accept your terms."

Next to him, Vok smiled. Grumblings from the various Klingons behind him indicated general acceptance of the idea, as well. That served to reaffirm Klag's faith in his crew's ability to win these contests.

"That is good." Me-Larr then reached into a pouch on his belt and removed a small stone carved with a rune of some sort on it. "When we speak before the *anlok*, our words are binding for the rest of the days."

Quaint, Klag thought disdainfully. "We are Klingon warriors. We need no such rituals. When a warrior gives his word, then it shall be so."

Me-Larr squinted. "Even when that word is given to an enemy?"

"Of course."

"Odd. An enemy is the last person one would speak the truth to, I would think."

Again Klag laughed. "Perhaps for some. But if your

enemies are honorable, then they deserve to hear the truth from your mouth. And if they are not honorable, then they do not deserve to be spoken to at all." He added, "I speak the words of Kahless, our greatest warrior from times past. It is from him that our way of life, our code of honor, derives."

"He was, I'm sure, a great fighter, Captain Klag. Now, let us discuss the contests. Then we may continue our fight in earnest."

CHAPTER EIGHT

Kornan stared at his captain from across Klag's desk. "Contests, sir?"

"Yes. A hunt, marine combat, defending territory, strength, and hand-to-hand combat. Our people against the San-Tarah."

Shaking his head, Kornan said, "Sir, surely we can defeat these people."

"No. Oh, we could, perhaps, succeed in taking the planet, especially once General Talak arrives, but we will not defeat them. I have looked into their leader's eyes, and I have seen into the San-Tarah's hearts. They are true warriors. They have sworn that they will willingly cede themselves to the Empire if we defeat them." Klag stood up. Kornan noticed that the captain did not stumble as he rose—the first time the captain had done so in Kornan's sight since he signed on. "Think of it, Commander. How often has a single ship been responsible for bringing an entire civilization into the Empire—and without a shot being fired?"

"Perhaps." Kornan shifted from foot to foot. "But it is not—not standard procedure."

Klag threw his head back and laughed the throaty laugh that Kornan—indeed, that everyone on the *Gorkon*—had come to associate with his commanding officer. "You think your captain has gone mad, is that it, Commander?"

In fact, Kornan had been thinking that very thing. But Klag was far too popular among the crew—and Kornan too unknown a quantity to all save the unreliable Leskit—for him to challenge the captain's authority.

"You may speak freely, Commander," Klag said. "Whatever you say now in this room shall meet with no reprisals. Speak your mind."

Kornan blinked. He had not expected this. Nor was he entirely sure the offer was genuine. One of the first commanders he served under on the *Rotarran* would often give his crew members permission to speak freely, then kill them on the spot for insubordination.

But no, he thought after catching a glance of the Order of the *Bat'leth* medallion affixed to the captain's cassock. *Klag is an honorable man. He will keep his word.*

"I question the wisdom of this course of action. We have nothing to gain by these contests and everything to lose. This planet is teeming with the very resources the chancellor's orders said we needed most: kellinite, koltanium, uridium, and so much more. Our wisest course would be to leave orbit and alert the general. Whether or not we can defeat the people, we can still take the planet—which is, after all, our primary mission."

Klag regarded Kornan for several seconds. The commander found that he could not read the expression on Klag's face.

Then the captain started to pace across the room. "Tell me, Commander, did Leskit ever regale you with the tale of the *Gorkon*'s first mission to the planet taD?"

Shrugging, Kornan said, "He mentioned it in passing. Why?"

"The *jeghpu'wI'* of that world, the al'Hmatti, were in many ways similar to the Children of San-Tarah." Klag seemed to be staring now at a point beyond Kornan on the wall behind him. "They had grown restive, no longer willing to live under the the flag of the Empire. They used the massive deployment of forces during the invasion of Cardassia against us, successfully, if temporarily, dethroning the Klingon overseers." Klag turned to stare right at Kornan. "Even after we took the planet back, the unrest remained for four years. When the *Gorkon* brought Ambassador Worf there to deal with the situation, it was the opinion of both the ambassador and your predecessor, Commander Drex—" and here Kornan noticed a slight curling of Klag's lips "—that the al'Hmatti would never yield, even if we wiped them all out. So an alternative solution had to be found."

Again, Klag started to pace. Pointing at the padds on his desk, as if the reports they carried represented the San-Tarah themselves, he said, "Those people are like that as well. Yes, we might be able to suppress them with the troops we have on board. Certainly we would be able to bring them down once Talak and his fleet arrive, even taking this planet's insane properties into account. We could fight them, but we would simply be going through the motions—the outcome of this battle has already been decided. The Children of San-Tarah, even more than the al'Hmatti, will die as a species before they allow themselves to be taken by force."

"If they are weak, then they *should* die."

Klag smiled. "I agree—if they *are* weak, but I do not believe they are. You have seen the scans Toq made of the planet, heard Vok's report on the engagement on the surface. With no warning, at night, they were able to fend off a hundred warriors—with an *organized* attack. They have no farms, no merchants, no indication of anything save a pure warrior ethic. They don't even have a word for technology. They literally live off the land—and this land provides them with plenty."

Moving closer to Kornan, Klag spoke now in a quieter, more intense tone, his deep voice going even deeper. "We call ourselves a 'warrior culture,' but in truth that only means that warriors hold the highest place in our society. But the San-Tarah live the ideal that we only aspire to. No politics, no commerce, no—" He hesitated, then smiled. "No compromise."

The captain then went back to his desk and sat down. "If we continue with proper procedure, as you suggest, we will be doing the Empire a disservice. Even if we managed to subjugate the San-Tarah for a little while, they would be ever against us, ever opposed to us. What Me-Larr has given us is a way that benefits them *and us*. Now, instead of fighting a war with a predetermined outcome, we battle for a cause where we know not what will happen. And if we are victorious— and I believe this crew to be more than worthy and easily capable of defeating even these fine warriors—then the San-Tarah will become part of the Empire *willingly*. These are pure warriors of a kind even Kahless would envy. The Empire can only benefit from having them be part of it, and can only lose if they continue to oppose us."

Kornan found himself speechless. After a moment, he finally said dryly, "Obviously the captain—has given this a great deal more thought than I."

At that, Klag once again reared his head back and laughed heartily. "Well said, Commander, well said!" Again, Klag rose from his chair, and again, he did not list to the right. "Now then, have Lokor, Toq, and Rodek meet with us in the wardroom in one hour. I wish to assemble a list of *Gorkon* personnel best suited for the tasks ahead of us." Klag grabbed a padd from his desk and handed it to Kornan. "The first contest is the hunt, and it begins at first sunrise tomorrow."

Gazing down at the padd's display, Kornan saw that the contest required one representative from each side to hunt a *san-chera*. Vok had scanned a drawing that one of the San-Tarah made of the animal in question: it looked, at first glance, like an overgrown *targ*. Based on the size of the stick figure drawn next to the beast, it was twice the size of a Klingon, and differed from a *targ* in three important ways: it had shaggier fur, four tusks instead of two, and six legs rather than four. The extra set of legs were in the center, and Kornan assumed that it increased the beast's speed. *No wonder hunting it is considered a challenge.*

Kornan remembered several mess-hall conversations and smiled. "I believe I know who will be best for this contest, Captain."

Toq moved silently westward through the thick foliage of San-Tarah, holding his prize *gIntaq* spear, trying to catch a scent of the *san-chera*. The thickness of the underbrush that snapped against his leg, the lack of a proper trail for him to follow, the sounds of the beasts crawling across the branches, all served to remind him of his first hunt, back on Carraya.

Toq was born and raised at a compound on a planet in the Carraya Sector—that was, in fact, where he got the spear. At the time, he had used it for farming—but at the time, he had thought his home to be something else entirely. On Carraya, Klingons and Romulans lived in peace. Toq had been told that his parents and the other adults had come there to get away from the endless war between their peoples. It wasn't until the arrival of Ambassador Worf—then a Starfleet officer, who had come to Carraya for reasons of his own—that he learned the truth. Toq's parents and the other adult Klingons had been taken prisoner after a Romulan attack on the Khitomer outpost. The Romulans had not permitted them to die, and the Klingon Empire would not bargain with the Romulans for their lives. A Romulan commander named Tokath took pity on them and set up the compound.

Carraya was a place for dishonored Klingons to live out their lives, with the rest of the galaxy thinking them dead in order to spare their families from the same dishonor. But their children were not told of their heritage, denied knowledge of who and, more importantly, what they were. Worf had taken Toq on a hunt, showed him how to scent his prey, how to stay downwind, where best to strike. They had successfully stalked and killed a beast that day, and Toq had reveled in it. Never before had he felt as *alive* as he had on that hunt with Worf.

At least, up to that point. Worf had left Carraya and taken with him any who wished to leave, on the proviso that they never reveal the truth about the prison camp. Toq was conveyed to Federation space by a Romulan supply ship, and thence to the Klingon Empire, with Worf claiming that the children were the survivors of a years-old crash. An old friend of Worf's family, Lorgh, made *R'uustai* with Toq, bringing the young man into Lorgh's own House.

The first thing Toq asked was to be permitted to go hunting with Lorgh.

Although he would never be able to re-create the sensation of joy he felt upon that first hunt with Worf, Toq had, in the years since, gotten much better at it. Now he could look back and see how clumsy he was on Carraya. He had not moved silently enough, then, barreling through the bushes and distressing the branches, leaving an obvious trail behind him. He became a most proficient hunter, encouraged by Lorgh, and had even entered a few professional competitions. Had not the siren call of the Dominion War led him to a different vocation, that of officer in the Klingon Defense Force, he might have gained tremendous renown.

Now, at last, he was able to combine his two greatest joys into one. He hunted for the honor of the *Gorkon* and the glory of the Empire.

Somewhere else in the forest, one of the Children of San-Tarah, a female named Ur-Gan, also hunted. They had both left from the San-Tarah's first city, moving in separate directions. Toq was given the scent of a *san-chera* that had been captured the night before but not yet slaughtered. Both Toq and Ur-Gan had the same task: Seek out and subdue a *san-chera* and bring it back to the first city by second sundown. If both succeeded, the hunter who brought down the largest beast would be declared winner. If neither did, they would start again the next day.

Toq heard a slithering noise overhead, and caught a vaguely reptilian scent. *Perhaps some manner of snake,* he thought, putting it out of his mind. Vermin such as that only distracted.

One thing Toq knew for sure was that he had to find as large a *san-chera* as he could. Ur-Gan had the upper hand, after all—she knew the terrain, she knew which animals were most dangerous, and she knew the signs of a *san-chera*'s passing: what it ate, what it wouldn't eat, what plants it would use, how it would mark its territory.

The first professional competition of Toq's had taken him to HuDyuQ. He was transported to the peak of a mountain and told to subdue the first animal he came across. He was told nothing about the local fauna— such as the fact that the smallest beast he was likely to find on that mountain would be thrice his size, and that it had been known to eat Klingons—but he not only succeeded in the hunt, he was among the top fifty in the competition's history for both size and speed of the capture.

And at least here it isn't so cold....

The biggest variable in hunting in an alien environment was how the prey would react to the unfamiliar scent of the hunter. After all, no Klingon had ever visited San-Tarah until yesterday. What Toq did not know—and, given the apparent paucity of alien visitors to this world, nobody knew—was whether the beast would avoid the strange new scent or investigate it.

In order to minimize this variable, Toq had dressed in a *So'HIp*—a one-piece outfit that altered its coloring to blend in with the background—and covered himself in dirt and mud and grass from the ground around him. The former meant he was visually the same combination of brown and green as the local flora, and the latter served to mask his scent as much as possible.

The wind shifted. Toq scented his prey. It didn't smell especially large, but it was a start.

Moving around one bush and hiding behind another one, Toq got a glimpse of a *san-chera* that was half as big as Toq himself. Its tusks barely stuck out of its mouth. A *mere pup*, Toq thought. It stood on its middle and rear legs and batted at a tree with its front paws, dislodging the ripe fruit.

Toq had two choices: take the easy kill and go back to the first city, hoping that Ur-Gan would find nothing or something smaller, or follow this one to better prey.

Smiling, Toq thought, *That is no choice at all. The day has barely begun. Surely I will find more worthy prey than this—and surely Ur-Gan will find something that at least has some meat on its bones.*

So the young second officer of the *Gorkon* bided his time, waiting until this pup led him to an older sibling, perhaps.

Having knocked down several fruits, the pup got down on all sixes and started gnawing on its meal, spitting out the seeds. The smell of the fruit juice combined with the scent of the *san-chera* made Toq's mouth water, but he did not move. This close, any movement, even to retrieve his water bottle from one of the pouches on his thigh, might alert the pup to his presence, and that he could not afford.

As he observed the pup dining, Toq wondered how the Children of San-Tarah would rule if he brought back multiple *san-chera*. *Would quantity make up for quality?* But no, Me-Larr had been very specific back at the first city. Whoever brought back *the* largest *san-chera* would win the day.

I hope you come from good stock, young one.

After eating parts of several fruit, the pup apparently grew bored with its repast, and started licking its paws clean.

Then the wind shifted again. Toq realized in an instant that he was downwind of the pup.

Sure enough, the pup raised its head up from its grooming. It looked around for a second, then turned its head right at the bush behind which Toq hid.

Toq, for his part, did not move. He willed himself to be as still as the statues in the Hall of Warriors.

The pup looked around a bit more, then loped off at a dead run on all sixes.

Now, truly, the hunt had begun. Unsurprisingly for a creature with six limbs, the *san-chera* moved very fast. Luckily for Toq, this was a young one, so its legs were short and not fully developed, slowing it down somewhat. The wind had not shifted, but Toq hardly needed a scent to track this prey. The pup barreled through the underbrush with all the clumsiness of youth, combined with the security of being near the top of the local food chain. It had no need for stealth.

When the wind did shift, Toq still did not pick up the scent immediately. *They* are *fast*, he thought as he moved through the brush, now taking less care himself to be subtle. After all, the *san-chera* knew he was near.

He slowed down when he caught the scent again, however. Spying a clearing up ahead, Toq looked around and found a tree that had grown in a manner suitable for climbing. Strapping the spear to his back, he shimmied up the trunk, ignoring the pricks of the smaller branches into his dirt-encrusted *So'HIp*, which did not protect his skin as well as his uniform did.

Coming to roost on a thick, outlying branch, Toq peered down at the clearing. Reaching into another thigh pouch, he removed a pair of binoculars that gave him a closer view.

The pup had, as expected, returned to the proverbial nest. A *san-chera* that was over twice Toq's size was nursing six baby *san-chera*—these had no visible tusks and were smaller than Toq's arm—and grooming two others that were about the same size as the pup. The mother wasted no time in turning her attention to grooming the pup, still covered as it was in fruit juice.

Toq bided his time. He would not kill a mother in the midst of feeding and caring for her young. There was no honor in such a kill—and no sense, either. The mothers were needed to keep the population alive so there would be subsequent hunts, and besides, only a fool took on a mother protecting her children.

The question is, do san-chera *fathers remain after childbirth—or even remain after conceiving the children? And if so, will this father return before the second sundown?*

Two hours passed before Toq got his answer. The infants had finished suckling and were now sleeping curled up against the stomach of the mother—three on either side of the mother's middle legs. The mother was also asleep, with the three pups gadding about the clearing, climbing trees and batting sticks and rocks at each other.

Just as Toq was about to give up and take his chances by bringing all three pups back to the first city, he caught another scent—similar to those of the *san-chera* before him, but far stronger. Seconds later, he heard the powerful six-legged strides of an approaching beast.

The sound was enough to wake the mother; the infants slumbered on. The three pups evinced no interest either way.

When the creature came into sight, Toq couldn't help but grin—and it took all his self-control to keep from laughing with joy.

The *san-chera* that lumbered into the clearing was about three times Toq's size. Covered in shaggy black fur that made him stand out even more against the green-and-brown flora, he ambled toward the mother, holding the remains of a small, four-legged animal in his mouth.

Standing between the male and the infants, the

mother looked at the male somewhat expectantly, to Toq's eyes. The male opened his mouth, dropping the animal in front of her, then nudged it toward her with one massive paw. Toq saw now that his upper tusks extended past his head, with the lower tusks extending almost to the ground (at least while he was on all sixes). His delivery complete, the male turned and stomped off the way he came.

By this time, the three pups decided to get involved. They circled the corpse while the mother sniffed it more closely. Then she leaned down and ripped out a chunk of meat with her bottom tusks.

Toq was, at this point, content to leave them to their meal. He had the scent of the giant male, and he was not about to give him up. It was possible that Ur-Gan would find a *san-chera* bigger than this, but Toq was not about to lay odds that he himself would.

Hoping that the beast was maintaining its leisurely pace, Toq moved as quickly as he could without disturbing his surroundings too much. He was upwind of the *san-chera*, but that could change at any moment. The pup's reaction to Toq's unfamiliar odor might well have been unpredictable, but Toq was willing to bet his spear that the large male would see him as a threat and act accordingly.

Of course, Toq thought with a grin, *he'd be right*.

Toq slowed once he realized that he had lost the scent. Then he heard the sound of running water. Less than a minute later he found himself at the edge of a stream, and spied the *san-chera* swimming in it. For such a massive creature, he disturbed the water surprisingly little, moving economically and almost silently.

What made Toq a superior hunter more than any other factor was his aim. He had reasoned early on in his training with Lorgh that the best way to subdue prey was to stab it through an eye. At worst, you blinded the creature, at least partially; at best, you killed it with a direct blow to the brain through one of the weakest parts of the outer portion of any living being's body.

The difficulty was in actually attaining the eye-shot, so Toq had dedicated himself to improving his aim, which was naturally quite excellent. Even as a boy on Carraya, he could hit targets no one else could even come close to. Now, after years of honing his skills, he could shoot the wings off a *glob* fly at half a *qell'qam*, and he was fairly sure he could throw his spear through the eye of the *san-chera* from the distance he was at now.

He aimed along his arm and waited for the creature to turn around.

The wind shifted.

Moving with a speed that belied his bulk, the *san-chera* turned around in the water, roared so loudly that Toq's teeth rattled, and leapt out of the water straight at the young Klingon.

Toq did not move until he threw the spear.

The *gIntaq* flew through the air, and lodged in the *san-chera*'s shoulder. The animal didn't even seem to notice, as it arced straight for Toq.

The Klingon's training was superb. Without even having to think about it, Toq fell backward, intending to roll with the blow and use the *san-chera*'s momentum to kick the creature behind him.

Sadly, the *san-chera*'s momentum was considerable, primarily due to its tremendous mass. Toq's legs were simply not powerful enough to perform the maneuver. The beast landed on top of Toq, pinning the Klingon to the ground, the claws of its front paws tearing into his *So'HIp* and chest.

Even as the pain seared through his upper body, Toq reached for his *d'k tahg* in its thigh pouch. All he needed was to free his right arm enough to plunge the blade into the creature's head.

The creature, for his part, sniffed Toq, as if verifying that he was, in fact, an alien—or perhaps that he was edible. Then the *san-chera* moved to bite Toq's head off.

However, Toq had taken advantage of those precious seconds. Lorgh had trained him well, including in ways to focus past pain, to disregard its presence. Toq did so while the *san-chera* performed its olfactory inspection. Then, with a mighty jerk of his right arm that flayed several layers of skin off his biceps as it ripped out from under the *san-chera*'s claws, Toq freed his right hand and plunged the *d'k tahg* it held into the side of the *san-chera*'s head.

The impact caused the *san-chera* to wave his head around and around. He screeched with sudden pain, hot breath steaming onto Toq's face. Yellow liquid—the creature's blood, presumably—spurted out, covering Toq's already-muck-encrusted form, as well as the bushes and ground around them.

Then the creature fell dead. Right on top of Toq.

The Klingon wasn't sure how long it took him to wriggle out from under the massive creature, but he managed it. He looked down at his person, found a bit of cloth from his *So'HIp* that was not covered in the *san-chera's* yellow blood, and ripped it off. Then he removed the *d'k tahg* from the animal's head and cleaned it with the cloth. After resheathing his personal weapon, he then, with his left hand, yanked out the spear and cleaned it as well. He would give them proper care when he transported back up to the *Gorkon*, but this would do for the time being—enough to keep the blood from drying and caking on the blade, thus dulling it.

Toq awkwardly strapped the spear to his back with his left hand, then looked down at himself and the *san-chera*.

He was covered in dirt and mud and water. He was bleeding profusely from his chest and right arm, his own blood mixing in with the yellow ichor of the *san-chera* that covered most of his body. It felt like at least eight ribs were bruised or broken. All feeling had fled from his right arm, and he was fairly certain that several teeth had come loose. His *So'HIp* had been torn to ribbons, and was now taking on the colors of the blood that covered what was left of it.

It was the best he had felt in years.

Still focusing past the pain that he knew intellectually was in his entire chest and right arm, he leaned down, grabbed the *san-chera* by the scruff of the neck with his left hand, and pulled.

The beast did not move.

Toq closed his eyes. He put the pain aside, as Lorgh had taught him. He gathered his strength.

He was a Klingon. He had defeated his prey. Now he must take it back and claim the prize. The captain, the ship, his crewmates, the Empire were all counting on him. The moment Worf had taken him on his first hunt seven years ago led him on a road that brought him to this place, and his greatest triumph as a hunter. He would not fail now.

Screaming his rage, his anger, his determination to the heavens, he again grabbed the *san-chera* and pulled.

This time, the dead creature was lifted from the ground.

Resting the creature's head on his shoulders, Toq started walking eastward, dragging the *san-chera* behind him.

Hours passed in a haze. The first of the suns set. Toq trudged through the underbrush. Recalling that this planet, according to his scans, was rich in koltanium, he occasionally wondered if the *san-chera* were made of that superdense ore, so heavy was the weight of the prize on his back.

But he continued onward.

His legs felt like bricks. He had no idea how he managed to keep them moving. All feeling had fled from his chest, right arm, neck, and stomachs. It was as if he were a head floating over two legs, somehow carrying the weight of a massive animal that seemed to grow heavier with each second. Indistinct brown-and-green shapes that he assumed were trees and bushes swam in his field of vision, but he simply trudged past or through them, uncaring. What energy he had was devoted solely to the task of moving forward.

Finally, he arrived at the first city of the San-Tarah— what the natives called their Prime Village. Klingons and Children of San-Tarah both stared openmouthed and silently at him. Or perhaps the roar of blood in his ears drowned out whatever they might have been saying.

In the center of the Prime Village stood Me-Larr and other members of their Ruling Pack. Klag and B'Oraq were also present. The latter rushed to Toq's side as soon as he dropped the *san-chera* at the feet of his captain.

"I bring you the prize, Captain. May it bring honor and glory to our—"

Toq found himself unable to continue speaking. Or standing. He collapsed to the ground.

As B'Oraq ministered to him, Toq caught sight of another *san-chera*. Its shaggy coat was a light brown. It had been decapitated, its head resting on a pike not far from the body.

It was also but three-quarters of the size of the *san-chera* Toq had subdued.

Me-Larr spoke, and even through his exhaustion and the pain that he could no longer keep in check, Toq heard the astonishment in the alien's voice. "You have brought down the *chera-mak*."

"What is the significance of that?" Toq heard Klag ask.

"It is the greatest of the *san-chera*. It has even been known to eat the flesh of the Children of San-Tarah.

Our cubs tell stories of the *chera-mak* to frighten each other. It had been believed unconquerable."

"You will find, Me-Larr, that the Klingon Empire considers nothing unconquerable—simply not yet conquered."

"Perhaps, Captain Klag, perhaps. In any event, the first contest goes to you."

Toq thought he heard a cheer of "Victory!" as he fell unconscious, but he wasn't entirely sure....

CHAPTER NINE

Leknerf sighed as the scanner picked up six more *grapok*-sauce stains on the mess hall's rear bulkhead. *At this rate*, he thought, *I'm going to be here all night*.

Quartermaster had, of course, chosen the night after both *gagh* and *racht* had been served for dinner to be the one when the mess hall got its regular scrubdown. This meant that Leknerf would be spending most of the night seeking, locating, and destroying any *grapok*-sauce stains before they had the chance to draw vermin. Other sauces were easier to clean up because they tended to spill in clumps. But, since *grapok* sauce was favored for the serpentine foodstuffs, it tended to spatter in little droplets all over the place. Most of the stains couldn't even be seen with the naked eye—especially given how maddeningly dark Klingons kept their rooms—hence the need for a scanner to find them all.

Gripping the stain remover with one tentacle, the

elderly Pheben examined the readout with one of his three eyestalks to verify that it was set for *grapok* sauce, then placed the device on the wall and activated it. Seconds later, all the sauce in the immediate vicinity had been reduced to its component atoms.

Still, as jobs went, it could have been worse. At least Leknerf had a place to sleep, regular meals, and a steady if small paycheck. It was better than some *jeghpu'wI'* could hope for. As natives of worlds conquered by the Klingon Empire, *jeghpu'wI'* occupied the lowest stratum of Klingon society. Even Houseless nonwarrior Klingons had higher places by virtue of being of the right species. All *jeghpu'wI'* could hope for was work that was beneath even the lowliest of Klingons.

However, Leknerf had little to complain about—especially now. With the end of the Dominion War, assignments to Defense Force vessels were much less risky than they had been. Many of Leknerf's friends had suffered the same fate at the hands of the Jem'Hadar that the *grapok* sauce had at Leknerf's own tentacles during those terrible two years. Leknerf had been lucky in that most of his assignments had been to space stations and planetside bases. He didn't draw a shipboard job until the last few weeks of the war, and that vessel made it through with barely a scratch.

As Leknerf turned one of his eyestalks to the scanner to search for more sauce stains, the sound of the messhall door opening reached his ear. A second eyestalk swiveled toward the noise to see Commander Kurak enter. Leknerf's objection to the intrusion died on his tongues. For one thing, while he could sometimes get the crew to stay out of the mess hall during a cleanup period, he had no chance of ever convincing an officer to abide by that rule. Quartermaster, perhaps, could keep one of them out, but not a lowly *jeghpu'wI'* maintenance drudge.

Besides, Leknerf *liked* Kurak. She was one of the few Klingons on the entire ship who even paid attention to him, and the only one of those who was ever nice to him.

"Greetings, Commander," he said. Phebens' two-tongued mouths meant they pronounced the Klingon language with a noticeable lisp, though Leknerf had made an effort to curtail that lisp as much as possible—if for no other reason than to avoid the inevitable gibes from Klingons on the subject.

"Hello, Leknerf. I'm sorry for intruding on your cleaning, but I crave some *rokeg* blood pie."

"Of course, Commander," he said as the scanner picked up some more droplets of sauce in the seam between bulkhead and deck. *That's going to be a challenge for the remover,* he thought as he applied the device.

"Computer, activate replicator, authorization Kurak *wa'maH Soch chorgh vagh.*"

The replicator in the center of the mess hall, shut down at this late hour in the midst of the second shift, hummed to life at the sound of Kurak's voice and access code.

"*Rokeg* blood pie." She turned to Leknerf. "Would you like to join me?"

"I can't, I'm afraid. Quartermaster said this place had to be spotless by the time first shift starts or he'd slice off a tentacle."

Kurak snorted. "That's novel. I would've thought he'd just threaten to kill you."

"No, ma'am. Quartermaster says *jeghpu'wI'* don't get honorable deaths."

Walking over to a table proximate to Leknerf's location, holding a plate with an entire blood pie occupying its center, Kurak said, "Typical."

"Suits me, ma'am. He cuts off a tentacle, it grows back. He kills me, I pretty much stay dead."

"Your tentacles grow back?" Kurak asked as she sat. "I didn't know that."

Leknerf didn't have anything he could really say in response to that, so he moved on to the next set of stains—this time it was bloodwine, which was halfway up the bulkhead and on the ceiling. Leknerf had long since abandoned trying to figure out how the stains in the mess hall came about. His imagination just wasn't that good, and, on the few occasions where he'd found out, the reality was far more bizarre than anything he could come up with.

After a moment, Kurak spoke through a mouthful of pie. "I have to admit, Leknerf, I envy you sometimes."

"Can't imagine why, ma'am," Leknerf said honestly while he waited for the remover to vaporize the bloodwine.

"Your tasks are simple, your responsibilities nonexistent. There are times when I crave that even more than I'm craving this blood pie right now." She took another bite.

"I suppose, ma'am, but at least you can leave whenever you want."

"Not really."

Leknerf frowned. "How's that?" The scanner found more *grapok* sauce in a corner. Leknerf set the remover back to sauce from bloodwine and applied it.

"Family obligations. Right now, I am the only able-bodied member of my House who can serve, so I must do so. I had hoped that the war ending would have relieved me of that, but I am not so fortunate." She took another bite of pie. "It could have been worse, I suppose. We could have lost the war."

Wincing at the bits of blood pie that were shooting onto the floor because of Kurak's talking with her mouth full, Leknerf said, "Suppose that could be viewed as worse, yeah."

"You disagree?"

The remover finished with the sauce. "From my point of view, ma'am, the difference between cleaning up after Klingons and cleaning up after Jem'Hadar isn't much. In fact, it's probably easier, since I hear that Jem'Hadar don't eat."

Kurak laughed at that. "An excellent point." She stopped laughing, and let out a long breath. "I still wish sometimes—"

She cut herself off. "Wish what, ma'am?" Leknerf prompted. He really didn't care much what Kurak wished, but he enjoyed the pleasant conversation. He had so few of them, after all.

"You're familiar with what's happening down on the planet?"

The scanner located an upended plate of heart of *targ* that had gotten wedged under one of the tables. Leknerf started moving chairs aside. "I've heard people talking about it. Some sort of competition between us and the aliens down on the planet. I heard Lieutenant Toq won the first one."

"Yes, a hunting exercise. I'm told the animal he captured made a fine feast."

One eyestalk turned toward Kurak, signaling Leknerf's surprise. "You weren't there?"

"All things being equal, I'd rather stay on the ship. The last thing I want to do is leave those imbeciles under my command alone in the engine room."

"Ah." Leknerf, having cleaned up the heart of *targ* remains, slithered over to the dirty-plate bin. A mechanism would carry the dish he deposited there to the galley, where it would be cleaned.

"Unfortunately, the second contest is a different matter. It's maritime combat."

Leknerf had no idea what that meant, and said so.

Kurak chuckled, spitting more pieces of the blood pie onto the floor. "I suppose you wouldn't know. The aliens down there still use boats to travel across water."

"Boats?"

"Yes, vessels made of wood that are powered by the wind."

"Why not just swim?"

Again, Kurak chuckled. "It is difficult to move people in bulk that way."

"You'd know more about it than I would," Leknerf said, though he still didn't understand why you'd use one of those boat things when you could swim.

"Yes, and that's the point."

Now Leknerf was completely confused. "What do you mean?"

Kurak waited until she swallowed a piece of pie before continuing. "Long ago, Klingons also used wind boats. My family has several such—antiques in our possession. They've been restored, and my mother taught me how to operate them when I was a girl." Kurak smiled. "I always enjoyed that—taking one out onto the River of Tolnat. I haven't been back on a wind boat since before the war." The smile fell. "Now, several of my shipmates have been assigned to take one of these boats and engage in sea combat against the aliens. They're using a primitive projectile weapon." She shook her head. "There is a huge difference between navigating at sea and in space. Leskit has been assigned to do so, and he will get them all killed."

"I thought you Klingons liked dying in battle."

"Some do." She took another bite of pie. "But at the very least, they should die well. There is no glory in dying while making an idiot of yourself. And that is what they will do, unless—"

The scanner told Leknerf that the only stains left on this side of the mess hall were those recently made by

Kurak. "Unless what?" he prompted when Kurak's hesitation went on for several seconds.

"Unless I volunteer."

"So why don't you?"

Slamming her fist into the table, Kurak said, "Because I do not *want* to! I hate this ship, I hate the Defense Force, I hate this mission! I want nothing to do with any of it! I certainly have no interest in furthering the cause of this foolish combat ritual that the captain and the aliens have concocted." Then she leaned back in her chair. "And yet, the sea is calling to me. It would be an opportunity to enjoy myself for the first time since I joined the Defense Force, and probably the last chance I will have to do so before this obscene mission ends." Kurak looked up at Leknerf. "I do not know what to do."

To Leknerf's surprise, it seemed that Kurak was looking to him for advice. This took Leknerf aback, and he needed almost a full minute to formulate his reply. "Commander, you're looking for advice on how to choose. I'm *jeghpu'wI'*. I've never made a choice in my life. I just do what they tell me."

Kurak stared at the Pheben for several more seconds. Then, throwing her plate and what was left of the blood pie on the floor, she made a disparaging noise and stormed out of the mess hall.

Sighing, Leknerf slithered over to the plate and reset the remover for *rokeg* blood pie.

B'Oraq sat on one of the rocks that overlooked the large body of water—which the Children of San-Tarah simply called the Great Sea—munching on a local fruit and a piece of leftover *san-chera* from the night before. The twin suns baked the surface in refreshing heat, the wind blowing in from the sea to keep that heat from being overly oppressive.

Of the five contests, this was the one that B'Oraq was at once eagerly anticipating and dreading. The former because she'd seen wind boats—humans called them *Seyllng Slps*—when she was at Starfleet Medical. One of her classmates had taken her to a display at the Hudson River on Earth that was truly a glorious sight: travel with no propulsion save what nature provided.

The dread derived from her shipmates' near-total lack of experience with wind boats.

Only Kurak knew anything about such endeavors— *and wasn't that a surprise to one and all?* B'Oraq thought with a smile—and she was but one of ten who were assigned to the boat. In fact, Klag had put her in charge, despite the fact that Kornan, also, was given wind-boat duty and he outranked her. Kornan, however, was willing to accept the "demotion," given the engineer's proficiency.

"May I join you?"

B'Oraq looked up to see an older member of the Ruling Pack standing nearby—at least B'Oraq assumed her to be older, given the gray that flecked her otherwise brown fur. The doctor had not heard the alien approach, and even now, the San-Tarah kept a respectful distance.

Since an attack was unlikely under these circumstances, and there was plenty of room on the rock, B'Oraq said, "Yes." As the San-Tarah sat on the other end of the rock—as far from B'Oraq as possible—the doctor said, "I am B'Oraq, the ship's doctor."

"I am Te-Run, Elder of the Ruling Pack. I'm afraid I don't understand the word 'doctor.' "

"My purpose is to heal the injured, cure the sick."

Te-Run said nothing in reply to that; indeed, she said nothing at all. B'Oraq wondered why the old woman had chosen to sit with her.

Finally, B'Oraq spoke. "May I ask a question?"

"Yes."

"Why do you have these wind boats? I was under the impression that you lived off the land."

"During the warm times, we do. When the weather grows cold, prey is sparse, and the plants wither. Before that time, we go on the Great Hunt. Across the Great Sea are the *san-reak*." Te-Run bared her teeth. "They make the *san-chera* look like insects. One *san-reak* can feed all the Children of San-Tarah for an entire cold season. But it takes many hunters to subdue one, and they only live on an island across the sea."

Nodding in understanding, B'Oraq said, "So once a year, you use the wind boats to bring warriors to the hunt?"

"Yes."

"Then why the weapons? What are they called, *tallyn?*"

"Yes. The *san-goral* live in the Great Sea and will sometimes feast on its travelers. The *tal-lyn* are to protect the Children of San-Tarah from the *san-goral.*"

"Why not just hunt them?"

Te-Run made a noise. "The *san-goral* are not good

prey. They are more bone than meat, and the meat is foul-tasting. Besides, why waste time on unworthy prey when you go to hunt the *san-reak?*"

B'Oraq found she couldn't argue with the logic. However..."Did you warn Captain Klag or Commander Kurak about the *san-goral?*"

"No."

Frowning, B'Oraq asked, "Why not?"

"Your people are fighters. If they cannot recognize an opponent when they see it, they do not deserve the fight."

I guess I cannot argue with that logic, either, she thought.

"I find it odd, B'Oraq, that your sole purpose is to heal. Do not all your people know those arts?"

B'Oraq restrained herself from going into her long-practiced tirade on the subject of the appalling state of Klingon medicine. Her fight to change that had been an uphill battle from the moment she decided to study at Starfleet Medical Academy in the Federation, but it was not one that Te-Run was likely to appreciate.

Choosing her words carefully, she instead said, "Our people have a variety of views on the subject of healing. Some feel that treatment of injury is a sign of weakness. In addition, our technology has improved what we can do to heal. Use of it is—"

"Technology?" Te-Run interrupted. "Is that what allows you to fly among the stars?"

"Yes, and—"

The doctor's next words were swallowed by the ear-splitting sound of an explosion. One of the two wind boats had engaged its opponent with its *tal-lyn*. B'Oraq peered out over the dark blue sea and saw that the *Gorkon*'s wind boat had fired a shot. The *tal-lyn* fired a metal ball through a tube via exploding gases. B'Oraq had always thought that such weapons lacked appeal. They simply destroyed anything in their path, requiring neither skill nor precision. Energy weapons at least were quick and surgical, and bladed weapons actually required that the wielder know how to use them.

The *Gorkon* wind boat's shot also went very wide of its target. B'Oraq shook her head. Rodek and Morketh—the two primary gunners—were supposed to be in charge of firing the boat's two *tal-lyns*. B'Oraq would have thought that using such a weapon would be as easy for those two as firing a quantum torpedo. The awkwardness of it, however, was no doubt working against them.

"Your empire," Te-Run said suddenly. "How large is it?"

"It encompasses many planets across dozens of star systems. I'm not sure how to put it on a scale you'd understand."

"And if you win this contest, then we will become part of it."

"Yes." B'Oraq didn't add that the chance of the San-Tarah winning this contest was the only chance they had of not becoming part of it.

"I would like to learn more about your empire, if you don't mind my asking you questions."

"Not at all," B'Oraq said. She could understand why Te-Run would come to B'Oraq. Unlike most of her crewmates, B'Oraq was accustomed to dealing with different peoples as equals—it came with the medical degree.

"Good. I have many questions, and I will need to know the answers before the contest is over and you depart."

B'Oraq couldn't help but smile at that. "Oh?"

"Your people are soft," Te-Run said matter-of-factly. "You depend far too much on this—technology. I admit that some of you are fine fighters—and the one who captured the *chera-mak* is a hunter the likes of which I haven't seen in many seasons—but you *will* lose."

Tugging on her braid, B'Oraq said, "You're that sure?"

"I'm old, B'Oraq. Very soon, it will be time for me to run with the dead. You gain understanding the more seasons you see, and my understanding tells me now that you will lose. What is that?" The last question was asked while pointing at the pin at the end of B'Oraq's braid, resting on her right shoulder.

Peering down briefly at the pin, B'Oraq said, "That is the symbol of my House—I guess you could say it's the equivalent of my pack."

"So you function in packs as well? Interesting."

"Well, no, not really." B'Oraq blew out a breath, wondering if she was up for explaining the entire structure of Klingon society.

Her attempt to do so was cut off by the sound of another explosion. A large green creature had emerged from the water—surprisingly silently, since the scaled animal was larger than the wind boat—and the *Gorkon* wind boat fired both its *tal-lyns* at it.

"That's a *san-goral?*" B'Oraq asked.

"Yes."

Even as the *Gorkon* continued its assault, the San-Tarah wind boat maneuvered around to the *Gorkon* wind boat's flank. *No, no, you fools*, B'Oraq thought. The San-Tarah were using the distraction of the *san-goral*—which probably caught Kurak and her crew by surprise—to get in behind them.

As it happened, Kurak knew this, too. Even from here, B'Oraq could hear the engineer screaming. She was too distant to make out words, but the doctor knew that Kurak was not happy. *Then again, when is she ever happy?*

The San-Tarah's *tal-lyn* fired a fatal blow into the keel of the *Gorkon's* wind boat. The latter was now on fire and starting to sink.

"*QI'yaH*," B'Oraq cursed, and stood up.

The *san-goral* retreated back into the sea. Relative to where B'Oraq stood, the creature was behind the wind boat, so the doctor couldn't tell if it was wounded or not.

"It would seem that this contest is ours." Te-Run sounded more than a little smug at that.

Four Klingons abandoned ship, jumping into the water and swimming to shore. That still left six on board the boat, which continued to sink.

B'Oraq activated her communicator. "B'Oraq to Klag."

"*Klag. I see it too, Doctor.*"

"Request permission to have the *Gorkon* beam everyone off the wind boat and to me here on the shore."

"*That violates the rules of the contest,*" said another voice in the background. "*Unless you are conceding, Captain Klag.*"

The doctor could hear the anger tinging Klag's words as he said, *"Yes, we concede this contest, Me-Larr. Proceed, Doctor."*

"Thank you, Captain. B'Oraq to *Gorkon*."

"Toq."

"Lieutenant, I need the transporter room to beam any Klingons on the wind boat about half a *qellqam* in front of me to my position."

"Stand by, Doctor." A moment passed. *"We have determined a way to use the transporters for site-to-site beaming."* Another moment. *"We can do it, but we are having difficulty locking on to specific life-forms."*

"There are only six on board, Lieutenant. Do a wide-beam if you have to, but we need to get all six of them off of there, living or dead."

"If they are dead," Te-Run said, "what does it matter if you retrieve the bodies?"

"If possible, we commend the spirits of the dead who fall in battle to *Sto-Vo-Kor*. That requires the body. Once that is done, the body is but an empty shell that may be disposed of. And if they live, I must heal them."

"One does not survive a sea battle if one loses." Te-Run spoke with the assurance of an older person speaking to a child who did not know better.

B'Oraq found she was going to enjoy proving her wrong.

A few seconds later, the red glow of a transporter beam deposited Kurak, Leskit, Kornan, Morketh, Rodek, and a soldier B'Oraq didn't recognize in front of her. Morketh and the soldier were quite obviously dead—the former's head had been half caved in, and the latter's entire chest cavity was destroyed—but the others still lived. Rodek was unconscious, the others simply bleeding, so she attended to the gunner first.

Kurak was in the middle of shouting as the transporter effect died down. "—ilthy *petaQ!* How could you have been so unutterably stupid?"

"The boat would not maneuver in the way that we had been led—" Kornan started.

"Which is why I told you not to make that maneuver! The captain put me in charge for a reason. And then, when that—that *thing* appeared—"

Kornan interrupted by limping over to B'Oraq. "Why did you transport us?"

"Captain's orders," the doctor said quickly, not wanting to get into a protracted discussion. Rodek had a subdural hematoma and several chest wounds. One chamber of his heart was damaged. "I need to get him to the medical bay." She bandaged both wounds— they'd keep for a few minutes while she checked the others.

"I knew this was a mistake," Kurak said as B'Oraq did a quick examination. The doctor hated working without a hand scanner, but that technology was lost to her here. "I should never have allowed myself to let deficients such as yourselves ruin this for me."

Leskit snorted. "I wasn't aware that this was about your pride."

"The one joy I still had in my life was sailing, Leskit.

Now you've taken that away from me. I'll never be able to look at a boat again without thinking of how incredibly *stupid* you all are!"

"You'll be fine," B'Oraq said to the engineer. "I'll knit your broken arm back on the ship." As she examined Leskit, she heard footfalls.

"Report, Commander," Klag's powerful voice said. B'Oraq looked up to see that he, along with Me-Larr, had joined them.

Both Kurak and Kornan spoke at once.

"Report, Commander *Kurak,*" Klag said, cutting them both off.

"Your precious warriors were unable to follow the simplest instruction, Captain, and even when they didn't completely embarrass themselves, they were barely competent. All of which would have been forgivable and might have allowed us to still at least put up a fight, until that green *thing* came out of the ocean and then both Morketh *and* Rodek turned to fire on it, even though I only ordered Rodek to do so. Morketh deliberately disobeyed me and fired as well, leaving our flank exposed. I want him disciplined."

"A bit late for that," B'Oraq said as she put a pressure bandage on Leskit's leg wound. "Morketh is dead. So is that soldier. I haven't yet performed the ritual."

"Then I shall," Klag said.

Kurak snorted. "I wouldn't bother with Morketh. He does not deserve—"

"He died in service of the Empire!" Klag snapped. "He died doing his duty, and for that reason alone, he died with honor. That is all that matters, Commander. You would do well to remember that."

The engineer said nothing in reply.

Klag walked over to Morketh, pried his one remaining eye open, then looked up to the heavens and screamed, warning the warriors in the Black Fleet that another was crossing the River of Blood to join them in *Sto-Vo-Kor*. He then did the same for the soldier.

"Captain, I need to take the wounded back to the *Gorkon*," B'Oraq said after determining that Kornan's wounds were superficial.

"Very well," Klag said.

Te-Run spoke up, then. "That was the death ritual of which you spoke?"

"Yes."

"Interesting. Why did you not perform it for this one?" She pointed at Rodek.

B'Oraq smiled at that. "He is not dead."

"That is ridiculous. He bleeds from multiple injuries. He cannot possibly live."

"You are incorrect. He will live, and fight another day. *That* is the advantage that our technology gives us." She activated her communicator. "*Gorkon*, this is B'Oraq. Have Nurse Gaj meet me in the transporter room, then beam up five from this position."

"*Acknowledged. Stand by*," Toq said.

"Te-Run, I'll need you to step back. Our transporters aren't able to work as precisely on this world, and I need only these wounded to be near me."

"May I be permitted to go with you? I would like to

see this *Gorkon* of which you have spoken—and I would especially like to see how you can save the life of one who is dead."

That was not B'Oraq's decision to make. She turned to Klag, who was talking with Me-Larr. "Captain, do you—or Me-Larr—have any objection to Te-Run accompanying me back to the *Gorkon?*"

Klag smiled. "Not at all. I think it would be good for your people to see what becoming part of the Empire will mean."

"Ready to transport, Doctor," said Toq.

"Make that six from this position, Lieutenant. Energize when ready."

CHAPTER TEN

Krevor stood at attention as *QaS DevwI'* Vok addressed the twenty troops that were gathered in the clearing. They stood in one of the many forests that this planet was littered with. The first sun was just starting to be visible over the tree line, and the second sun would rise within the hour. Krevor squinted as the light flickered through the brown leaves.

The contest in which the fifteenth and three other squads were to engage was a common enough combat exercise. Many species had variations on it—humans called it "capture the flag," Tellarites referred to it as "defend the trough," and Andorians simply used an unpronounceable word with too many lisping sounds. One had to find a symbol of the enemy's power and capture it, all the while defending one's own symbol.

Between Vok and the line of troops was a circle of stones. Each stone had a character painted on it, and the circle's diameter was wide enough so that two Klingons could stand in it. In the center of the circle was another stone. Unlike the other bits of lettering, a translation had been provided for the character painted on this one: *prize*.

"Second Squad will scout ahead in search of the enemy prize," Vok said. "Fourth and Seventh Squads will defend the inner reaches, and also search. Fifteenth Squad will remain here and defend the prize."

Krevor was still not sure what she and her squad were doing here. The first had been assigned to remain at the "prime village," as the natives called it, to make sure that the Children of San-Tarah stayed true to their words, the third and fifth had both taken losses during the initial strike, and the sixth was wiped out in the same attack.

"*QaS DevwI'* Vok, request permission to speak." That was Wol, standing to Krevor's left at the end of the line of troops. If their Leader had shown any sign of her wound at the hands of the enemy, she no longer showed it. It was either a testament to the doctor's talents or to Wol's own fortitude. Krevor chose to believe the latter. Her own broken leg had been but a minor inconvenience, easily repaired, the lingering pain hardly worth acknowledging.

Vok grinned a very wide grin. "Granted, Leader."

"The fifteenth is honored by your assigning us to this glorious task, sir. But I have to wonder why the eighth was not given the honor. Surely, they have earned it."

Walking over to stand in front of Wol, Vok rested his right arm on his corpulent belly. "Honor is indeed earned, Leader, but by deeds and actions, not by numbers or accidents of birth."

Krevor started.

"You held the road," Vok added.

"Yes, sir."

Vok then turned to the rest of the gathered troops. "The aliens do not know where our prize is, and we do not know where theirs is. Let us show them that it is not just our bridge officers who are skilled in the hunt."

Several troops chuckled at that, including Krevor.

The first sun shone brightly as it moved past the top of the tree line. Krevor put up her arm to block out the worst of the rays. Next to her on the right, G'joth did likewise, cursing under his breath.

"Worried the sun will melt you, G'joth?" Krevor asked with a grin.

"No, just burn out my eye sockets," he muttered.

Vok turned and faced the forest. "It begins! To battle! *Qapla'*!"

All twenty troops cried *"Qapla'!"* in reply.

Then fifteen of them followed Vok into the forest, leaving Wol, Davok, G'joth, Goran, and Krevor to defend the prize.

Wol had brought a *bat'leth* this time, and she held it firmly in her right hand, using it to point. "Goran," she said, directing her weapon at the circle of stones, "I want you to stand right there and not move. You're our last line of defense. Even if those *toDSaH* get past everyone else, you're not to let any of them into the circle, is that understood?"

"Yes, Leader."

"That includes helping anyone. If I'm standing right in front of you being slaughtered by ten of those beasts, you're not to move from your post. You have no other duty but to keep the prize from enemy hands."

Goran nodded with almost childlike enthusiasm. "You can rely on me, Leader Wol."

Davok muttered, "Good to know we can count on *that*, at least."

"Something bothers you, *Bekk?*" Wol asked frostily.

"No, Leader, not a *thing* is bothering me. What could possibly be bothering me?" Davok started to pace, his small eyes squinting even more than usual, making him look to Krevor like a blind *grishnar* cat. "After nine weeks of tedium, we're now called upon to keep a bunch of primitives from stealing a rock. Surely, this is a glorious mission worthy of the finest warriors in the Empire."

"We're fighting to conquer this world," Krevor said. "It will be a great victory."

"By sailing in wind boats and stealing rocks?"

Krevor shook her head. "No, fool, by defeating our enemies!"

G'joth put a hand on Krevor's shoulder. "You're wasting perfectly good breath, Krevor. Arguing with Davok is like teaching a *targ* to sing opera—you waste your time and annoy the *targ*."

Snorting, Davok said, "I'm surprised *targ* singing isn't one of these mindless competitions."

"That's enough!" Wol said before Krevor could reply.

"Davok, cover the north flank. G'joth, the south. Krevor, go west. I'll take east."

"Yes, Leader," Krevor and G'joth said in unison. Davok simply took up a position in a northerly direction.

"This is still a waste," Davok muttered. "With nothing to lose, no sacrifice, there is nothing to gain."

"Ensign Morketh would disagree with you on that subject," Krevor said. "And many others almost died in the second contest. For that matter, Lieutenant Toq could have been killed by the beast he slew."

"Yes, but they're officers. They spend their time on the bridge pushing buttons. I'd expect foolishness like this to be a challenge for them. You notice that none of the troops on the wind boat were hurt."

"Actually," Wol said, "*Bekk* Moken from the twentieth died."

"Well, then he'll be the laughing stock of the Black Fleet," Davok said. "Of all the ways to get into *Sto-Vo-Kor*..."

G'joth sighed. "Davok, you're spoiling my concentration."

"What could you possibly be concentrating on? Even if they started the second the sun came over the trees, those primitives can't possibly have come this far yet."

"I'm concentrating on my song."

Goran shot G'joth a look. "I thought it was a novel."

"No, it was a poem," Krevor said.

Archly, G'joth said, "I have found that the epic poem is overrated as a form of self-expression."

Wol laughed. "It will be a *llm'rlq* before long."

Krevor frowned. "A what?"

"It's a type of human poem—a short form, only five lines. I heard one—during the war. They don't translate very well—it depends on rhymes in order to be appreciated."

"Five lines?" Davok said with disdain. "Typical of humans—everything of theirs is too small."

Krevor, however, noted that Wol hesitated. She wondered if she heard this human poetry at a time other than during the Dominion War. Frankly, Krevor was surprised that Wol had had any congress with humans. There was very little interaction during the war between ground troops among the different militaries. The only human she'd had any extended contact with in her life was the aide to Ambassador Worf when she served as the latter's bodyguard.

"Humans are small, it's true," Wol said, "and they can be incredibly fragile, but they're not weak."

"There are some humans who are able to overcome their weaknesses." Davok sounded grudging as he admitted this fact. "But they are not the majority."

"Ah," G'joth said, "and you've done an extensive survey of all humans, have you?"

"I've seen enough of them. I fought them at Ajilon Prime. It was before the war, when they abrogated the treaty because they were too squeamish to support our just invasion of Cardassia."

Chuckling, G'joth said, "As usual, you refuse to let facts get in the way of shooting your mouth off. We abrogated the Khitomer Accords."

"With reason!" Davok snapped. "We should never have renewed that treaty. Humans are soft, they have their precious replicators that allow them to live a life of ease, and they die far too easily. I know, I killed dozens of them at Ajilon, and they all screamed like old women."

G'joth looked toward Krevor. "Actually, he only killed four humans at Ajilon—though it's possible he's killed dozens of old women, and just got them confused."

Krevor laughed. "And yet, without those fragile, squeamish soft humans, we would have lost the war."

"Oh, so you believe the propaganda, then?" Davok said disdainfully. "That does not surprise me."

"Propaganda?"

Shaking his head, Davok said, "It never takes long for the new chancellor to wipe out the memory of the old. Gowron wasted no time in singing his praises at the expense of K'mpec, and Martok did the same with Gowron. Everyone speaks of the great deeds Martok committed as general, but it was Gowron who gave Martok his orders, *he* who led us down the path to victory. Martok simply took the final few steps, yet now he claims that he and the Federation, and even the Romulans, won the war together." Davok spit. "It was *the Empire* that kept us in the war. When the Breen entered combat with their weapon, it was the Empire that held the line. Even the defense against that weapon came from the Cardassians. Humans were *useless*, little more than cannon fodder."

Krevor couldn't believe what she was hearing. The last nine weeks had proven Davok to be a malcontent, but she hadn't thought of him as actively stupid until this moment. Still keeping her eye on the forest in front of her, she said to Davok, "And what of the troops who died at such disasters as Avinall VII? That was ordered by Gowron. Or the victories that were led by the Federation?"

Davok sneered. "Yes, well, a Houseless fool like you *would* fall for those lies, wouldn't you?"

Whirling around, Krevor unsheathed her *d'k tahg* with her right hand in a fluid motion. She still held her *mek'leth* in the left. "If I am a Houseless fool, Davok, what does that make you? On the *Gorkon*, after all, we are equals."

"We may both be *bekks*, Krevor, but if you truly believe that we are equals—"

"I am your Leader, Davok," Wol said sharply. "And I too am Houseless. I know that we are *not* equals, that, in fact, I am *your* superior. You would do well to remember that."

G'joth, who was grinning ear to ear, added, "Besides, Davok, it's not like you were *born* to the House of Kazag."

Unsheathing his own *d'k tahg*, Davok said, "I *earned* my place in Kazag!"

Krevor weighed the benefit of finding out how Davok came to be part of a House he was not born into against the detriment of having to listen to him tell it. *He was probably still noble born*, she thought with an envy that shamed her. Krevor was the unwanted daughter of an unworthy woman. A harlot from the Old Quarter of the First City, Krevor's mother left the bulk of the task of raising her daughter to her fellow whores and thieves. The only person who ever treated her as anything other than a burden was one of her mother's clients, a Defense Force soldier. For all she knew, that soldier was her father. When she reached the Age of Ascension, she left the Old Quarter—for which her mother was probably grateful—and enlisted. It had taken many years, but she had proven her worth on the battlefield more than once.

Now, having risen to a squad of the first among *QaS Devwl'*, she knew that this would bring her more glory still. If she lived, they would sing songs about what she and her shipmates did this day; if she died, she would go to *Sto-Vo-Kor*, a fate she would never have given herself hope to achieve in her formative years in the Old Quarter.

Nothing Davok could say about her status would change that.

"Quiet!" Wol said suddenly.

"I will not—" Davok started.

"I said, *quiet!*" Wol repeated in a shouted whisper, and Krevor knew why: the enemy was approaching. She picked up the scent of six—no, seven of the aliens approaching from above.

Immediately, Davok sheathed his *d'k tahg* and took out his *qutluch*. The scent of the enemy came from the north, and so Krevor moved around to stand by Davok, as did Wol. They spread out a bit to cover the maximum ground but still form a phalanx that the San-Tarah would be hard-pressed to get through. Wol also motioned for G'joth to stand his ground, just in case.

What intrigued Krevor was that the San-Tarah were coming through the trees—but she knew this only from their scent, not from any aural clues. They moved silently through the branches, not disturbing them any more than the wind did. *They know their territory.*

Perhaps they did not know about Klingons' superior olfactory capabilities. *But then*, she realized after a moment, *why should they?* The ones who learned of it during the *Gorkon* crew's initial attack did not survive to share that intelligence, and Krevor doubted that the captain would tell them of it now.

Good, she thought, the bloodlust rising within her, *let them charge into their destruction.*

"Eyes ahead," Wol said, "we want to be ready for their frontal assault." Wol grinned. The San-Tarah wouldn't be able to understand the words—there were no translators on the field of battle—but the aliens would think the Klingons were expecting a ground assault.

The scent grew closer; Krevor dared not look up to see if they were in sight, for that would give away their deception, but she knew they were close.

When they were close enough so that Krevor knew she would be able to see them if she looked up, Wol cried, "Davok, *now!*"

Davok threw his *qutluch* into one of the trees. A second later, a black-furred San-Tarah fell from one of the branches, the assassin's dagger protruding from its head.

Five of the remaining six aliens leapt down from the trees, howling in unison, their moment of surprise gone. Two headed toward Krevor, one straight for her, the other on an approach that would put it a few paces in front of her. Not concerning herself with the other one at first, she waited until the last second, then ducked backward and swung her *d'k tahg* in an arc toward the alien's neck. The blood spurted outward, covering Krevor's own face, even as her enemy fell to the ground, writhing in agony as the life poured out.

The smell of freshly spilled blood assaulted her nostrils, and she gave in to the fires within.

This, she thought as she turned and faced the other San-Tarah, who unsheathed one of those curved swords of theirs from a back harness, *is what I was meant for.*

She parried the San-Tarah's sword thrust with her *mek'leth,* then tried to go on the offensive. Her enemy was skilled, however, and would not allow her to do so—at first. Krevor focused her bloodlust, and kept only one thought in her mind: Kill the enemy. Within minutes, she was pressing forward, putting the San-Tarah on the defensive, before finally exploiting a weakness in one parry that allowed her to disarm the alien.

One thrust of the *mek'leth* later, the alien lay dead on the ground, bleeding from the chest.

Krevor had turned to find a new enemy when a projectile struck her from behind. She stumbled briefly, and found herself splattered with blood. Looking down, she saw the projectile roll along the ground, and realized with a start that it was Davok's head.

Looking up, she saw one of the San-Tarah standing over Davok's decapitated body, blood matting its gray fur, its sword stained with the *bekk*'s blood.

Whatever his flaws, Davok was her comrade, and she would avenge him, or die trying. Screaming, she leapt onto the gray-furred alien, tackling it. Even as they crashed to the ground, her enemy tried to swing its sword at her, and succeeded in cutting through the arm of her uniform, though not flesh. But the smell of Davok's blood only served to fuel her anger, as she plunged her *mek'leth* into the alien's chest.

She looked up. Three of the five who had leapt from the trees were dead. The other two sparred with G'joth and Wol, while Goran stood his ground in the circle. Wol seemed to be holding her own, so Krevor moved to aid G'joth.

As she did so, searing pain flared through her back— two blades sliced into her from behind. In one motion, she grabbed the hilt of her *d'k tahg* and unsheathed it, then thrust backward with the point at whatever was standing behind her. The tip of the blade struck something. Again, the pain flared as the blades were removed from her back.

Embracing the pain, allowing it to give her focus, Krevor turned around and faced her foe: a brown-and-white-furred San-Tarah with her *d'k tahg* hilt protruding from its belly. *The sixth one*, Krevor realized. *It must have leapt down from the trees.*

The *d'k tahg* did nothing to slow the alien down, as it attacked Krevor with impressive speed. Krevor parried the sword thrust with her *mek'leth*, then swung her blade toward its neck. The San-Tarah parried, and thrust downward, almost disarming Krevor, and bringing one of the sword's blades perilously close to Krevor's blood-soaked head.

Krevor reached up and grabbed the end of the blade with one gauntleted hand. The edges bit into flesh, but she was beyond caring about such trivialities as pain now. She yanked the blade out of the surprised hands of the San-Tarah and cast it aside.

Her enemy did not remain surprised for very long, instead attacking frontally. It leapt at her, tackling her, sinking its teeth into Krevor's neck as they fell to the ground.

The smell of her blood, the alien's blood, and Davok's blood intermingled with the matted fur and hot breath of her foe. Krevor screamed out in rage and joy and pain even as she stabbed the San-Tarah in the side with her *mek'leth*.

In its death throes, the San-Tarah tore a large chunk of flesh and muscle from Krevor's right shoulder with its teeth.

Blood covered Krevor from head to toe as she threw her dead foe off her with her left arm—her right arm was now utterly useless. She saw that Goran was now fighting two San-Tarah at once—and that both G'joth and Wol were down, possibly dead.

Krevor had no idea how much of the blood was her own or was Davok's or the San-Tarah's. It didn't matter, really. She knew that she would die soon. But she would take as many of her enemy with her.

Today is most definitely a good day to die.

Grabbing the San-Tarah's own two-bladed sword from the ground with her left hand, she charged at one of the two trying to get past Goran's massive form to the circle. Her thoughts as she decapitated the San-Tarah were not of the whorehouse where she was born, nor of the disdain of those around her as she worked her way through the ranks.

She thought only of *Sto-Vo-Kor* and the glory that awaited her as she died in battle, as a true Klingon.

Goran snapped the neck of the last of the seven San-Tarah who had attacked.

"Wol to Vok."

Krevor turned to see that Wol had managed to get up, though she bled profusely from a wound in her right leg.

"Vok."

"We have encountered seven Children of San-Tarah who attempted to claim the prize. They have failed, but we have taken losses. Davok is dead, G'joth may well be soon, I'm wounded, and Krevor is halfway across the River of Blood."

Angrily, Krevor said, "I can stand my post, Leader."

Wol smiled. "Of that I have no doubt, *Bekk.*"

"We are close to our goal," Vok said, *"but I will send two soldiers back to you. Well done, Leader. I knew I could count on the fifteenth to hold the line."*

As Wol cut the connection, Krevor asked, "What of G'joth?" Unlike his friend, the aspiring writer had been a comrade in more than just arms to Krevor.

The Leader limped over to G'joth's form. "He still

lives, but he is not conscious. He'll need to transport back to the *Gorkon.*" Then Wol made her way to where Davok's head lay, right beside one of the dead San-Tarah. Wol got down on her good knee, checked Davok's eyes, then screamed to the heavens.

Krevor and Goran both threw their own heads back and joined in the scream. Krevor found her voice failing her, even as the numbness spread from her right arm to her entire chest.

"I'm sorry," Goran said.

Turning to face the giant, Krevor asked, "Why?"

"I might've been able to save Davok, but I had to stay here." Goran sounded almost sad.

Wol walked over to the circle, using her *bat'leth* as a makeshift cane. "You have nothing to apologize for, Goran. You followed orders, and did your duty. If you had helped Davok, one of the other San-Tarah may well have claimed the prize."

Goran smiled, apparently happy from the reassurance from his Leader.

Krevor's vision swam, and not just from the blood that was now dripping into her eyes. *I will hold the line,* she thought, forcing herself to focus. More San-Tarah could come at any moment, after all.

"You have done well, Krevor," Wol said. "It has been the greatest of honors to serve with you."

"Thank you, Leader," Krevor said. "I—I feel the same."

"I do not speak those words lightly," Wol added. "I have known many great warriors in my time." She hesitated. "I was not always as I am now. Once I was Eral, daughter of B'Etakk of the House of Varnak."

A part of Krevor's mind registered surprise at this revelation. The rest of her mind was occupied with trying to figure out why she could no longer smell the blood. It was everywhere, after all, she should still be smelling it....

She managed to get out the word "What—"

"What happened to me does not matter. What does matter, *Bekk*, is that I have met beings from dozens of species, and I have seen Klingon society at its highest and lowest. Today, you have reminded me that the true heart of a warrior has naught to do with where that heart was born."

Krevor wanted to thank Wol for the words, but she couldn't make her lips work. Even Wol's voice was starting to sound almost hollow, and Krevor's vision grew worse.

Looks like we go to Sto-Vo-Kor *together, Davok,* she thought, and as she died she wondered if he'd be as argumentative in the next life as he was in this....

B'Oraq looked over the scanner readings for Rodek just as Klag entered the medical bay. Rodek was the only patient left—the other survivors of yesterday's disastrous sea battle had been discharged after treatment that took only a few moments once B'Oraq had access to working modern tools. Te-Run had transported back down to the planet after standing uncharacteristically quietly and with her tongue literally hanging out of the side of her mouth while B'Oraq worked on Rodek.

The Child of San-Tarah never actually admitted that she was wrong about Rodek's prospects, but clearly Te-Run was astonished by the fact that the gunner would live.

"Report, Doctor," the captain said.

"Lieutenant Rodek is stable. I've repaired the damage to his heart and his head, but he is still unconscious. At this point, it's just a matter of if and when he wakes up. What disturbs me is these readings in his hippocampus and the evidence of surgery."

"Oh?"

B'Oraq looked up at Klag. "The readings in his hippocampus are odd. I suppose it relates to the amnesia."

Klag nodded. Rodek had been in a shuttle accident near Bajor four years earlier that cost him all his memories prior to that moment. "What about the surgery?"

"It looks like his crest has been altered." She shrugged. "It's not unheard of, but usually not in officers from strong Houses. Usually people only get this kind of surgery to disassociate themselves from their family."

"I doubt that is the case here," Klag said with a snort, not sounding overly concerned. "You may ask him about it when he wakes up, if you wish. What of the others?"

If he's not going to care, no reason why I should. Though I am curious. In any event, the doctor had, as the humans said, bigger fish to fry. "Kurak, Leskit, and Kornan are all fit for duty."

"Good."

"Not particularly," B'Oraq said, turning angrily at

her captain. "Sir, if one of those *tal-lyns* had struck a bit closer, or if we hadn't beamed them off in time, we might well now be without the services of our first officer, chief engineer, and primary pilot. As it is, one of our gunners is dead, and I don't know when the other one will be fit to return to duty."

"We are warriors, Doctor, that sort of risk is—"

Angrily, B'Oraq said, "Yes, I *know* that such risks are part of combat, but there's also no need to be foolish about it."

Klag's face darkened. "Tread carefully, Doctor."

B'Oraq, however, was beyond caring if she angered her captain or not. *Let him kill me, I will be heard on this.* "Of all the contests, this was the one we were mostly likely to fail at. Kurak is the only crew member who has even *been* on a wind boat. The San-Tarah center one of their most important annual rituals around it—there was no reasonable way to expect that we would be able to defeat them in this. The other contests, certainly, but not this one."

"Do you truly think so little of your shipmates, Doctor?"

Save me from Klingon arrogance, B'Oraq thought. "In a hunt? In hand-to-hand combat? In a show of strength and power? I believe that the warriors of this vessel can overcome anything—and I have every bit of faith that we will triumph in the other contests, including the one going on down there now. But the sea combat was a loss, Captain. It was *guaranteed* to be a loss."

Slamming a fist onto an empty biobed, Klag yelled,

"What would you have me do, Doctor? Forfeit the contest? Is this the way we prove our mettle?"

"Of course not—but why commit valuable bridge officers to the mission? We're only nine weeks into a mission that could take years, with no chance of crew replacements in anything like a timely manner. Kurak, I can see, given her experience, but the first officer? The pilot? Both gunners?"

Klag scowled. "The contest called for a pilot and two who can fire weapons. I wanted the best we had. Only a fool goes into battle without his best weapons."

"I believe a more apt saying, Captain, is that only a fool fights in a burning house, and this one was practically burned to the ground before we arrived. Leskit's skills didn't prepare him for maneuvering in water, and any idiot can fire one of those *tal-lyns*. There are fifteen hundred expendable soldiers on board this ship, who swore to give their lives for the Empire. They should have been sacrificed on this contest, not the officers."

Klag's hand moved to his *d'k tahg* as he spoke in a quiet, slow voice. "Your objection has been noted. You will not speak of it again, or I will put you to death where you stand."

"Go right ahead," B'Oraq said. "Then you can heal the wounded yourself in your mad quest."

"My mad quest? We fight for the Empire, B'Oraq, not—"

"Yes, yes, I know, we engage in pure battle to preserve the spirit of what Kahless taught us. Kornan has gone on at great length on the subject. But I saw you on

Ty'Gokor when Captain Dorrek approached you. And I saw you after we received the report on Brenlek. Tell me, are you engaging in this contest as a return to proper Klingon values, or do you just want to one-up your brother?"

B'Oraq barely saw Klag move—one moment he was standing in front of her, smoldering, the next he had slammed the heel of his hand into her chest, sending her sprawling against the bulkhead. Before she could catch her breath, he pinned her to the bulkhead with his right arm, having unsheathed his *d'k tahg* with his left. The point of the blade was at her neck.

Despite the shooting pains in her chest and the sudden difficulty breathing, B'Oraq managed to say, "Go ahead and kill me, Captain—if I'm lying, you have every reason to."

Klag stared at her for several seconds, the fire in his eyes so intense that B'Oraq was not at all convinced that she would live to see the next minute. Not that she was afraid; she had dedicated her life to challenging her people's assumptions and habits. Every morning she woke up fully expecting a blade in her chest for her insolence before she went to bed that night.

"I also have every reason to kill you if you are insubordinate, Doctor. Do not *ever* forget that."

Then he broke her right arm.

After that, he walked toward the exit, leaving her to collapse onto the deck in considerable pain. "Keep me apprised of the lieutenant's progress, Doctor," Klag said as the doors ground open to allow him egress.

Somehow B'Oraq managed to get to her feet, using only her left arm for support. She walked over to the bone-knitter, and began the awkward task of applying it to herself.

It would seem, she thought, *that I was right. I rather wish I wasn't. If he is truly blinded by his need to prove himself superior to his brother, Morketh may not be the only officer we lose. . . .*

CHAPTER ELEVEN

Kurak had read the same paragraph of the technical journal eight times when the alert to her door sounded.

"Go away," she said, starting the paragraph for the ninth time. A plate of half-eaten *zilm'kach* sat in front of her, along with a mug of *raktajino* that had long since gone cold.

"It is Kornan," said the voice from the other side.

She sighed. "That changes nothing. Go away."

"I am still first officer of this ship, *Commander*, and I will enter your quarters with or without your consent."

Kurak let out another sigh as she turned off the display on the padd. The latest theories in warp-field technology—or was it antimatter injection?—faded from the screen. *I might as well get this over with*, she thought. *It's not as if I am getting any work done here. . . .*

"Enter."

The door opened to Kornan's muscular form. As

usual, he wore a sleeveless tunic, now showing off the scars on his arms. Normally, Kurak would find such a sight intoxicating, but knowing that he got those scars from their embarrassing bout of sea combat ruined the effect.

"What do you want, Commander?"

Kornan had the unmitigated gall to smile as he entered her quarters, the door closing behind him. "Why so formal? I was hoping to make up for what happened yesterday with that—inspection."

"If you and Leskit performed a mutual *Mauk-to'Vor* on each other, I might consider it a small step toward making up for what happened yesterday. That, however, is the only way you will be able to do so."

At that, Kornan stepped backward as if she'd struck him. "How dare you—"

"How dare you, *Commander!*" She stood, knocking her padd, the plate of *zilm'kach*, and the mug of cold *raktajino* to the floor. "Very little in this life has given me joy. Thanks to the stupidity of you and the other 'officers' on this *targ*pit of a ship, the one thing I still cherished as a fond memory has been soiled!"

Walking up to her and practically shoving his face against hers, Kornan said, "You might recall, *Commander*, that you volunteered for the mission. No one forced you to do so—no one even knew of your prowess with wind boats. You could have simply remained on board, and no one would have been the wiser."

Her crest almost scraping against his, Kurak almost screamed. "Perhaps I should have! But I didn't, and now my life, already a shambles, has been all but ruined." Kurak decided not to bother mentioning the role that Leknerf had played in her decision making. Bad enough that Kornan was so unrepentant in his role in this—she couldn't stomach the idea of his ridicule at her asking *jeghpu'wI'* for advice.

"No, Kurak," Kornan said, his voice now softer, "you could not have. Do you know why? It would have been the act of a coward. You are many things, but you are not the type of craven animal that hides her talents in order to avoid conflict. Even if you are more at home among data spikes than disruptors, your heart is still Klingon."

Kurak laughed in Kornan's face, then turned her back on him—two deliberate insults. "You know nothing about me, Kornan, and even less about my heart. Now, unless you have official ship's business, get *out* of my quarters!"

"Oh, I do have *business*, Chief Engineer. Lieutenant Toq has some theories he wishes to test involving traveling around the subspace eddies. You need to report to engineering to supervise the modifications to the navigation shields."

Gripping her right wrist with her left hand, Kurak said, "I am off duty until—"

"You are on duty when I *say* you are on duty, Commander, is that clear?" Kornan barked.

She whirled around. "Or what? You will kill me? Feel free." Then she smiled and walked back toward him. "Oh, but then you will *never* get me into your bed, will you? That has been consuming you all these weeks, hasn't it? 'How do I get Kurak into my bed? How do I harness that fire for myself?' " Once again, she brought her face close to his. His musk permeated her nostrils, but now she just found it repugnant. She whispered, "I guarantee that you will *never* succeed."

Scowling, he looked into her eyes with a stare of death. *A pity that stares do not match the reality.* But, though she had misread her own heart rather spectacularly, she had taken Kornan's measure weeks ago. He had wanted her from the moment he laid eyes on her, and it had taken her until now to realize that that, truly, was what appealed to her about him as well. Now, however, that she knew him to be the same sort of fool that littered the Defense Force, she had dismissed him as yet another who disgusted her by his very presence.

After a moment, he said slowly, "You will report to the engine room. *Now.*"

"As you wish, Commander Kornan."

She pushed past him, the door to her quarters opening. Then she stopped and turned around. "Feel free to stay if you wish. You may sit on my bed. But know this: It is the only circumstance under which you will get to experience it." She grinned. "Unless, of course, Leskit is an especially adroit storyteller."

With that, she headed to engineering. Her only regret was that she did not stay long enough to see the look on Kornan's face. It had made only a minor improvement in her mood, but she would take what she could get.

As she approached engineering, she saw Leskit

standing in the corridor. "Ah, there you are. Toq is waiting for us inside to go over the modifications."

Kurak sighed. She had been hoping to avoid Leskit for much the same reasons she was avoiding Kornan, but if they were performing modifications to the navigational shields, she supposed the ship's primary pilot needed to be present also.

As she started to move past Leskit into engineering, the lieutenant put a hand on her shoulder. "Kurak, a moment."

"Remove that hand, Lieutenant," Kurak said without looking at him, "or I will remove it for you."

Doing so, and putting both his hands up in a mock gesture of surrender, Leskit said, "Of *course*, Commander, my *humblest* apologies for soiling your person with my unworthy touch! I simply wished to convey something of a personal nature before we went about our business."

Kurak had to force herself to keep from smiling. *That's the Leskit I know.* But it was also the Leskit she was still, dammit, furious at. "I have no wish to discuss anything personal with you."

"No discussion will be involved—as I said, I just wish to convey something."

Resigning herself to the inevitable, Kurak again grabbed her left wrist with her right hand and let out a growl for good measure. "Get on with it, then."

Leskit took a long breath, one so deep it made the Cardassian neckbones he wore rattle. "I have always prided myself on my ability to steer any vehicle in the Empire. Yesterday proved me wrong. I made a fool of myself, and contributed to our defeat—and, it would seem, hurt you personally as well. I regret that, and therefore offer my life in recompense." Standing up straight, speaking formally, he said, "Kurak, daughter of Haleka, I am yours to do with as you will."

This time Kurak was unable to hold back the laugh.

Leskit grinned. "My imminent death amuses you, Commander?"

"No, *you* do." She shook her head. "I *should* kill you, truth be told, but as irritating as you are, and as much as I would love for you to pay for what you did yesterday, Ensign Koxx is even worse than you at navigating the subspace eddies. At least I know *you* will keep the ship in one piece."

Bowing, Leskit said, "The commander is too kind."

She leaned in close. "Don't make me regret the decision, Leskit."

"The last thing I would ever wish to do, Kurak, is make you regret anything. I remain yours to do with as you will." He grinned. "*Whatever* that might be."

"I'll keep that in mind," she said dryly. *I don't know what it is about this old fool, but I cannot seem to retain any anger toward him.* "Now come, let us see what obscenities you and Toq wish to perform upon my engines."

B'Oraq returned to the medical bay from dinner to find Toq sitting by Rodek's bedside. Rodek was no longer the ward's sole occupant. *QaS DevwI'* Vok and his troops had succeeded in capturing the prize of the San-Tarah even as the Klingons successfully defended against the San-Tarah's attempt to do likewise, so the third contest had resulted in a victory for the *Gorkon*. However, as with all true victories, a price had been paid. Several warriors, including Krevor, Klorga, H'Na, and Davok, had died, and several others had been wounded. Wol, G'joth, Maris, and Trant were among the latter, and they all lay in biobeds.

The doctor had come back from the evening meal to check up on her healing limb, which was still a bit sore after her discipline at the captain's hands, and do her rounds.

Toq looked up. "Nurse Gaj let me in," he said by way of explanation.

Holding up a hand, B'Oraq said, "It's all right, Lieutenant. I was wondering why I didn't see you at the secondary bridge in the mess hall."

"You have healed all the damage to Rodek, yes?"

"Yes." B'Oraq nodded as she walked to her supply cabinet. "Unfortunately, at this point, it's more or less up to him. He has to fight to stay alive—and to regain consciousness—or give up and die."

Toq turned back to his crewmate. "He would never give up. Rodek may be a passionless bloodworm, but he is still a Klingon. When he awakens, I want his first sight to be of me." Then Toq looked over at the doctor. "And if he *does* die, I wish to be the one to commend his spirit to *Sto-Vo-Kor*."

"Feel free to stay as long as you want, Lieutenant," B'Oraq said with a smile. She grabbed a scanner and looked over her arm. It seemed to be almost completely mended. *If only I can do the same for the captain*, she thought. She then grabbed a padd and started making rounds. *Now we'll see how many of them ask when they can be discharged as soon as I'm in earshot.*

"When may I leave, Doctor?" Wol asked as soon as B'Oraq approached her biobed.

That's one. "In the morning, Leader. I don't want you to put any weight on your leg until then."

Wol spoke with the belligerence that most of her people showed to B'Oraq's profession. "I can return to duty, Doctor."

"Which you wouldn't be doing until morning in any case, so you may as well stay here." Satisfied with the current biobed readings that Wol's healing was proceeding apace, she moved on to G'joth.

The older warrior was entering something on a padd, and barely looked up at B'Oraq. "You're doing fine, G'joth," she said. "You may go now."

"Fine," G'joth muttered.

Odd. G'joth is usually more voluble than this. "Is something wrong, *Bekk?*"

"Why should anything be wrong?" G'joth snapped. "Davok and Krevor died noble deaths defending the Empire and are probably arguing about something in *Sto-Vo-Kor* now."

"That is to be expected, G'joth. You should know that as well as anyone."

"Yes, I know, I've served for many years—but for the last ten, Davok has been by my side. We've been together at dozens of posts. Now he's dead."

Wol actually chuckled at that. "You didn't even *like* Davok."

Again, G'joth snapped. "He was my *friend*. I don't care if he's in *Sto-Vo-Kor*—or maybe in *Gre'thor* as punishment because he was such a pain in the crest—but the point is he is there and not here. Who am I supposed to argue with now?"

B'Oraq tugged on her braid. "Isn't that a little selfish?"

"Why can't I be selfish? I think after serving this damned Empire and this damned Defense Force for all this time, after giving up my life for it, I am entitled to be selfish when my friend dies!"

"Tell you what, G'joth," Wol said, "tomorrow in the mess hall when we come off duty for dinner, I promise to say something incredibly stupid, and then you can excoriate me for it."

"It won't be the same," G'joth muttered. Then he actually let out a bark of laughter. "No offense, Leader, but you're incapable of saying something as stupid as Davok would say."

Wol grinned. "I have an entire day to practice, I am sure I can come up with something."

Laughing, B'Oraq said, "I, at least, have faith in you, Leader."

At that, Wol scowled.

"In any case, *Bekk,* you can finish your opera in the mess hall or in your bunk or wherever you wish." She pointed at G'joth's padd. "That *is* the opera you're working on, yes? Or, no, wait, it's a novel now."

Her scowl returning to a grin, Wol said, "Now it's a song."

"Actually, it's done. And it's not a song anymore." As he stood up from the biobed, he handed the padd to B'Oraq.

"Oh?" B'Oraq took the proffered padd. The words, *qaStaHvIS may' Hegh jup; qaSpa' may', ngeD ngoDvam qawmeH Qu'; qaSpu'DI' may', QatlhchoH*, shone on the display.

" 'In battle, friends die. It is easier to remember this before the battle than after.' " She smiled and handed the padd back to G'joth. "Actually, *Bekk*, that's rather profound."

G'joth snorted. "Davok would have hated it."

"In that case," Wol said, "it's the best possible tribute to him you could write."

Then G'joth laughed. B'Oraq thought it to be a good sound, and was silently grateful to Wol for provoking it. There was an old human cliché that laughter was the best medicine, but B'Oraq had found it often to be the case, even with Klingons.

"You are probably right, Leader," G'joth said.

B'Oraq gave G'joth an encouraging look. He nodded in return and departed the medical bay.

She then moved on to Maris. The soldier snarled at her. "When can I leave this place? And if the answer is anything other than now, I will kill you."

And that's two. As it happened, there was no reason not to discharge Maris, either. His wounds were considerably greater than G'joth's, but they were all in the chest and arms, and sitting thrashing about in bed probably wouldn't make them heal any faster. "We are both fortunate, *Bekk*—the answer is, in fact, now."

"Good." Maris bared his teeth and growled as he got up, no doubt secure in the knowledge that he had intimidated the *yIntagh* of a doctor into letting him go. *Let him think that*, B'Oraq thought wearily. *It's not worth trying to convince him otherwise.*

Maris stopped and turned toward his comrade. "Oh, and Trant? I've changed my mind. I hate the beard." With that, he left.

"Stupid *petaQ*," Trant muttered as B'Oraq walked over to him. At her arrival, he said, "Obviously, I cannot leave any time soon, but may I at least move further from *him?*" He pointed at Toq as he spoke. Trant's legs were still encumbered by bandages that were facilitating the healing process after they'd been shredded by one of the San-Tarah—according to what B'Oraq had heard, that same San-Tarah cut a swath through the seventh, killing Klorga and H'Na and wounding Trant and Maris, before Leader Avok drove his *d'k tahg* into the enemy's heart. Shortly after that, *QaS DevwI'* Vok was able to claim the prize and win the victory.

"What's wrong with Lieutenant Toq?" B'Oraq asked in response to Trant's question.

Keeping his voice low, the *bekk* said, "He has been spending all his time in here talking to Lieutenant Rodek. Rodek is *unconscious*. He cannot hear a word the lieutenant is saying, but the rest of us can. I have heard about how Toq hunted the *san-chera* three times.

Now he discusses ship's business. Bad enough to be stuck in this place for days, but listening to talk of modifying the navigation shields with our madwoman of a chief engineer will make my head explode."

B'Oraq smiled. "I'll see what I can do about moving you farther away. Or you could ask Toq to keep his voice down."

Trant went pale. "I would rather not come to the lieutenant's attention." Interestingly enough, the *bekk* shot a look at Wol, of all people, as he spoke. Obviously, he was not willing to put himself in the position of offending, and therefore challenging, a superior officer when his legs didn't work and he could not adequately defend himself. Instead, he just turned over on the biobed, facing away from Toq and Rodek.

After a quick check to see that Trant was healing nicely—and might even be able to return to duty in less than the three days she had originally predicted—she went over to Rodek's bed.

Toq looked up at her. "We were supposed to celebrate."

"What?"

Indicating Rodek with a nod of his head, Toq said, "He and I were going to celebrate my victory. The hunt for the *san-chera* was a great day for me."

"Yes, I understand you were telling Rodek all about it."

Toq scowled. "What do you mean?"

"Some of your fellow inmates have overheard you."

Proudly, Toq said, "It is a story worthy of being retold."

"I'm sure it is." B'Oraq smiled encouragingly. Rodek's

vital signs hadn't changed since before dinner. "In fact, I'd like to hear it." If Trant didn't have the courage to confront Toq directly, the doctor wasn't about to make his life any easier.

"Of course, Doctor," Toq said as B'Oraq moved one of her guest chairs over to the other side of Rodek's biobed and sat down. "I began by changing into my hunting clothes. A warrior should take pride in his uniform, but this called for a different approach…"

Klag watched as the bodies burned.

Me-Larr had invited him to the Prime Village to observe the Children of San-Tarah's funerary rites. The San-Tarah fighters who fell in battle to Klag's warriors yesterday were, as Me-Larr had put it, being sent to run with the dead. The bodies were laid side by side on a pallet made of wood. Several tree branches were piled beneath the pallet and lit on fire. According to Me-Larr, the branches were from one of their sacred trees, so considered because of the ease with which it burned.

It also gave off a scent while burning that Klag found pleasant, and which served as a palliative to the wretched smell of burning flesh and fur that made the entire Prime Village reek like some human's kitchen.

As the flames climbed higher, consuming the bodies of the fallen, Me-Larr gave a lengthy speech. Klag's translator rendered it—it went on about the San-Tarah's gods, whom they referred to as the *el-mar*—but he found it pointless. *All this is ritual nonsense*, he thought. *Their spirits have been released. The rest is pomp and foolishness.*

When Me-Larr finished his speech, he howled, and all the San-Tarah around him joined in the howling. The sound was glorious, a cacophony that was in near-perfect unison and harmony.

They should have just done this, Klag thought. The howl was a pure sound, even more so than the death scream that Klingons used when a warrior fell. Hearing this—no, *feeling* it, the sound made his ribs vibrate, it was so intense—Klag was more moved by the nobility of these deaths than he was by Me-Larr's speech or the flames that consumed the empty shells of their bodies. The captain was almost tempted to join in the howl himself, but he knew that his own inability to do so properly would only spoil the effect.

The howls died down. The flames continued to crackle, smoke rising to the sky alongside the echoes of the howls. Me-Larr turned to his people and said, "They now run with the dead. The *el-mar* smile down upon them and bring them everlasting conflict—as we all shall someday."

With those words, the ceremony seemed to have ended. The Children of San-Tarah who had gathered started to drift off to their own concerns. Me-Larr and the older member of the Ruling Pack, Te-Run, both approached Klag.

"Te-Run tells me," the leader said, "that you also commend your dead to the next world."

"We have two afterlifes," Klag said. "The honored

dead cross the River of Blood to *Sto-Vo-Kor*, where our warriors join the Black Fleet to fight for eternity. The others—the dishonored, the unworthy—ride the Barge of the Dead to *Gre'thor*."

"And the *el-mar* consider this just?" Me-Larr spoke as one trying to glean information, not pass judgment.

Klag still had a hearty laugh at the very idea. "Hardly. We have no gods, no *el-mar*. Klingons bend their knee to no one, whether they be divine or mortal. Our Empire remains strong because we are beholden only to ourselves."

Te-Run asked, "What of this Kahless you spoke of before?"

"Kahless is the greatest Klingon who ever lived. He gave us our warrior's code, led us out of barbarism and into lives of glory and honor."

"But he was not a god?"

"No. Klingons once had gods, but we killed them." Klag smiled widely.

Me-Larr shook his head. "I do not understand. If the *el-mar* do not factor in your lives, then who maintains *Sto-Vo-Kor* and—what was the other place?"

"*Gre'thor*." Klag looked upward. "Who commands suns to go nova? Who keeps worlds spinning on their axes?" He looked at the two aliens. "And who cares? They are there—that is all that matters."

"It makes no sense," Me-Larr said. "Who decides who goes to *Sto-Vo-Kor* and who goes to *Gre'thor*?"

"Klingons decide that when they choose to live their lives with—or without—honor. Heroes cross the river, cowards ride the barge. It is the way of things."

Te-Run finally spoke. "And some of your dead don't die at all."

"What do you mean?"

"I saw your Dr. B'Oraq bring one of your fighters back from the dead. I have lived a very long time, Captain Klag, and seen many things that none would easily believe possible, but I have never seen the like of what I saw on your ship."

Unable to resist, Klag said, "There are benefits to being part of the Klingon Empire."

Me-Larr bared his teeth. "Perhaps. But in order for us to reap those benefits, Captain Klag, you must win one more contest."

"Indeed." Klag looked up to see that the second sun was nearing its apogee. "It is almost time for the next one. Shall we proceed?"

"Yes."

As the three of them walked toward the clearing where the contest of strength would take place, Klag thought about Te-Run's reaction to B'Oraq's work. "You might be interested to know that I once lost my right arm in battle."

Me-Larr's head whirled toward Klag at that. "You have both arms, Captain Klag."

"Yes. But Dr. B'Oraq was able to provide me with a new arm that serves me as the old one did."

"How is that possible?"

Chuckling, Klag said, "I am afraid I can no more tell you that than I can explain why suns go nova. But such procedures are simplicity itself for us."

The two San-Tarah said nothing in response, but Klag could see that they were thinking about his words.

Then Klag's communicator sounded. He activated it. "Klag."

It was Kornan. "*Captain, we have succeeded in penetrating the subspace interference locally. We can send a report to General Talak.*"

Klag hesitated. Briefly, he wondered if Kornan had timed this deliberately, then dismissed it. *Kornan isn't that subtle.* Besides, Klag had ordered Kornan and the rest of the bridge crew to find ways to circumvent the subspace eddies that were so vexing them.

However, the last thing he wanted was for General Talak to come in and spoil his triumph. Besides, his anger at B'Oraq notwithstanding, the doctor had been correct, at least in part, that Klag had a great desire to one-up his younger brother. Dorrek's idea of filial piety had been inconsistent at best, and he had disgraced the family name. Like their father, Dorrek had gotten away with it so far, but Klag would prove himself to be the better of the sons of M'Raq.

Kornan then added, "*We have also received a report from General Talak. It is three days old, but the conquering of Brenlek continues. The general reports that his forces will be occupied there for at least a week.*"

Klag smiled. Whether Kornan knew it or not, he had just made Klag's day. Brenlek was far enough distant that, without the communications relays that were throughout Empire territory, it would take at least half a day for any message to reach Talak's flagship from here.

Combined with the amount of time left needed to secure Brenlek, that meant there was no chance of Talak interfering.

"Send the general a message explaining what we are accomplishing here, Commander. Include both your logs and mine on the subject, as well as any reports made by Lieutenant Toq, Commander Kurak, and *QaS DevwI'* Vok on the three contests thus far."

"*I doubt there's much useful from Commander Kurak, sir.*"

Klag laughed. "An excellent point. And we lost that one in any case. Just the contests in which we were victorious, then."

"*The message will go out within the hour, sir.*"

"Good."

"*Lieutenant Toq also has a theory as to the nature of the subspace eddies, sir.*"

"Oh?"

"*He believes that they are the by-products of a battle fought with subspace weapons some time within the last century or two.*"

That got Klag's attention. Subspace weapons were unpredictable. Both the Empire and the Federation agreed to a ban on the research or development of such weapons as part of the Khitomer Accords. It had not been as difficult a concession as one might think—such weapons carried risk to the wielder as well as the target. Klag had always preferred a weapon that would do what he expected it to do when he expected it to, and many other warriors shared that preference. Even the Romulans, Cardassians, and Breen had abided by the ban. The only use of such a weapon in the quadrant that Klag was aware of was by the Son'a a year ago, and that was an isolated incident.

"Make sure that is mentioned in the report we send to General Talak and to Command," Klag said. The other exploring vessels needed to be aware that there might be a spacefaring power in the Kavrot Sector that employed such weaponry.

"Yes, sir."

"Out."

Me-Larr bared his teeth at Klag. "I was correct—you do wish to take us without aid from one of your other packs."

"We are Klingons. Though we understand the need to fight in groups, to rely on others to watch your back, we also know that a triumph is sweeter if it is achieved alone. If I require General Talak's help, I will not hesitate to ask for it—but I would prefer never to have to ask for it, to achieve victory on my own."

Te-Run made an odd noise. "That is a foolish attitude."

"Perhaps. But it has served us well."

After a moment, Me-Larr said, "Captain Klag, what your subordinate mentioned about the strange forces that make your technology fail—there are stories of a battle that took place in the sky dozens of generations ago. When it was over, we could no longer see the stars."

Nodding, Klag said, "That fits with Lieutenant Toq's theory. The subspace eddies—those strange forces—are hampering our use of technology. They are also not natural phenomena." The captain smiled. "If you ever encounter those people again, you should thank them. It is the residue of their battle that makes your planet defensible. It is the only reason why this contest has come about."

"Then we are grateful, Captain Klag."

"As am I." At the surprised looks on the two San-Tarah's faces, Klag chuckled. "This contest is far more satisfying to me as a warrior than a simple battle would have been. Here, we are truly testing our mettle against a worthy foe. If we had not been restricted by the subspace eddies, we never would have learned the true nature of your people. And when we defeat you, and you join the Empire, we will be better for it. That would not have happened without those eddies."

They arrived at the clearing. Klag saw one Klingon and one San-Tarah standing there. The former was *Bekk* Goran, who had stripped to the waist, and wore only *mok'bara* pants. Obviously the latter had been specially made, as Klag didn't think such clothes—or, in fact, *any* clothes—were mass-produced in the *bekk's* size. Klag had been in shuttlecraft that were smaller than Goran. Lokor had assured Klag that Goran was the best for this contest, which was one of strength, and looking upon the *bekk*, the captain was sure that Lokor had made the right choice.

Next to him stood a Child of San-Tarah who was as to the other San-Tarah as Goran was to ordinary Klingons—or as Toq's *chera-mak* was to ordinary *san-chera*.

She stood almost as tall as Goran, though she had nowhere near Goran's width. Like Goran, she appeared to be made up almost entirely of muscle.

Behind the two contestants sat two large, flat-topped boulders, positioned about two meters apart. On top of them was a lengthy, thick wooden plank, and on top of the plank sat a small black rock. Its size notwithstanding, it was obviously of a weight that put a considerable strain on the plank.

Although he had no scanner with which to confirm it, the rock almost had to be laced with, or perhaps entirely composed of, koltanium, one of the densest terrestrial ores ever encountered. Koltanium had hundreds of construction applications, and its presence on this world was yet another reason why Klag sought to plant the Empire's flag on it.

He turned to look at the two members of the Ruling Pack. "Are we ready to begin?"

"It would seem so," Me-Larr said. He turned to address all those present. "The fourth contest is one of strength. Each side has chosen a champion who will lift the plank carrying the rock from the Sacred Mountain. Whoever holds the rock longest shall be the winner. The Children of San-Tarah have chosen Fe-Ruv. Captain Klag of the *Gorkon* has chosen *Bekk* Goran. As they presently have triumphed twice to our one, the *Gorkon* may have the first chance at victory—for if the day is won by *Bekk* Goran, the *Gorkon* will have won, and the Children of San-Tarah will forevermore be part of the Klingon Empire. If Fe-Ruv should be the victor, then the fate of our people will be decided by a sword-fight within the circle."

By the strength of Goran's back, we will have this day, Klag thought.

For as long as Goran could remember, he was always the biggest and the strongest.

Though born on Qo'noS, he had spent most of his childhood on the prison planet of Rura Penthe. His parents worked as administrators there, and so Goran had grown up on that ice planet, surrounded by prisoners and the few other children of the prison's workers. Unfortunately, there was a fast-growing, never-ending supply of the former (a sentence to Rura Penthe was almost always for life) and precious few of the latter. Most children left the frozen wastes as soon as they reached the Age of Ascension, leaving Goran mostly friendless.

Of course, being the biggest and the strongest didn't do much to endear him to his fellow children either. He had never lost a fight, not even to those older than he was. This tended to anger the older ones, who then picked more fights, often in larger and larger groups.

Goran won those fights, too. It wasn't even difficult for him. Everyone was so small and fragile, and he was so big and strong, it was hard for him *not* to lose. No one could hurt him, but he could hurt others easily.

Once he was old enough, he too could have left, but he saw no reason to when such a lucrative career awaited him in the prison itself. Overseers were always needed, especially in a prison population as contentious as that of Rura Penthe, unburdened as they were by having anything to lose.

Besides, he was more comfortable around prisoners. When he was around ordinary people—like the other children or the adults who ran the prison—they all looked up at him in fear. He spent all his life looking at either the tops of people's heads or at faces filled with fright. At least when prisoners looked at him that way, it was natural. Prisoners were *supposed* to fear guards, after all.

So he took that as his vocation. Goran's natural talent for banging people's heads together proved quite useful. And when that didn't work, he had the disruptor.

Father had given Goran the disruptor when he reached the Age of Ascension. "This disruptor has been in our family for three generations. My grandfather served with *Dahar* Master Kor. He fought the legendary Kirk and Ambassador Spock in a great struggle on Organia during the last great Federation War. Grandfather said he shot several dozen Organians with this weapon, and also fired on Ambassador Spock with it, though obviously he did not kill him."

"Why not?" Goran had asked the top of Father's head.

Laughing, Father had said, "Because Ambassador Spock is still alive, boy. Don't interrupt. Anyhow, Grandfather passed this on to my father, and he passed it on to me. I want you to have it now."

Goran proudly took the disruptor. He had heard many stories about *Dahar* Master Kor, from his campaigns at Organia and the Delta Triangle to his great victories at Klach D'Kel Brakt and the Korma Pass. To think that his own great-grandfather served with such a legend...

Shortly after that, Goran began his career as a guard, and the same disruptor pistol that had almost killed Ambassador Spock was used to keep many a prisoner in line.

Until the scandal, anyhow.

To this day, Goran wasn't sure of the details. All he knew was that his parents had done something horribly wrong involving deals with prisoners and letting people escape—or maybe it involved stealing money. The representative from the High Council who had ordered Goran's parents to be arrested and taken away to trial tried to explain to Goran more than once, but he had never been able to fully comprehend it all, instead just staring at the top of the representative's head with his mouth hanging open, trying not to feel foolish.

What he did know was that they could not allow Goran to keep working at Rura Penthe—especially after his parents were sentenced to serve the rest of their lives there. Had Goran been of a turn of mind to appreciate irony, he might have laughed at that. Instead, he was just confused. All he'd known all his life was keeping prisoners in line and winning fights. What could he do elsewhere?

The representative from the High Council proposed a simple solution: to join the Klingon Defense Force as a soldier. After all, in the Defense Force, they always needed ground troops, whose job was similar to his prison guards' duties of banging heads together and shooting people with his disruptor.

As an added bonus, he learned how to use edged weapons. He owned both a *bat'leth* and a *tik'leth*—he had taken them off prisoners who, after all, didn't need them anymore—but had never been trained in their use. One of his fellow soldiers on his first posting showed him how to fight with them, though Goran had been able to put only some of the *bat'leth* techniques to good use, as it was, for Goran, pretty much a one-handed weapon. His hands were so much larger than average that to use both hands to grip the weapon meant a fatal sacrifice of dexterity. However, the *tik'leth* was something he took to fairly easily, with its single grip and long, wide blade. And he already knew how to use a disruptor. Even if it wasn't regulation, his superiors usually didn't mind, as long as it didn't misfire.

His first posting was to the *I.K.S. Nipak*. The ship won every campaign it fought after Goran came on, and the squads he served in always got through alive. Goran continued to never lose a fight. There were times where his shipmates were not all victorious, but his personal fights always resulted in victory. He was bigger and stronger than anyone, after all.

Best of all, on those rare occasions where he saw people's faces instead of the tops of their heads, they didn't look upon him with fear. He was their comrade-in-arms, a fellow warrior who was going out to die for the Empire.

Or, in Goran's case, fight for the Empire. He didn't fancy the idea of dying. Dying meant you lost, and

Goran never lost. That was one of the few good things about being the biggest and the strongest.

During the Dominion War, he was transferred to the *Ki'tang*. True to form, even when his crewmates lost, Goran was victorious. The *Ki'tang* was the only Klingon ship to survive the attack on Chin'toka, and also was the ship that found a way to resist a deadly Breen weapon. However, the *Ki'tang* was eventually destroyed at Nramia—but it was while the ground troops were on Nramia, so Goran once again lived, and the planet was taken from the Dominion.

Now he served on the *Gorkon*, and his good fortune continued. His squad held the road during the initial attack, and his squad defended the prize yesterday. Now, once again Goran was called upon.

He liked Captain Klag. He liked the *Gorkon*. And he wanted to win, mainly because he didn't know what it was like to lose and never wanted to find out.

All he had to do was hold up a rock.

When given the instruction to go ahead by Captain Klag—who was watching, along with several of his shipmates and several more of the natives—Goran bent over and squeezed his massive frame into the space between the two flat-top rocks, bracing his shoulders against the plank.

Then he slowly started to stand up.

The wood pressed against his back and shoulders, putting pressure on his spinal ridges.

He started to straighten his knees.

The pressure on his spine and shoulders intensified.

The plank did not move.

Goran refused to accept this. Once he fought off fifteen Kreel. Or maybe it was nine. Goran had always had trouble counting, but in any case, there were a lot of them. And he killed all of them without getting a scratch. During the war, he killed dozens of Jem'Hadar soldiers, and none of them had ever been able to do more than wound him.

He could damn well lift a rock. Even a heavy one.

Again, he started to straighten his knees.

The plank rose into the air. Goran reached up to balance the plank with his massive arms.

His knees were now straight, but he remained hunched over, making his back and neck as flat as possible so he could keep the plank flat.

Then he stood still.

For some, this might be the difficult part. Now that he had his balance, after all, it was simply a question of endurance. Physical endurance was not a problem for Goran. Mental endurance was another thing altogether. But Goran had spent his formative years as a prison guard. He was used to standing still and staring straight ahead and not doing anything. The actual number of opportunities to bang heads together or shoot people were few and far between. By the time prisoners made it to Rura Penthe, they were broken, and those who weren't, well, the planet itself would take care of that in fairly short order. Some guards, of course, liked to pick fights with inmates, but Goran had never been one for that. If drawn into a fight, he was in it for keeps, but he never started fights. It seemed wrong, somehow, what with him being so big and strong.

So he started to think.

Mostly Goran thought about his friends. Who his friends were would change from time to time—lately, the number included the fellow members of Fifteenth Squad. He liked them very much. He was also sorry that Krevor and Davok had died. He wanted to help them as they fought, but Leader Wol had ordered him to stay where he was to defend the prize, and that was what he did. After the battle was over, the Leader told him that he had done the right thing. By keeping the natives from claiming the prize, he kept Krevor and Davok's deaths from being in vain.

Goran had been very pleased when the Leader told him that. He was still sad at the deaths of Krevor and Davok, but at least they had died well. Father had always told him that it was important to die well.

Of course, Father died on Rura Penthe. One of the inmates didn't like Father's face, and so stabbed him in the eye with an icicle. Mother died of an infection a year later. That wasn't, as far as Goran knew, dying well at all. But it was hard to die well in prison, he supposed.

The plank pressed down on his spine. Pain started crawling through his thick neck. His arms grew heavier. Goran might have been big and strong, but even he had his limits. So lost in his thoughts of Krevor and Davok and Mother and Father had he been that he had no idea how much time had passed.

A wave of dizziness and nausea overcame him, and the *bregit* lung he'd eaten started to well up in his throat. An acidy taste filled his mouth. Goran had had a hearty meal before beaming down to participate in the contest, joined by Leader Wol and G'joth—and even *QaS DevwI'* Vok had partaken of a portion of the feast, which pleased Goran greatly. Vok was a good warrior, and Goran was happy to be serving under him.

A second dizzy spell forced Goran to lose his footing, and he almost stumbled forward. That would mean losing the rock, however, so he managed to straighten himself out, keeping the rock on the plank.

The pressure now was like nothing Goran had ever felt. It was as if someone had placed the entire *Gorkon* on his back. Black spots started to form in front of his eyes. He tried to blink them away, but that just made more of them appear.

I can't lose. I must hold the rock. I am the strongest.

Eventually, however, his knees gave out, and he stumbled to the ground. The rock fell off the plank, and slammed into the ground, forming a wide divot in the dirt.

"Impressive," the head of the natives said. "You lasted longer than any other. Twenty-six thousand four hundred and two seeds passed into the basket."

Goran sat upright and tried to figure out what that meant.

Dr. B'Oraq came up to him and asked him how he felt.

"I am fine. My back and neck hurt." He looked at the head native. "What does that mean?"

Klag answered when the native hesitated. "It means, *Bekk*, that you held a koltanium rock on your back for over seven hours. Congratulations. You have served me well."

That was what Goran wanted to hear. He started to get up, but B'Oraq put a small hand on his big shoulder.

"Not so fast, *Bekk*. You're severely dehydrated, and there's probably half a dozen ligaments out of alignment. I take it you don't want to beam back to the *Gorkon* until after Fe-Ruv takes her turn?"

Goran blinked. "I cannot leave until the battle is over."

"That's what I thought." She injected him with one of her devices. "This will help with the dehydration." Then she handed him a small bottle. "So will this. Drink it."

Taking the bottle, Goran removed the top and started pouring the contents into his mouth. The chill of the ice-cold liquid reminded him of Rura Penthe as it washed the acid taste out of his mouth.

It took two natives to put the plank back on the two flat-top rocks and six more of them to put the koltanium rock back on the plank.

Then the other native—what was her name? Fe-Ruv?—bent down and stood between the rocks just as Goran had.

Then she stood up.

Goran was annoyed. She did not struggle as he had. She simply rose and the rock rose with her.

As she did so, Goran saw something he had been too busy focusing on his own efforts to notice. One of the natives upended a thin-necked bottle into a harness over a thickly woven basket. The bottle was full of large seeds, but the bottle's neck was so thin that only one seed could pass through at a time. The seeds passed through at a rate of about one per second.

Finally Goran realized that it was a timekeeping device. The number of seeds that fell into the basket denoted the number of seconds that first Goran and now Fe-Ruv had hefted the koltanium rock.

Goran was very proud of how he had worked that out.

Then he glanced over at his foe and saw the expression on Fe-Ruv's face.

Most of the inmates of Rura Penthe were not Klingons. Goran had therefore gotten very good at reading the faces of many alien races—particularly ones who tried to appear stronger than they truly were. It was a survival skill in a place like Rura Penthe, and he had seen aliens who were very good at it and ones who were very bad at it. Goran didn't know much, but he knew when someone was attempting to look strong.

Fe-Ruv was trying desperately to look strong.

She stumbled around, losing her balance more than once. Goran was sure she'd fall over within the first half-hour, and then it would all be over. The *Gorkon* would win the contest, and it would all be because Goran was the biggest and the strongest.

He liked that idea very much.

But eventually, Fe-Ruv got her bearings. Eventually, she kept her balance.

She stood still.

Hours passed.

One of the San-Tarah brought some food to the spectators—some kind of dried, salted meat. Someone told him it was the remains of the *san-chera* that Lieutenant Toq had hunted. Goran found it rather tasty. Toq, too, had won a great victory, so Goran thought it was good that he got to feast on Toq's triumph while waiting for his own to become a reality.

One of the two suns was starting to disappear behind the trees. B'Oraq came over, then, to ask how Goran was doing.

"I am fine. How much time has passed?"

"Almost seven hours."

This did not make Goran happy. Fe-Ruv was no longer trying to look strong. She looked strong all on her own, in fact.

And now it had been seven hours.

Then he heard it.

Fe-Ruv's tongue had been hanging out of the side of her mouth for quite some time—at least an hour. Now Goran heard heavy panting coming from that mouth, and her tongue hung out even farther. She was starting to weaken.

Again, she started to stumble.

Goran's heart sang. Soon she would drop the plank or fall to the ground. Then once again he would win!

Finally, she fell.

As she collapsed to her knees, the rock fell off the plank and embedded itself in the ground once again.

"Twenty-six thousand eight hundred and seventy-seven seeds passed through the screen," the head of the natives said. "Victory belongs this day to the Children of San-Tarah."

Goran's mouth fell open. He was so shocked he could not summon the energy to close it.

He lost.

In his entire life Goran had never lost before.

But now some strange alien had proven herself stronger. She held the koltanium for over four hundred seconds longer than he had.

He lost.

"Tomorrow we will have the final contest—a sword-fight in the circle." The native leader bared his teeth. "I, Me-Larr, Head of the Ruling Pack, shall represent the Children of San-Tarah."

"And I, Captain Klag, son of M'Raq, shall represent the *Gorkon*." The captain smiled. "As it should be."

Goran barely acknowledged the words. He lost.

He did not know what to do.

CHAPTER TWELVE

Te-Run stood before the Ruling Pack on the night before the final contest. Even as Fe-Ruv was triumphing over the alien *Bekk* Goran, a pack had gone on the day's hunt and brought back a fine *san-rellik*, which had served as the evening meal. Several members of the *Gorkon* crew had joined the feast, including the healer B'Oraq and the hunter Toq. The latter was asked to tell the story of his subduing of the *chera-mak*, a story that, Te-Run was sure, would be told at feasts for the next several generations regardless of the outcome of the contest.

She had asked Me-Larr for permission to speak before the Pack after the feast ended and the Klingons departed, which Me-Larr had granted. In truth, asking was a formality. Te-Run had more than earned the right to speak before the Pack whenever she pleased.

The Ruling Pack gathered in the Meeting Hut. Each of them took their place, lying on their stomachs. The heads of many *san-reak* decorated the walls of the hut, testament to Great Hunts of the past. Me-Larr lit a fire with the wood from the Sacred Tree, and pronounced the gathering to have commenced.

Then Te-Run spoke.

"Tomorrow, the fate of our world will be determined. For many generations, we have heard the stories of the beings who fought wars in our skies and blotted out the stars. For many generations we have wondered if other beings would come from the sky. Now they have come, and they have changed everything."

Ga-Tror laughed and said, "Not if Me-Larr is victorious tomorrow."

Several of the Pack joined in the Fight Leader's laugh, but Te-Run was not among them. *Young, ignorant fool.* "You are incorrect, Ga-Tror. The change has already been made, and even if Me-Larr is victorious and Captain Klag takes his ship away never to return, everything has changed. Because we know that they are there. *And they are better than us.*"

"You speak madness, old woman," Ga-Tror said.

"Mind your place, Ga-Tror!" Me-Larr stood up as he rebuked the Fight Leader. "Te-Run is the oldest and wisest of us, and I have never known her words to be mad."

Respect returned to Ga-Tror's voice. "I am sorry, Me-Larr, but these Klingons are simply beings like us."

"No, they are not," Te-Run said emphatically. "I have been to their ship. I have seen what they are capable of. Whatever the beings from the sky did to blot out the stars also hampers their technology. Many of their tools do not function here. And that is all that has saved us, because without that, their weaponry could eliminate the Prime Village from the sky without their ever setting foot on our grounds.

"And there is more. Say Me-Larr does win tomorrow and they go away. We will be denied the use of their technology."

"What need do we have of it?" Ga-Tror asked.

"One of their fighters, Rodek, was on the sea. He received a grave injury to his head."

"So he is dead," Ga-Tror said. "What of it?"

Te-Run bared her teeth. "No. He is not. He lives and breathes on the *Gorkon*. I have seen it. I have been to a place they call a medical bay. They have healing arts far beyond anything we could imagine."

"She speaks the truth," Me-Larr said. "Captain Klag told us of his right arm, which he lost in battle. It was replaced with a new one."

"That is impossible," Ga-Tror said, and several grumblings from around the circle indicated that the others thought this claim to be dubious as well.

"You all saw Toq on this night," Te-Run said. "And you saw his wounds after he brought the *chera-mak* to us. Was there any sign of those wounds tonight?"

Even Ga-Tror found himself speechless.

"Exactly. They can fight with even more passion, more skill than we because they know they can be healed. Imagine what we could do with those arts."

Me-Larr stood up. "We will do nothing with those

arts if I am victorious tomorrow. And if you are asking me to lose deliberately—"

"I would never make such a perverse request!" Te-Run also stood up, her claws extending in outrage. "But our actions tomorrow will have greater consequences than the immediate. And there is something else."

Sitting back down, Me-Larr prompted, "Yes?"

"We have been fortunate in that the Klingons are sensible folk, who share many of our ways. But Captain Klag and his fighters have spoken of other worlds, other species, other peoples. Not all of them will be as wise as Klingons, nor have their sense of propriety and of right and wrong. We may well be vulnerable to them. If Me-Larr is victorious tomorrow, then we must turn our thoughts to how we may defend ourselves against others who may come from the sky to destroy us. These Klingons were the first. Or perhaps those who blotted out the stars were the first, but their war prevented them from taking advantage of us. Either way, though, I do not believe that they will be the last."

An insistent beeping sound awoke G'joth. He was awake in an instant, and, out of habit, he called up for Davok to awaken. He had done this every day for years; without that, Davok would sleep straight through and miss his morning duty.

"Davok, you old *toDSaH*, wake up or—"

He stopped himself. Davok was dead. G'joth would never have to make the idiot get up again.

With a heavy sigh, G'joth climbed out of his bunk

and down the ladder. He passed Krevor's old bunk. *She's dead, too.* G'joth and Krevor had shared bunks once, a few weeks into the mission. She was an agile lover—or as agile as possible, given the space limitations in the bunks—and G'joth wished he had asked her for a second coupling. He wasn't entirely sure she enjoyed it as much as he did, though, and he speculated that she probably found him too old. Such speculation was enough to discourage him from making that request for more.

Now he'd never know.

Leader Wol was fishing out a disruptor from her belongings. "Leader," he said out of respect.

"G'joth. We have guard duty. Each of us has been assigned to one of the weapons lockers."

This didn't surprise G'joth. When squads suffered losses in the midst of a campaign, they were often given simple shipboard duties for a day or two until soldiers were reassigned. Two others from lesser squads would eventually be given positions in the fifteenth.

But G'joth doubted that either of them would be so entertainingly cantankerous as Davok. Or as much fun as Krevor.

G'joth then noticed that Goran's bunk was empty. "Where's the big man?" G'joth asked.

Wol shrugged. "I was discharged from the medical bay five minutes ago. He wasn't in his bunk when I got here." She looked up suddenly. "Do you smell something?"

"Yes," G'joth said, getting a whiff of some kind of incense. Then he heard footfalls—very loud footfalls that could only belong to one person on the *Gorkon*.

Sure enough, Goran approached. He was carrying *adanji* incense in one hand, a *mevak* dagger in the other, and wearing a robe that was about three sizes too small for him and looked to be constricting his ability to breathe.

"You must be joking," G'joth said.

"*Bekk*, what are you doing?" Wol asked, though she must have known.

"I claim the right of *Mauk-to'Vor*. I know family is supposed to perform it, but I have no family. At least, if I do, I don't know where they are. So I'm asking you, Leader, to kill me."

Through clenched teeth, Wol said, "*Bekk*, you will take that absurd robe off, get into uniform, and report to Armory Number Three immediately, is that clear?"

"You don't understand! I lost!"

"So what?"

G'joth shook his head. "Goran, Klingons lose all the time. It is nothing to be ashamed of if you fought your best and didn't give in to cowardice."

"I—I didn't do that."

"Commander Kurak lost the naval contest, Goran," Wol said. "She didn't think it cause to kill herself."

"Well, she's an officer, she should expect to make a *targ*'s ear out of *real* combat," G'joth muttered.

"G'joth!"

He looked at Wol. "Well, it's true! All officers are good for is getting us killed!" He turned to the oversized *bekk*. "Look, Goran, you fought your best. That's all that matters. At least you're still alive, so you have a chance to win again. Krevor and Davok are dead, and they're not coming back. They don't have the same chance you do."

"But—but I've never lost before."

G'joth blinked. "Really?"

"Really."

For only the second time since he woke up in the medical bay and learned that Davok and Krevor were dead, G'joth laughed. "If there's one thing I've learned, Goran, it's that, no matter what you're good at, there's always someone better. Sometimes a lot of someones. I, for example, now know that there are hundreds—no, thousands of Klingons in the Empire who are better than I am at composing an opera."

"Or writing a novel," Wol added.

G'joth laughed again. "Yes, or writing a poem or a song. However, that is hardly grounds for death." He put a hand on Goran's tree trunk of an arm. "It just means I need to focus on what I'm good at."

Goran looked confused. "But what I'm good at is fighting and being biggest and strongest. I *lost* at that!"

Wol said, "Then you'll just have to make sure it doesn't happen again. But you will not perform the *Mauk-to'Vor*. To request it under these circumstances is cowardly—and there will be no cowards in my squad, is that understood, *Bekk*? Krevor and Davok died glorious deaths. I expect you to do the same—with a weapon in your hand and a song in your heart, not hiding behind a ritual intended to restore honor to one who has lost it."

"Besides," G'joth added, "it's not like you lost at fighting. You did well at that two days ago."

Goran nodded. "That's true."

"Now then," Wol said, "you have one minute to get out of that robe and back into uniform. You have duties to perform."

"You can rely on me, Leader," Goran said, removing the robe.

Sighing, G'joth cast a glance up at the two empty bunks that used to belong to Krevor and Davok. *It's nice to know that we can rely on something.*

After discharging Leader Wol from the medical bay, B'Oraq had beamed straight down to San-Tarah. She had spent a great deal of time during the previous night's feast answering questions about medicine, and she promised to return at first sunrise and give a demonstration in basic first aid. In preparation, she had dug out her old copy of *The Starfleet Survival Guide*—a graduation present from one of her classmates at Starfleet Medical—and used it as a reminder of the first-aid classes that the Academy gave to all first-year cadets.

B'Oraq was appalled when she discovered that the Children of San-Tarah didn't even know how to make a splint for a broken bone. Apparently such an injury usually led to the offending limb being cut off or simply healing badly—and eventually resulting in what they referred to as the Green Death.

As she demonstrated on one San-Tarah volunteer using two branches from a nearby tree, she thought,

Gangrene. They're dying of gangrene. It's an obscenity. The next time I think Klingon medicine is primitive, I'm going to remind myself of this place.

Her demonstration came to an end just as the captain beamed down from the *Gorkon*. The timing was deliberate, as all of her students wanted to see the final contest. Indeed, dozens had arrived that morning—and were continuing to arrive—from other villages as word had spread throughout the continent of the contests, and how the fate of the world was now being decided by death-duel in the circle.

To B'Oraq's considerable dismay, Klag beamed down holding a *bat'leth*.

She almost ran to her captain's side. "Sir, may I have a word with you?"

"Be quick, Doctor." Klag spoke coldly, apparently still angry about her questioning of his motives in the medical bay days ago. "I have a battle to win."

"Really? Then why are you holding a *bat'leth*?"

Klag snorted. "You would have me use a slingshot, perhaps? The San-Tarah swords are formidable weapons, Doctor. I will require a *bat'leth*."

"Captain, we've only *begun* the *bat'leth* drills. It will be months before you're back up to your old levels." Remembering Morr's admonition after the holodeck session, B'Oraq thought that estimate was generous, but she was pushing her luck as it was, and wasn't eager to have her arm broken again. "I think you'd be better off using a *mek'leth*."

"Doctor, I have the utmost respect for you as a physician. However, you are my doctor, not my *qownSlor*," he said, using the human term for a ship's psychologist, "nor an expert in armed combat. This is the second time you have advised me in matters outside your purview. There will not be a third."

"There has not been a first!" B'Oraq tugged agitatedly on her braid. "Your state of mind while commanding the *Gorkon* is very much in my 'purview' as ship's physician, Captain, and as for your choice of weapon, it is my opinion as the surgeon who performed the transplant procedure on your arm that you are not yet ready for full use of that arm. That includes a death-duel with a *bat'leth*. My advice to you *as your doctor* is to use a *mek'leth*—or perhaps a *tik'leth*."

Klag smoldered, and B'Oraq prepared for an attack that she suspected would result in far more than a broken arm.

However, the attack did not come. "Your advice is noted, Doctor. But a one-handed weapon is a poor match for the San-Tarah sword. It must be a *bat'leth*."

Before B'Oraq could object further, Klag turned his back on her—a deliberate insult—and walked away.

We will lose this planet, and our commanding officer, to your foolish pride, Captain. She looked around at the Children of San-Tarah to whom she had taught the most rudimentary of first-aid skills, and thought about how much more she could teach them. *And these good people will lose their only chance to receive the benefits of our rule.*

* * *

When she came off-shift, Leader Wol entered the security office. The office was a small, cramped space occupied solely by a desk piled high with padds. Lokor sat at that desk, reading three padds at once and entering data into a terminal.

Wol's encounters with the security chief of the *Gorkon* had been minimal. She had heard the same rumors as everyone on board, of course—that Lokor was secretly a member of Imperial Intelligence. Most of the troops believed it, but Wol did not. Back in the days when she was a true highborn Klingon, she had met several agents of I.I. Wol had no doubt that there was at least one I.I. agent on board the *Gorkon*, and there were probably several; she had just as little doubt that they were not in positions so—well, *obvious* as chief of security.

G'joth had told her his own theory, that Lokor was part of a group of Defense Force personnel who were dedicated to wiping out I.I. completely. "Fanatical devotees of Kahless," he had said, "who find any actions taken by a covert group to be inherently dishonorable." Right after he shared this, Davok, naturally, had declared it the most idiotic thing he'd ever heard.

Lokor's intense black eyes did not look up from his work as he spoke. "I assume you're here to return the *adanji* that *Bekk* Goran stole."

Wol stopped short halfway through the doorway. "Well, yes, actually. How did you know—?"

"Nothing happens on this ship that I am not aware of, Leader." Now Lokor looked up at her. "You would do well to remember that."

Right there and then, Wol decided that Lokor had started the I.I. rumors himself. "If that's the case, why didn't you stop Goran?"

Lokor shrugged. "I was prepared to if it became necessary. Three of my deputies were stationed near your bunk area. If you were unsuccessful in your endeavor to relieve Goran both of the *adanji* and of the notion that he was a candidate for *Mauk-to'Vor*, they would have moved in. Your actions made it unnecessary."

Wol walked into the office. "My actions shouldn't have had anything to do with it, Lieutenant." She cast about for a place to put down the pot of *adanji*, but found none on the cluttered desk. "If Goran did steal this *adanji*—" and until this moment, she hadn't known of the theft, she simply thought Lokor was the sensible person to dispose of the incense "—then should he not be held responsible?"

"Probably," Lokor said with a nod that caused his intricately braided, waist-length hair to almost bounce. "But the punishment would have been to reassign him to the lowest-ranked squad and give him the lowest duties for a month. I think that's a waste of the *bekk*'s talents. Besides, the fifteenth has suffered enough losses on this campaign." Lokor smiled, baring unusually sharp teeth. "Wouldn't you agree?"

"Perhaps," Wol said cautiously.

"You've done very well as Leader, Wol. Vok was wise to give you the position. Though I have to admit, there is little in your service record to indicate why he would think you worthy of it."

That immediately put Wol on edge. *What does he know?* She chose her words carefully. After coming so far, she would not do well to make an enemy of the chief of security. That was as dangerous in its own way as making an enemy of the captain.

"Vok saw things not apparent in the records." If Vok could read between the lines of what happened on Mempa IX, so perhaps could Lokor.

The security chief leaned back in his chair and fixed Wol with a penetrating gaze. "Then there are things not in any records. At least, not any public ones. Of course, one finds all manner of interesting things in public records. For example," he held up one of his padds, "I was reading this account from the Homeworld about the mysterious disappearance of Eral, daughter of B'Etakk, several turns past. This Eral was a member in good standing of the House of Varnak. That House no longer exists, though I understand that they had a rather large reward posted for information regarding Eral's whereabouts for a time. She was obviously a very valued member of that House, and they missed her very much."

Wol started. She hadn't known about any reward.

After a moment's thought, though, she realized that it didn't surprise her. Father wanted her to disappear, after all. If anyone could find her, he would want to know about it, so he would use the reward as a way of closing any holes in her disappearance that might crop up. Anyone who tried to claim the reward would no doubt find themselves on the wrong end of Father's hired *qutluch*.

Was Lokor fishing for information? She dismissed that thought immediately. *He wouldn't be having this conversation with me if he didn't already have all the information. He's waiting to see how I respond to it.*

"Lieutenant, you are speaking of a highborn woman. I can assure you, I would never have dealings with such a person. That I leave to those like yourself. I am content to serve the Empire in my own way. No doubt this Eral woman is dead from one of those silly romantic intrigues that plague such foolish women. Probably made the mistake of falling in love with a man beneath her station. I understand that women of your class do that sort of thing often."

Again, Lokor smiled. "Not as often as you might think. In any case, Leader, it is my considered opinion that you are twice the woman that the daughter of B'Etakk was. Never let anyone tell you otherwise."

Wol allowed herself to relax, if only marginally. For the time being, at least, Lokor was not making an enemy, just providing a warning. He was armed with information about her she would probably not want made public. He would not use it against her now, but it was there if he needed it.

Lokor cleared several padds away to make room for the box of *adanji*. Wol set the box down. "Thank you, Lieutenant."

With that, she turned and left, and wondered how she could turn Lokor's knowledge to her advantage. For one thing, he might know the specifics of who from

Varnak died when the House was dismantled—and, possibly even the true parentage of all of them....

Klag stood in the circle, gripping his *bat'leth* with both hands.

The circle was approximately six meters in diameter, its circumfrence marked by a simple line in the dirt drawn with a stick. *Primitive*, Klag thought, *but effective*. A crowd of many hundreds of San-Tarah had gathered, not to mention dozens of *Gorkon* crew. Klag had granted leave to any of the first shift who wished to observe their captain's moment of glory, and many had taken him up on it, including Toq and Leskit. The sole exception Klag had made was Kornan, and that only because *someone* needed to run the ship. The commander, to his credit, understood, and further arranged with Toq to set up a communications relay that would transmit the contest to the monitors on the *Gorkon* for all to see.

Te-Run stood at one edge of the circle, and as soon as she raised her arms, all the Children of San-Tarah grew silent. It took a few more seconds for the Klingons to get the hint, but they quieted as well.

"This is the final contest. It is fitting that the fate of our world will rest upon the leader of our Ruling Pack. If Captain Klag is victorious, then we shall willingly become part of the Klingon Empire, and we will be forever changed. If Me-Larr is triumphant this day, then the Children of San-Tarah shall attempt to live on as we have always done."

Interesting choice of phrase, Klag thought. *"Attempt" to*

live on? Perhaps Te-Run sees the benefits of adding her peo-
ple to the Empire. Good. It will make it that much easier for
them when I win.

"The combatants will remain within the circle and fight. The fight will end when one of them is defeated or when one of them steps outside the circle—and not before. Do you both understand these conditions?"

"I do," Me-Larr said.

"Yes," Klag said, eager to get on with it.

"Then begin."

Klag turned to face his foe, holding his *bat'leth* in a simple defensive posture. Me-Larr held his sword upright, elbows bent inward, keeping the blade close to him. Klag noted that the blade's curvature allowed Me-Larr to hold the sword near his head without risking injury to his protruding snout.

Me-Larr swung his sword, and Klag parried it easily, the metal striking metal with a clanging sound that echoed off the surrounding trees. They each backed away a step. Klag then swung his *bat'leth*, and Me-Larr parried. Again, the sound reverberated; again, they each backed away. They were simply taking each other's measure.

They continued, each making progressively bolder strikes, then pulling back. The San-Tarah's double blade provided a flexibility with types of strokes, which made up for the limited range of those selfsame attacks. Klag found himself on the defensive in short order, but he had allowed it on purpose. He had never fought against this weapon, and he needed to know how his foe would use it.

As it happened, the strokes were fairly wide ones, but strong. What they lacked in unpredictability—a sufficiently skilled opponent could see most of them coming a *qelIqam* away—they made up for in sheer power.

One such stroke from Me-Larr to Klag's right proved difficult to parry. Klag almost lost his footing as he thrust the *bat'leth* out and to his right to stop it. Me-Larr then took another swing to Klag's left. The San-Tarah's speed was impressive given the ungainliness of the sword, and Klag was barely able to switch arms so that he could parry this blow also.

This time, though, Klag was able to do more than block the stroke—he redirected it downward. Me-Larr didn't lose his grip, but he did lose control of the sword for a moment. In that instant, Klag brought his left arm upward, striking Me-Larr in the snout with the back of the *bat'leth* blade. As the San-Tarah stumbled backward, Klag moved to strike him in the chest, but Me-Larr was barely able to block the blow.

Now Klag was on the offensive, hitting Me-Larr with a continuous barrage. His foe seemed to be slowing with each parry—unfortunately, so was Klag. They had been going at it for the better part of an hour now, based on the passage of the suns overhead. In particular, Klag found that he was hurting right at the point of the connection between his father's right arm and his own right shoulder.

He drove Me-Larr to the edge of the circle, and the San-Tarah obviously realized his position, since his posture became more aggressive, then. Me-Larr refused to give any more ground.

Then Klag made his first mistake. Me-Larr thrust weakly at Klag's left. Klag parried it with ease, but it left his right side wide open for a second—which Me-Larr took advantage of. Klag managed to get his *bat'leth* over in time to block the second curved blade, which kept the first straight blade from penetrating too far into his side. But penetrate it did.

First blood to Me-Larr.

Klag cursed himself. It was an obvious feint that Me-Larr had made. *I fell for it like a novice.* He hadn't done anything so foolish since—

Since Father taught Dorrek and me how to use our bat'leths *as boys.*

Back then, the sons of M'Raq were inseparable. Even as Me-Larr harried him with a series of strikes, Klag smiled grimly at the bittersweet memory. They had only been born a year apart, though they looked very little alike—Klag taking after M'Raq, Dorrek after their mother—but they might as well have been twins for all the time they spent together. They learned to hunt and fight together, they both studied to become officers in the Defense Force together, they even chased the same women.

It wasn't until M'Raq escaped from the Romulans and came home that the rift opened between them.

If you had told the young Klag that they would grow up to each command one of the finest ships in the fleet, his heart would have sung with joy. It was only fitting that each command a mighty vessel. But when the news of Dorrek's posting to the *K'mpec* came, Klag was filled only with disgust that his once-worthy brother now filled the same role as he. Dorrek had, Klag knew, lost sight of what it meant to be a Klingon.

He swore that the final blow in this battle with the Children of San-Tarah would be his. And then he would show Dorrek, show General Talak, show *everyone* that his was the heart of a true warrior.

Toq watched with glee as Klag and the San-Tarah leader fought. Neither of them gave in—whenever one got the upper hand, it didn't last long. The fight took them all around the circle, and sometimes to its very edge, but neither combatant ever came close to stepping over the line that would end the match.

"This is truly amazing," he said to Leskit. They stood side by side amidst a group of Klingons and San-Tarah who were crammed together, each trying to get a better view of the proceedings. "I know about the captain's skills, but this is the first time I've seen one of the San-Tarah in action."

Leskit shot him a look. "Really? Oh, yes, well, you would not have seen the other hunter in your contest."

"No, only the results. And I have heard the stories from the troops, but still. This Me-Larr is a worthy foe."

A voice sounded from behind Toq. "He is a superior foe."

Toq was about to come to the defense of his captain against the slander of the San-Tarah, but when he turned around, he saw that it was *Bekk* Morr, the captain's own bodyguard, who had spoken.

That, if anything, angered Toq more. "You dare speak ill of the captain?"

"I do not do so happily, Lieutenant, believe me." Indeed, Morr's voice sounded pained, as if he'd been forced to eat dead *gagh*. "I had hoped that I was mistaken, that he had regained his skills, but he has not."

Leskit shrugged. "His form looks excellent to me."

"Parts of his form are, yes. All his one-armed and one-handed maneuvers are those of a champion. But anytime he uses both hands or must switch, he is awkward like a novice. In particular, he is vulnerable on his right side."

"I haven't noticed it slowing him down," Toq said defensively.

"It would not, at first. But the longer this goes on, the more glaring the weakness will become—and if the San-Tarah is as worthy a foe as he appears to be, then he will find ways to exploit it."

As if to lend credence to Morr's words, Me-Larr began a barrage of attacks, all downward strokes, first to Klag's left, then his right, left, right, left, right in rapid succession. Klag succeeded in blocking each one, though.

"Bring your right up farther," Morr whispered.

Much as Toq hated to admit it, he saw that Morr was right. The captain's right arm—the one he'd had replaced—was not as strong to defend as his left. Me-Larr's strikes on that side came very close to getting through.

Then Klag surprised everyone by blocking a left

strike, not with his *bat'leth*, but with his left arm. The San-Tarah sword cut into his gauntlet, though Toq didn't think it made it all the way through to the skin. Klag then swung his *bat'leth* around with his right arm to Me-Larr's exposed right side. Me-Larr managed to avoid the worst of the thrust, ripping his sword out of Klag's arm, but the *bat'leth* still tasted blood.

"That was foolish," Morr said.

"I agree," Leskit said, pointing at the darkening stain on Klag's left gauntlet. "See? It penetrated. His left arm will weaken, and it was the stronger of the two."

Angrily, Toq said, "Captain Klag defeated a dozen Jem'Hadar with the use of only one arm!"

"Yes, with a *mek'leth*—a weapon you can use one-handed. You don't show up for a gunfight with a *d'k tahg*." Leskit snorted. "And it was only seven Jem'Hadar."

Klag struck another blow that Me-Larr was unable to parry, but did dodge. Unfortunately for the San-Tarah, even with the dodge, it struck his right leg. As he moved back further, he stumbled to the ground.

"Now it will end," Toq said confidently.

Klag lifted his *bat'leth* for the killing blow. Toq could see the fire in the captain's eyes and knew that he could not lose.

However, even as he brought it down, Me-Larr somehow managed to position his sword over his chest, blocking the blow. The deafening sound of colliding blades echoed back and forth throughout the forest, as did the cheers of the Children of San-Tarah, who no doubt momentarily thought their champion lost. Me-

Larr had caught the *bat'leth*'s two front blades between his two blades, then twisted his arms so that the *bat'leth* shifted to the right. The captain was unable to keep his grip on the weapon, and it flew off to the side.

Fortunately, it did not fly far—still within the circle—and Klag was able to get to it in very short order. It did, however, give Me-Larr time to regain his footing.

Leskit smiled at Toq. "Care to revise your statement, Lieutenant?"

Toq spit at the ground at Leskit's feet. "You may have no faith in our captain, Leskit—"

"I am extremely confident that Captain Klag will wage this battle with all the skills at his disposal," Leskit said in that overbearing, sardonic tone of his.

Again, Toq spit at his feet.

Meanwhile, Klag bent down to the ground to grab the *bat'leth* with his left hand and then swung it upward in one smooth motion. Me-Larr parried the strike easily, but it left him vulnerable to a kick to the stomach from the captain.

That led to a flurry of attacks from Klag. Toq smiled, noting that the captain was wielding the *bat'leth* with his right arm, and mirroring the very same right-left attack that Me-Larr had used.

Toq winced when one thrust that should have come did not—it was as if the captain's right arm suddenly seized up and stopped working. Based on the look of surprise on Klag's face, the sudden dysfunction of his limb was neither planned nor expected. Me-Larr took advantage, naturally, and sliced upward, catching Klag in the belly.

However, Klag was able to punch Me-Larr hard in the snout with his left fist. Me-Larr stumbled backward, briefly addled, blood pouring from his mouth.

"Now, Captain, kill him!" Toq cried.

To his shock, Klag did not administer the killing blow. It was a perfect opportunity—all he had to do was run the alien through with his *bat'leth*. Instead, the weapon sat uselessly in his right hand.

Then Klag grabbed the *bat'leth* out of his right hand with his left and swung it, but by then Me-Larr had recovered.

Morr shook his head. "His right arm is useless. And his left is still bleeding. If Klag is not victorious in the next half-hour, he will not be."

"I am sure that they thought the same of Kahless and Lukara at Qam-Chee," Toq said with a snort.

"I do not wish to—"

Leskit interrupted Morr. "Both of you be quiet! There is a reason why the songs aren't written until *after* the battle is over. Right now, we are privileged enough to watch two masters at work. Enjoy it, will you?"

Morr let out a long breath. "I apologize, Lieutenant, I simply—fear that I have failed in my duty to protect the captain."

At once, Toq realized the reasons for Morr's constant harping on Klag's inadequacies. Klag had been taking his *bat'leth* drills with Morr. Toq remembered the pride that Lorgh had taken in Toq's hunting lessons, and his feelings of personal failure whenever Toq did something wrong, as if that failure reflected on Lorgh's abilities as a teacher more than Toq's inadequacies as a student. Morr appeared to be feeling much the same thing.

"The captain took us on this path, *Bekk*," Toq said quietly. "It is only fitting that he be the one to take the final step. You have done everything you can, and there is no shame in it."

"Listen to the boy, Morr," Leskit added with a smile. "He's smarter than he looks."

A cheer went up from the gathered Klingons, and Toq looked back into the circle.

Klag had struck another blow, this to Me-Larr's shoulder.

Pain tore through Me-Larr's left shoulder as the Klingon sword penetrated fur, flesh, and bone. His right leg burned even as it started to go cold. Gripping the hilt of his sword in his right hand, he desperately kept up a defense. His breaths came in shallow rasps that sent needlelike pains through his chest, his tongue lolling out the side of his mouth. The salty taste of blood filled his mouth from the tooth that had loosened from his foe's blow to his head.

Captain Klag was a magnificent, if flawed, opponent. What he lacked in skill, he made up for with sheer tenacity and ferocity. The mightiest Child of San-Tarah could not hope to surpass the passion with which this Klingon fought.

The weapon Captain Klag used helped considerably. Me-Larr had been told that Kahless—that revered figure in the Klingons' history—had forged the first of these weapons, which they had named a *bat-lett*. Its versatility amazed Me-Larr. The weapon was suited to be held one-handed or two-handed, horizontally or vertically, straight ahead or cradled against the curve of one's arm. Me-Larr thought it the finest weapon he'd ever seen, and he wondered if there was any way the Klingons could leave some of them behind after the contest was over.

The thought was, of course, pure foolishness. *They will hardly reward the one who defeats their leader.*

Even as feeling drained from Me-Larr's left arm, he thought he saw an end in sight. He had spent the entirety of the fight watching Captain Klag, and discovering the pattern of his swordplay. Several times, Me-Larr had deliberately let the Klingon get the upper hand in order to better study his maneuvers. Truth be told, Captain Klag also earned the upper hand with no help from Me-Larr on many occasions. But Me-Larr had been able to find several weaknesses, and he now had determined a means to use it against his worthy opponent.

Assuming I live long enough to implement it. It had been many seasons since Me-Larr had fought for so long alone. Many Great Hunts had lasted longer than this, of course, but there he was one among many. Few of his bouts in the circle had been so grueling, certainly none of the recent ones. He could feel his limbs slowing down, felt his very life drain with each effort to make his body move, and those efforts taking longer each time. *I feel like I'm older than Te-Run. . . .*

His only solace was that he could see the same thing happening to Captain Klag. The Klingon had taken to avoiding using his right arm, which only improved Me-Larr's chances, especially as the blood seeped from the wound in the captain's left.

What he needed to do was get Captain Klag to commit to a thrust that led with his right arm. For whatever reason, those thrusts tended to come up short, and were easily parried. Me-Larr needed to set up one such thrust so he could disarm his foe.

Dimly, he registered the cheers of both his people and the Klingons. He was too fatigued to make out the words, but he heard both his name and Captain Klag's being called out. Out of the corner of his eye, he could see that the size of the crowd watching them had not noticeably diminished, even though the contest had gone on for much of the day.

The fate of our world is in my hands, he thought as he made a conservative feint to his right, leaving his left side vulnerable.

Leading with his right hand, Captain Klag thrust downward toward Me-Larr's left side.

Me-Larr parried easily, catching the Klingon's blade—which would not have reached Me-Larr's side in any case—between the blades of his own sword right at the spot where Klag's right hand held it. Then he twisted his wrists.

The weapon went flying out of the Klingon's hands and out of the boundaries of the circle. Me-Larr heard the snapping of bones in Captain Klag's right hand even as he slammed the hilt of his sword into the Klingon's jaw, sending his opponent down to the ground.

Almost instantly, the crowd went quiet.

Me-Larr stood over his fallen foe. "The battle is over, Captain Klag. You may not retrieve your weapon without violating the circle. You are at my mercy. Do you concede the battle?" To accentuate the point, Me-Larr cradled the Klingon's neck between the two blades of his sword. One slice in either direction would cut his throat.

The head of the Ruling Pack of the Children of San-Tarah watched the eyes of his foe as they vacillated between furious and respectful.

Speaking slowly, with the fury Me-Larr saw in his eyes tingeing his voice, Captain Klag said, "You have won this battle. I die with my eyes open. I ask only that you kill me quickly."

A part of Me-Larr wished to do it. It was, after all, the fitting end to the fight. *But, no.* He removed the sword from Captain Klag's neck. "I would sooner cut down the Sacred Tree than I would deny your noble crew their leader. You have been more than just to us, and are truly the greatest foes we have ever fought. Tales of your prowess will be told at feasts until the end of time." He threw his sword to the ground. "I grant you your life, Captain Klag, for you have earned that and more. But your people must leave San-Tarah immediately and never come back."

The Klingon leader rose to his feet. His eyes still smoldered, but Me-Larr sensed that the anger was at himself for losing. Lending credence to this were the

CHAPTER THIRTEEN

Klag sat in his office on the *Gorkon*, reviewing the record of the final swordfight against Me-Larr that had been transmitted to the ship. It was the third time he had watched it since he and the rest of the crew had beamed back up and left orbit. They had not departed the star system yet, pending a response from General Talak to Klag's report. Toq had requested they remain a bit longer to finish mapping out the subspace eddies—the knowledge that they were caused by subspace weapons in a long-ago space battle had proven helpful to Toq in determining their pattern, interestingly enough.

Besides, Klag was not yet ready to leave this place.

The door chime rang, and Klag said, "Enter."

B'Oraq came in, looking confused. "You sent for me?"

"Yes, Doctor." Klag had gone to the medical bay

after the fight yesterday so his wounds and broken bones could be healed, but he and B'Oraq had not spoken beyond what was necessary to accomplish his treatment. Indeed, Klag had spoken very little that was not absolutely necessary to perform his duties yesterday.

When Klag said nothing further, the doctor prompted, "Your hand is recovering?"

"It is fine." Klag blew out a breath and gave B'Oraq a smile. This seemed to confuse the doctor, and she tugged on that braid of hers. "This is an irritating habit of yours."

"Sir?" The doctor sounded understandably apprehensive.

"Actually, two irritating habits. The first is the way you constantly tug on that braid."

"I don't tug on my braid."

Klag smiled. "Yes, you do. But far more irritating is your habit of always being right. Seven months ago, you told me I would be wise to replace my right arm. I dismissed your idea out of hand as ridiculous. Yet I came to realize the value of having two working limbs, and was able to try to restore my family's honor in the bargain when you grafted my father's arm onto me. Yesterday, you told me that I was not yet ready to fight with a *bat'leth*, and again I dismissed you. Watching my performance against Me-Larr, I am once again forced to concede that you were right and I was wrong."

"I—Captain, I do not—"

Klag held up a hand. "Say nothing. I simply wished to acknowledge it. I thought you deserved that much. I let my pride get in the way of what was best for the Empire. I should have chosen a different weapon."

"Or perhaps a different champion?"

Shaking his head, Klag said, "No. The original decision to engage in these contests was mine, and it was my word that was given to Me-Larr that we would abide by it. I could not ask anyone else to stand in my place."

Kornan's voice then sounded over the intercom. *"Bridge to Klag."*

"Klag."

"Incoming message from General Talak. The time delay is approximately thirteen hours."

"Put it through to me here." He looked up. "You are dismissed, Doctor."

B'Oraq nodded and took her leave. She did, Klag noticed, have a small smile on her face. *Triumphant, perhaps?* Klag thought. *Well, she's earned it. I should know better by now than to underestimate her.*

As she walked toward the door, her hand moved to tug on her braid, then stopped. She stared at her hand for a moment as if she'd never seen it before, shook her head, and continued back out onto the bridge.

Klag laughed, then activated his terminal's viewscreen.

General Talak's face appeared, and Klag forced himself to remember that respect for the rank was of more importance at present than his lack of respect for the person. Still, he was grateful that this was a recorded message. After the exertions of the past day, Klag would have been hard-pressed to avoid his instinctive reaction of hatred to the very sight of the general's white-haired, brown-bearded, gray-eyed self with the crest that matched the hated Kargan's.

"*Captain Klag, I have reviewed your reports. While I appreciate your admiration for these primitives, I do not appreciate your attempts to speak on the Empire's behalf, nor do I see any reason for the future of the Empire to be governed by words spoken to those who deserve only to be jeghpu'wI'. Regardless of the outcome of this ridiculous 'contest' that you and these people have concocted, San-Tarah is a world that must come under our flag. Brenlek will be fully conquered within three days of your reception of this message. You are to hold station at San-Tarah and await the arrival of the task force in five days' time. I expect a full map of the subspace eddies and a tactical analysis of how best to secure the planet given the limitations presented by those eddies by the time the fleet arrives. San-Tarah will become part of the Empire within the next two weeks. I will contact you again when the task force is en route. Out.*"

Klag stared openmouthed at the now-frozen image of Talak on his screen.

He replayed the message again, convinced that he could not have heard the words properly. It was impossible to believe that a Klingon had spoken them—and, his unfortunate relationship to the late Captain Kargan notwithstanding, Klag had never before doubted that Talak was a Klingon.

Madness, he thought after a second viewing of the

general's message. *Absolute madness. I am a captain of the Klingon Defense Force—of course I "speak for the Empire," especially on a mission such as this. And even if I were not, I gave my word to Me-Larr and his people. That is all that matters.*

He activated his intercom. "Commander Kornan, report to my office."

Kornan entered after a few moments. Klag noted that the first officer wore the scars of his wounds proudly.

Rather than try to explain things, Klag simply played the general's message again.

"As you can see, Commander, we have a decision to make."

The words were as much a test for Kornan as anything. *Will he agree with the general or will he follow his Klingon heart?* After ten weeks, Klag found he still did not entirely know if Kornan's heart truly was Klingon.

The first officer hesitated before finally speaking, and he did so slowly. "As I see it, Captain, we have two choices. The easiest choice, and the one with least risk to the crew, is to follow General Talak's orders. None will think poorly of us if we do so, and it would give us a planet rich in resources that would be of great service to the Empire."

"All compelling arguments. And our second choice?"

"Keep our word to the San-Tarah and go against General Talak's orders. Take up arms against a task force that may be as many as a dozen ships, depending on how many are left behind at Brenlek. We would probably die, and possibly in disgrace if the truth of what happened here is suppressed."

A *very cynical attitude*, Klag thought, *but not an unjust one*. If Talak could so easily cast aside the word of a Klingon captain, there was obviously no end to his dishonorable behavior.

"A fine summary of the dilemma, Commander."

"Thank you, sir."

"What is your opinion of General Talak's statements?"

Kornan started. "I would not presume—"

"I order you to presume." This was no time to be playing games. If Klag was to go through with what he planned, he had to have Kornan on his side. Their only chance of triumph was to present a united front. Even as weak as he seemed to be, Kornan *was* the second-in-command, and as such was potentially either his most useful asset or his most dangerous enemy. Klag vowed that Kornan would not walk out of this office alive unless he was the former. After all, Toq was next in line for the first officer's position, and Klag *knew* he could count on him.

Again, Kornan spoke slowly. "The general's words are peculiar, but not completely surprising. His mandate is to expand the Empire, and to add worlds that will make us stronger."

Not good. "So you believe we are made stronger by casting aside the very tenets that we fight every day to preserve?"

"I simply wish to present the captain with what I believe to be the general's viewpoint, sir."

Slamming a fist down on his desk, Klag rose from his chair, walking around to stand face-to-face with the commander. "I *know* the general's viewpoint! That is not what I am asking, Kornan. Tell me what *you* think."

Klag looked into Kornan's space-black eyes, and Klag saw only befuddlement and confusion there. His left hand moving to his *d'k tahg*, Klag resigned himself to the inevitable—

—until the look in Kornan's eyes changed. It was, oddly, not one of resolve, but of resignation.

"As I told you when I first reported on board, sir, years ago, I lost my way. I had always followed an honorable path, but I found only despair and defeat in my wake. There were many days on the *Rotarran* when I seriously considered taking my own life, knowing full well that it would trap me in *Gre'thor* for eternity. But what did it matter? The *Rotarran* in many ways *was* the Barge of the Dead. I would simply be eliminating the final step."

Kornan started to pace across Klag's office. "But then we at last were victorious. We defeated the Jem'Hadar, rescued the *B'Moth*. I had found my way." He turned back to Klag. "Here, again, I am lost. I had thought myself ready for the challenges of being first officer, but I have failed in every regard. That I still live is a testament to your patience." He barked a laugh. "Or perhaps a sense of masochism on your part, I cannot say for certain. I have become unsure of everything, to a degree I have not felt since those dark days on the *Rotarran*." Kornan let out a long breath. "But I do know this: Whatever we do, we will lose. If we follow the general's orders, we prove ourselves to be worthless as Klingons. If we oppose the general's orders, we will be destroyed, and posthumously denounced as traitors. No matter what we do, the dishonorable path will rule in the end." Kornan let out a long breath. "If that is the case—"

Klag tightened his grip on the hilt of his *d'k tahg*.

"—then I would prefer to die with honor than live with the betrayal we would be committing. I have seen enough darkness in my time, and I'd rather sneak out of *Gre'thor* than be denied *Sto-Vo-Kor*."

Klag stared at his first officer for several seconds.

Then he threw his head back and laughed.

Either Kornan was a far better actor than Klag gave him credit for, or he had finally shown his worth as the *Gorkon*'s second-in-command. Klag left his *d'k tahg* sheathed.

"Well said, Commander, well said." He clapped Kornan on the shoulder. "But you are assuming one thing in your worst-case scenario—that we will face General Talak alone."

Sounding dubious, Kornan said, "Sir, I doubt the Children of San-Tarah will be of much aid."

"Do not be so sure of that—remember how they routed us our first night here—but that is not of whom I speak."

Then Klag removed a medallion from his uniform, one that had been there for the past ten weeks, since they departed from Ty'Gokor.

Toq stood over the pilot's console while Leskit put several course paths on the screen. He was fairly sure he had mapped out all the subspace eddies, and now he had conscripted Leskit to aid him in working out ways to navigate them. "That is probably the most efficient path through them, assuming you've finally gotten all of them," Leskit said, pointing at one of the courses.

Smiling, Toq said, "There is only one way to find out."

"No need. Kurak already wishes to disembowel me, I'd prefer not to give her further cause by taking the *Gorkon* into one of these eddies again."

Toq laughed. "Next time, do not volunteer for a mission you are ill equipped to serve on."

Leskit fingered his crescent-shaped beard. "I had believed it to be the same theory as piloting an airship. How was I to know that—"

Unable to resist, Toq said, "You had brought a *d'k tahg* to a gunfight?" The pilot looked up and scowled at Toq, who just laughed again.

"Watch your tongue, boy, or someone will cut it out." Leskit, however, spoke with a grin.

Returning the grin, Toq said, "That's 'Second Officer Boy' to you, Lieutenant. I take it that you have not been able to work your charms on our chief engineer as you once did?"

"Sadly, no. A pity—she seems like she could use it."

Toq barked a laugh. "She *always* seems that way. For that matter, she still seemed that way after you two had your tryst during your first tour. It does no good. She remains the most ill-tempered she-beast I have ever seen."

Leskit grinned a wide grin. "You'd be amazed what a she-beast can do under the right circumstances."

At that, they both laughed heartily. Toq clapped his hand on Leskit's shoulder. "Very true. Transfer those course changes to my station."

Toq then walked back to the operations console. As he did so, he heard Grint, the ensign who had been assigned to the gunner's position until Rodek was fit to return to duty, talking with the *bekk* at the cloaking-control station. "We should never have lost to them," Grint said.

"I do not see why we do not simply bombard them from orbit," the *bekk*, who was no more than a boy, said. "They would be easy prey."

"The captain *did* give his word," Grint pointed out.

The *bekk* growled. "Perhaps he should not have done so to such primitives."

Giving the child a sharp look, Toq said, "Are you questioning the captain now, *Bekk?*"

"I merely speak hypothetically," the *bekk* said quickly, returning to his station.

Grint turned to Toq. "I still cannot believe that we lost to such animals as that."

"The beast that I hunted and slew was an animal, Ensign," Toq said. "The Children of San-Tarah are *warriors*. There is no shame in losing to a foe if the foe is worthy."

"Maybe—but winning is still better."

Toq smiled. "That is certainly—"

He was interrupted by the rumbling sound of the captain's office door opening. Toq turned to see Commander Kornan exit.

"Lieutenant Toq," Kornan said, approaching the operations station, "we have been given new orders. You are to complete the mapping of the subspace eddies and create battle plans for fighting within them."

Toq looked quickly over at Leskit, who looked as confused by the order as Toq felt. Turning back to his superior, Toq said, "We have already mapped them, Commander, and Lieutenant Leskit and I have come up with several flight scenarios. I will begin creating tactical ones immediately."

"See that you do. And prepare to address intraship as soon as the captain enters the bridge."

"Yes, sir." Even as Toq spoke, Kornan sat at his station and entered commands into his console.

Grint leaned over to Toq. "What is happening?"

"I have no idea," Toq said honestly as he prepared the bridge cameras for shipwide communication. Then Klag entered. "But I suspect we will gain an inkling in a moment." To the captain, he said, "Intraship ready at your command, Captain."

"Proceed."

Toq activated the comm link.

Standing at the fore of the bridge between the

viewscreen and his command chair, Klag addressed the bridge crew directly; Toq had arranged that his face and words would be carried to every monitor on the *Gorkon*. Those monitors were in every cabin, corridor, workstation, and bunk, and could not be turned off, so there was no chance of anyone missing the announcement.

"This is Captain Klag. What you are about to see is a communiqué I received from General Talak regarding the situation on San-Tarah—a situation which we had all believed to be resolved."

At Klag's signal, Kornan then keyed in the message from Talak. Toq's eyes went wide in surprise. Communications from Command were very occasionally shared with senior staff—*never* with the entire crew. *Whatever is happening, it is of great consequence....*

Then Toq saw the message, and felt his stomachs try to meld together into one. The young lieutenant had always had nothing but respect for General Talak until this moment.

"Are we oath-breakers, then?" Klag said when the general's obscene message was done. "Do we cast aside all that Kahless taught us, everything that makes us who we are, simply because it may seem easier for us to do so? Perhaps that may be sufficient for some, but *not* on my ship."

Several members of the bridge crew rumbled their approval—even, Toq noticed, the boy at cloaking control.

"Kahless slew his brother because he went back on his word, and I will do no less now. We fought against the Dominion to preserve our way of life. If we go back on our word to the Children of San-Tarah, we become no better than the Vorta and their changeling masters. Worse, we become Jem'Hadar—mindless, soulless, honorless automatons who know nothing of glory. I say we are more than that."

"Yes!" cried the ensign at fire control. "We are Klingons!" cried the one next to her at damage control.

"I say that we will defy this general who would have us betray our very souls."

Toq was among the many who repeated the cry of "Yes!"

"If there are any who object, who feel that we should not disobey the orders of our superiors, speak now—so we may strike you down as the honorless cowards you are!"

More cheers. "Strike them down!" "We go with honor!"

Toq smiled. Anyone on the bridge foolish enough to have that point of view was at least not quite so foolish as to say so out loud.

Then Toq started to sing. He had first learned the song as a lullaby on Carraya, only to be told later by Worf that it was a victory song. He had been in no shape to sing it after his own capture of the *chera-mak*, but he started it now:

"bagh Da tuH mogh, chojaH Du'rHo."

When he reached the refrain—a repetition of the phrase "don't speak"—the entire bridge crew joined in.

"yIja'Qo', yIja'Qo', yIja'Qo'."

At the start of the second verse, the speakers crackled with the sound of more singing. Toq imagined that the very bulkheads vibrated with the tumult of warriors rejoicing. If vacuum could carry sound, Toq had no doubt that General Talak himself would have been able to hear it at Brenlek.

> *majaq u'tugh*
> *jIDaq majun*
> *pa'Daq cha'baH*
> *bu'raq tlhuQa'*
> *tep lagh negh'uH*
> *mughoto' tu'*
> *yIja'Qo'*
> *yIja'Qo'*
> *yIja'Qo'*

When the second refrain ended, a great cheer went up on the bridge. Toq and Grint head-butted, as did several others.

"Fear not!" Klag cried over the din, and his words served to quiet down the bridge once more. "We will not face the honorless general alone. Over a thousand years ago, the Order of the *Bat'leth* was formed by the Lady Lukara after Kahless ascended to *Sto-Vo-Kor*— both to spread his word and to enforce his doctrine. Today, the call will go out once more. Again, the Order of the *Bat'leth* will serve to remind the galaxy of what it means to be a Klingon!"

Klag walked over to Toq and handed him a data

spike and his Order of the *Bat'leth* medallion. He indicated the medallion first. "This will allow you to send a tight-beam communication to anyone else in the Order. I want you to send the message encoded on this." He held up the spike.

Toq remembered Chancellor Martok's words on Ty'-Gokor—or, rather, he remembered B'Oraq telling him Martok's words in the medical bay, since Toq himself was unconscious for the ceremony itself. In particular, he remembered that the Order had not been called to this function for many turns. Even as he prepared the transmission to Klag's fellow inductees, Toq wondered how many of them would actually reply to this call to arms.

And what if none do?

He shook his head. *It does not matter. We are Klingons. Our captain gave his word, and if we must die in order to defend it, then that is what we must do.*

Toq sent the message.

Thirteen Klingon Defense Force vessels orbited the planet Brenlek. Led by the *I.K.S. Akua*, a *Vor'cha*-class battleship under the command of General Talak, the rest of the task force included six birds-of-prey, two *K'Vort*-class heavy cruisers, and three of the new *Karas*-class strike ships—plus one Chancellor-class warship, the *I.K.S. K'mpec*, which had discovered the planet in the first place.

Within the *Akua*, Talak sat in his cabin, surrounded by padds reporting on the progress of the conquering of

Brenlek. They remained unread, for Talak's mind was in another place entirely.

Specifically, a solar system that was two days' travel from here, where an unworthy animal had at last made the error that Talak had been waiting for ever since the Battle of Marcan V, ever since that one-armed *petaQ* had claimed credit for a victory that was rightly Kargan's, ever since he spit on everything Klingon by performing arcane surgeries with the still-warm corpse of his father. Klag's very existence was an affront to Talak, and the fool had finally provided the opening through which Talak would gladly slide his *d'k tahg*.

He opened a secure communication to the captain of the *K'mpec*.

"*Dorrek.*"

"On Ty'Gokor, I told you that we would speak again when the time was right, Captain. In reply, you said you would provide whatever aid you could to prove your older brother to be the cowardly *toDSaH* you and I know him to be."

"*And I will gladly fulfill that promise.*" Talak could hear the glee in Dorrek's voice. No doubt, suffering as the younger brother of such filth, Dorrek's pain had been, in its own way, as great as Talak's. Greater, perhaps, since the general at least had the security of his position and the nobility of his House to comfort him. Dorrek could not even take refuge in that, with the way Klag had soiled their House's name.

"The time *is* right, Captain."

"Then I will keep my word."

"Good. When Brenlek is tamed, we will proceed to a world called San-Tarah, and there secure glory for the Empire *and* achieve our greatest desire."

"It will be a great day, General. Qapla'!"

"Qapla'!"

Talak cut the communication, then leaned back in his chair and thought about how much pleasure he would take from plunging his *tik'leth* into Klag's chest....

To be continued in

STAR TREK: *I.K.S. GORKON* BOOK 2: HONOR BOUND

GLOSSARY OF KLINGON TERMS

Most of the language actually being spoken in this novel is in the Klingon tongue, and has been translated into English for the reader's ease. Some terms that don't have direct translations into English or are proper nouns of some kind have been left in the Klingon language. Since that language does not use the same alphabet as English, the transliterations of the Klingon terms vary depending on preference. In many cases, a more Anglicized transliteration is used instead of the *tlhIngan Hol* transliterations preferred by linguists (e.g., the more Anglicized *bat'leth* is preferred over the *tlhIngan Hol* spelling *betleH*).

Below is a glossary of the Klingon terms used. Anglicized spellings are in **boldface**; *tlhIngan Hol* transliterations are in ***bold italics***. Please note that this glossary does not include the names of locations, people, or ships. Where applicable, episode, movie, or novel citations are given where the term first appeared. Episode citations are followed by an abbreviation indicating show: TNG=*Star Trek: The Next Generation*, DS9=*Star Trek: Deep Space Nine*.

adanji *('aDanjI')*

An incense that is used in the *Mauk-to'Vor* ceremony. [First seen in "Sons of Mogh" (DS9).]

bat'leth *(betleH)*

Curved, four-bladed, two-handed weapon. This is the most popular handheld, edged weapon used by Klingon warriors owing to its being favored by Kahless, who forged the first one. The legendary Sword of Kahless now held by Chancellor Martok is a *bat'leth*, and most Defense Force warriors are proficient in it. [First seen in "Reunion" (TNG).]

bekk *(beq)*

A rank given to enlisted personnel in the Defense Force. [First referenced in "Sons and Daughters" (DS9).]

bok-rat liver, stewed *(boqrat chej)*

Food made from the liver of a *bok-rat*, apparently cooked to some degree, making it unusual among Klingon foods. [First seen in "Soldiers of the Empire" (DS9).]

bregit lung *(bIreQtagh)*

Food made from the lung of an animal, presumably a *bregit*. [First seen in "A Matter of Honor" (TNG).]

chech'tluth *(chechtlhutlh)*

An alcoholic beverage best served heated and steaming. The word seems to derive from the verbs meaning "to drink" and "to get drunk." [First seen in "Up the Long Ladder" (TNG).]

chorgh

The number eight.

Dahar Master *(Da'ar)*

A warrior who has attained legendary status in life. [First referenced in "Blood Oath" (DS9).]

d'k tahg *(Daqtagh)*

Personal dagger. Most Defense Force warriors carry their own *d'k tahg*; higher-born Klingons often have them personalized with their name and House. [First seen in *Star Trek III: The Search for Spock*.]

gagh *(qagh)*

Food made from live serpent worms (not to be confused with *racht*). [First seen in "A Matter of Honor" (TNG).]

gIntaq

A type of spear with a wooden haft and a curved, two-bladed metal point. [First seen in "Birthright Part 2" (TNG).]

glob fly *(ghIlab ghew)*

Small, irritating insect with no sting and which makes a slight buzzing sound. [First referenced in "The Outrageous Okona" (TNG).]

grapok sauce *(gha'poq)*

Condiment, often used to bring out the flavor in *gagh* or *racht*. [First seen in "Sons and Daughters" (DS9).]

Gre'thor *(ghe'tor)*

The afterlife for the dishonored dead—the closest Klingon equivalent to hell. Those who are unworthy spend eternity riding the Barge of the Dead to *Gre'thor*. [First mentioned in "Devil's Due" (TNG).]

grishnar cat *(ghISnar)*

Small animal, apparently not a very vicious one, though with perhaps a predilection for trying to sound fiercer than it actually is. [First referenced in "The Way of the Warrior" (DS9).]

Habnagh

A type of stone indigenous to Qo'noS. Often used in the construction of statuary. [First referenced in *The Brave & the Bold* Book 2.]

jatyIn

According to legend, spirits of the dead that possess the living. [First mentioned in "Power Play" (TNG).]

jeghpu'wI'

Conquered people—more than slaves, less than citizens. This status is given to the natives of worlds conquered by the Klingon Empire. [First used in *Diplomatic Implausibility*.]

Mauk-to'Vor *(ma'to'vor)*

A death ritual that allows one who has lost honor to die well and go to *Sto-Vo-Kor* by being honorably killed by a Housemate or someone equally close. [First seen in "Sons of Mogh" (DS9).]

mek'leth *(meqleH)*

A swordlike one-handed weapon about half the size of a *bat'leth*. [First seen in "Sons of Mogh" (DS9).]

mevak dagger *(mevaq)*

A ceremonial weapon used in the *Mauk-to'Vor* ceremony. [First seen in "Sons of Mogh" (DS9).]

mok'bara *(moqbara)*
Martial art that focuses both the body and the spirit. [First seen in "Man of the People" (TNG).]

petaQ
Insult with no direct translation. Sometimes anglicized as *pahtk*. [First used in "The Defector" (TNG).]

pipius claw *(pIpyuS pach)*
Food made from the claw of an animal. [First seen in "A Matter of Honor" (TNG).]

Qapla'
Ritual greeting that literally means "success." [First used in *Star Trek III: The Search for Spock*.]

QaS DevwI'
Troop commander on a Defense Force vessel, generally in charge of several dozen soldiers. Roughly analogous to a sergeant in the modern-day army. [First used in *The Brave & the Bold* Book 2.]

qell'qam
Unit of measurement roughly akin to two kilometers. Sometimes anglicized as *kellicam*. [First used in *Star Trek III: The Search for Spock*.]

QI'yaH
Interjection with no direct translation. [First used in "Sins of the Father" (TNG).]

qutluch
A weapon favored by assassins, one that leaves a particularly vicious wound. [First seen in "Sins of the Father" (TNG).]

Qu'vatlh
Interjection with no direct translation.

racht *(raHta')*
Food made from live serpent worms (not to be confused with *gagh*). [First seen in "Melora" (DS9).]

raktajino *(ra'taj)*
Coffee, Klingon style. [First seen in "The Passenger" (DS9).]

ramjep **bird**
Avian life-form indigenous to Qo'noS that only comes out in the dark, and is sometimes served as food. Name literally means "midnight." [First referenced in *Diplomatic Implausibility*.]

rokeg blood pie *(ro'qegh'Iwchab)*
Food apparently made from or with the blood of an animal, possibly a *rokeg*. [First seen in "A Matter of Honor" (TNG).]

R'uustai *(ruStay)*
Literally, "the bonding," this is a ritual that allows an orphan to join another House. [First seen in "The Bonding" (TNG).]

Soch
The number seven.

So'HIp
Literally "uniform of hiding," this is a camouflage outfit that changes color in order to blend with the background of the environment the wearer is currently inhabiting.

Sto-Vo-Kor *(Suto'vo'qor)*
The afterlife for the honored dead, where all true warriors go, crossing the River of Blood after they die to fight an eternal battle. The closest Klingon equivalent

to heaven. [First mentioned by name in "Rightful Heir" (TNG).]

taknar gizzards *(taqnar)*

The contents of the belly of an animal, served as food.

targ *(targh)*

Animal that is popular as a pet, but the heart of which is also considered a delicacy. [First seen as a pet in "Where No One Has Gone Before" (TNG) and as a food in "A Matter of Honor" (TNG).]

tik'leth *(tIqleH)*

An edged weapon, similar to an Earth longsword. [First seen in "Reunion" (TNG).]

toDSaH

Insult with no direct translation. Sometimes anglicized as *tohzah*. [First used in "The Defector" (TNG).]

vagh

The number five.

wa'maH

The number ten.

yIntagh

Epithet with no direct translation.

zilm'kach *(tlhImqaH)*

Food made from something orange. [First seen in "Melora" (DS9).]

ABOUT THE AUTHOR

Keith R.A. DeCandido has written a wide variety of *Star Trek* material in an equally wide variety of media: novels, short fiction, comic books, and eBooks. That material includes the *Star Trek: The Next Generation* novel *Diplomatic Implausibility* (which introduced the *I.K.S. Gorkon*), the *Star Trek: Deep Space Nine* novel *Demons of Air and Darkness* and the follow-up novella "Horn and Ivory" in *What Lay Beyond* (both part of the ongoing series of post-finale *DS9* stories), *Star Trek: The Brave and the Bold* (a two-book series that covered all five TV shows and also included Captain Klag and the *Gorkon*), the *TNG* comic book *Perchance to Dream*, the novel *The Art of the Impossible* (part of the *Star Trek The Lost Era* miniseries), the *DS9* short story "Broken Oaths" in the *Prophecy and Change* anthology, the *Star Trek: New Frontier* short story "Revelations" in the *No Limits* anthology, and several *Star Trek: S.C.E.* eBooks (a monthly series, co-developed by Keith, of adventures featuring the Starfleet Corps of Engineers; the first sixteen have been reprinted in the volumes *Have Tech, Will Travel*; *Miracle Workers*; *Some Assembly Required*; and *No Surrender*). Forthcoming forays into the *Star Trek* universe include *Tales of the Dominion War* (an anthology of short stories edited by Keith, due in the summer of 2004), a two-book *Star Trek: The Next Generation* story focusing on Ambassador Worf in the time leading up to *Star Trek Nemesis*, and more adventures of the *I.K.S. Gorkon*.

Keith—whose work has been praised by *Entertainment Weekly*, TrekNation.com, *TV Zone*, Cinescape.com, *Dreamwatch*, and *Publishers Weekly*, among others—has also written novels, short stories, and nonfiction books in the universes of *Buffy the Vampire Slayer*, *Gene Roddenberry's Andromeda*, *Farscape*, *Doctor Who*, *Xena*, Marvel Comics, and more. He is the editor of the groundbreaking *Imaginings: An Anthology of Long Short Fiction*, his original novel, *Dragon Precinct*, will be published in 2004, and his original short fiction can be found in *Murder by Magick*, *Urban Nightmares*, and *Did You Say Chicks!?* Keith, who is also a musician and an avid New York Yankees fan, lives in the Bronx with his girlfriend and the world's two goofiest cats. Learn too much about Keith at his official Web site at DeCandido.net, join his fan club at KRADfanclub.com, or just send him silly e-mails at keith@decandido.net.

Look for STAR TREK fiction from Pocket Books

Star Trek®

Star Trek®: The Original Series

Star Trek: The Next Generation®

Novelizations

Far Beyond the Stars • Steve Barnes
What You Leave Behind • Diane Carey

#1 • Emissary • J.M. Dillard
#2 • The Siege • Peter David
#3 • Bloodletter • K.W. Jeter
#4 • The Big Game • Sandy Schofield
#5 • Fallen Heroes • Dafydd ab Hugh
#6 • Betrayal • Lois Tilton
#7 • Warchild • Esther Friesner
#8 • Antimatter • John Vornholt
#9 • Proud Helios • Melissa Scott
#10 • Valhalla • Nathan Archer
#11 • Devil in the Sky • Greg Cox & John Gregory Betancourt
#12 • The Laertian Gamble • Robert Sheckley
#13 • Station Rage • Diane Carey
#14 • The Long Night • Dean Wesley Smith & Kristine Kathryn Rusch
#15 • Objective: Bajor • John Peel
#16 • Invasion! #3: Time's Enemy • L.A. Graf
#17 • The Heart of the Warrior • John Gregory Betancourt
#18 • Saratoga • Michael Jan Friedman
#19 • The Tempest • Susan Wright
#20 • Wrath of the Prophets • David, Friedman & Greenberger
#21 • Trial by Error • Mark Garland
#22 • Vengeance • Dafydd ab Hugh
#23 • The 34th Rule • Armin Shimerman & David R. George III
#24-26 • Rebels • Dafydd ab Hugh
   #24 • The Conquered
   #25 • The Courageous
   #26 • The Liberated

Books set after the series
   The Lives of Dax • Marco Palmieri, ed.
   Millennium Omnibus • Judith and Garfield Reeves-Stevens
      #1 • The Fall of Terok Nor
      #2 • The War of the Prophets
      #3 • Inferno
   A Stitch in Time • Andrew J. Robinson
   Avatar, Books One and Two • S.D. Perry
   Section 31: Abyss • David Weddle & Jeffrey Lang
   Gateways #4: Demons of Air and Darkness • Keith R.A. DeCandido
   Gateways #7: What Lay Beyond: "Horn and Ivory" • Keith R.A. DeCandido
   Mission: Gamma
      #1 • Twilight • David R. George III
      #2 • This Gray Spirit • Heather Jarman

Enterprise®

Novelizations
    Broken Bow • Diane Carey
    Shockwave • Paul Ruditis
    The Expanse • J. M. Dillard

By the Book • Dean Wesley Smith & Kristine Kathryn Rusch
What Price Honor • Dave Stern
Surak's Soul • J.M. Dillard
Daedalus • Dave Stern

Star Trek®: New Frontier

New Frontier #1-4 Collector's Edition • Peter David
No Limits • ed. by Peter David

#1 • House of Cards
#2 • Into the Void
#3 • The Two-Front War
#4 • End Game
#5 • Martyr • Peter David
#6 • Fire on High • Peter David
The Captain's Table #5 • Once Burned • Peter David
Double Helix #5 • Double or Nothing • Peter David
#7 • The Quiet Place • Peter David
#8 • Dark Allies • Peter David
#9-11 • Excalibur • Peter David
    #9 • Requiem
    #10 • Renaissance
    #11 • Restoration
Gateways #6: Cold Wars • Peter David
Gateways #7: What Lay Beyond: "Death After Life" • Peter David
#12 • Being Human • Peter David
#13 • Gods Above • Peter David
#14 • Stone and Anvil • Peter David

Star Trek®: Stargazer

The Valiant • Michael Jan Friedman
Double Helix #6: The First Virtue • Michael Jan Friedman and Christie
    Golden
Gauntlet • Michael Jan Friedman
Progenitor • Michael Jan Friedman
Three • Michael Jan Friedman
Oblivion • Michael Jan Friedman

Star Trek®: *I.K.S. Gorkon*

Diplomatic Implausibility • Keith R.A. DeCandido
The Brave and the Bold, Book Two: "The Final Artifact" • Keith R.A.
 DeCandido

#1 • A Good Day to Die • Keith R.A. DeCandido

Star Trek®: Starfleet Corps of Engineers (eBooks)

Have Tech, Will Travel (paperback) • various
 #1 • The Belly of the Beast • Dean Wesley Smith
 #2 • Fatal Error • Keith R.A. DeCandido
 #3 • Hard Crash • Christie Golden
 #4 • Interphase, Book One • Dayton Ward & Kevin Dilmore
Miracle Workers (paperback) • various
 #5 • Interphase, Book Two • Dayton Ward & Kevin Dilmore
 #6 • Cold Fusion • Keith R.A. DeCandido
 #7 • Invincible, Book One • David Mack & Keith R.A. DeCandido
 #8 • Invincible, Book Two • David Mack & Keith R.A. DeCandido
Some Assembly Required (paperback) • various
 #9 • The Riddled Post • Aaron Rosenberg
#10 • Gateways Epilogue: Here There Be Monsters • Keith R.A. DeCandido
#11 • Ambush • Dave Galanter & Greg Brodeur
#12 • Some Assembly Required • Scott Ciencin & Dan Jolley
No Surrender (paperback) • various
#13 • No Surrender • Jeff Mariotte
#14 • Caveat Emptor • Ian Edginton & Mike Collins
#15 • Past Life • Robert Greenberger
#16 • Oaths • Glenn Hauman

#17 • Foundations, Book One • Dayton Ward & Kevin Dilmore
#18 • Foundations, Book Two • Dayton Ward & Kevin Dilmore
#19 • Foundations, Book Three • Dayton Ward & Kevin Dilmore
#20 • Enigma Ship • J. Steven and Christina F. York
#21 • War Stories, Book One • Keith R.A. DeCandido
#22 • War Stories, Book Two • Keith R.A. DeCandido
#23 • Wildfire, Book One • David Mack
#24 • Wildfire, Book Two • David Mack
#25 • Home Fires • Dayton Ward & Kevin Dilmore
#26 • Age of Unreason • Scott Ciencin
#27 • Balance of Nature • Heather Jarman
#28 • Breakdowns • Keith R.A. DeCandido
#29 • Aftermath • Christopher L. Bennett
#30 • Ishtar Rising, Book One • Michael A. Martin & Andy Mangels
#31 • Ishtar Rising, Book Two • Michael A. Martin & Andy Mangels
#32 • Buying Time • Robert Greenberger

Star Trek®: Invasion!

#1 • First Strike • Diane Carey
#2 • The Soldiers of Fear • Dean Wesley Smith & Kristine Kathryn Rusch
#3 • Time's Enemy • L.A. Graf
#4 • The Final Fury • Dafydd ab Hugh
Invasion! Omnibus • various

Star Trek®: Day of Honor

#1 • Ancient Blood • Diane Carey
#2 • Armageddon Sky • L.A. Graf
#3 • Her Klingon Soul • Michael Jan Friedman
#4 • Treaty's Law • Dean Wesley Smith & Kristine Kathryn Rusch
The Television Episode • Michael Jan Friedman
Day of Honor Omnibus • various

Star Trek®: The Captain's Table

#1 • War Dragons • L.A. Graf
#2 • Dujonian's Hoard • Michael Jan Friedman
#3 • The Mist • Dean Wesley Smith & Kristine Kathryn Rusch
#4 • Fire Ship • Diane Carey
#5 • Once Burned • Peter David
#6 • Where Sea Meets Sky • Jerry Oltion
The Captain's Table Omnibus • various

Star Trek®: The Dominion War

#1 • Behind Enemy Lines • John Vornholt
#2 • Call to Arms... • Diane Carey
#3 • Tunnel Through the Stars • John Vornholt
#4 • ...Sacrifice of Angels • Diane Carey

Star Trek®: Section 31™

Rogue • Andy Mangels & Michael A. Martin
Shadow • Dean Wesley Smith & Kristine Kathryn Rusch
Cloak • S.D. Perry
Abyss • Dean Weddle & Jeffrey Lang

Star Trek®: Gateways

#1 • One Small Step • Susan Wright
#2 • Chainmail • Diane Carey
#3 • Doors Into Chaos • Robert Greenberger
#4 • Demons of Air and Darkness • Keith R.A. DeCandido
#5 • No Man's Land • Christie Golden

#6 • Cold Wars • Peter David
#7 • What Lay Beyond • various
Epilogue: Here There Be Monsters • Keith R.A. DeCandido

Star Trek® The Lost Era

The Sundered • Michael A. Martin & Andy Mangels
Serpents Among the Ruins • David R. George III
The Art of the Impossible • Keith R.A. DeCandido
Well of Souls • Ilsa J. Bick

Star Trek® Omnibus Editions

Invasion! Omnibus • various
Day of Honor Omnibus • various
The Captain's Table Omnibus • various
Double Helix Omnibus • various
Star Trek: Odyssey • William Shatner with Judith and Garfield Reeves-Stevens
Millennium Omnibus • Judith and Garfield Reeves-Stevens
Starfleet: Year One • Michael Jan Friedman

Star Trek® Short Story Anthologies

Strange New Worlds, vol. I, II, III, IV, V, and VI • Dean Wesley Smith, ed.
The Lives of Dax • Marco Palmieri, ed.
Enterprise Logs • Carol Greenburg, ed.
The Amazing Stories • various
Prophecy and Change • Marco Palmieri, ed.
No Limits • Peter David, ed.

Other Star Trek® Fiction

Legends of the Ferengi • Ira Steven Behr & Robert Hewitt Wolfe
Adventures in Time and Space • Mary P. Taylor, ed.
Captain Proton: Defender of the Earth • D.W. "Prof" Smith
New Worlds, New Civilizations • Michael Jan Friedman
The Badlands, Books One and Two • Susan Wright
The Klingon Hamlet • Wil'yam Shex'pir
Dark Passions, Books One and Two • Susan Wright
The Brave and the Bold, Books One and Two • Keith R.A. DeCandido

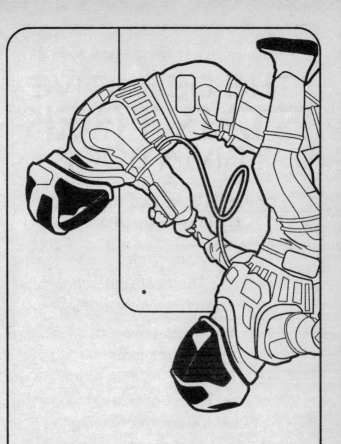

STAR TREK®
THE STARFLEET SURVIVAL GUIDE
AVAILABLE NOW... FOR THOSE WHO PLAN AHEAD.

STSG

STAR TREK®

STARGAZER: OBLIVION

MICHAEL JAN FRIEDMAN

In 1893, a time-traveling Jean-Luc Picard encountered a long-lived alien named Guinan, who was posing as a human to learn Earth's customs.

This is the story of a Guinan very different from the woman we think we know.

A Guinan who yearns for oblivion.

Available Now

STSO.01

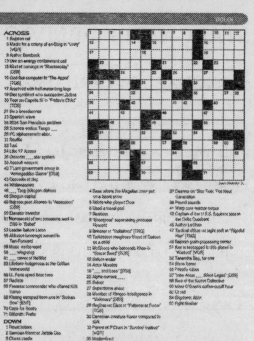